HOLY OIL

Jonathan Thomas Stratman

Front cover design: Celina Hicks

Editor: Billie M. Judy

The characters in this book are fictitious, and any resemblance to actual persons is coincidental.

~For Billie~
There are quiet moments,
still summer afternoons
with windows open
and faint distant chirps
of children playing,
that the world slows
like breath held
or a heartbeat
that hesitates.
And that's how I think of you,
think of our days of easy grace,
how we're held in the midst
of this life
together.
And how my next breath
is always you.
And my next heartbeat.
And my quiet moments.
All you.

CHAPTER 1

On September 24, Peter Senengatuk, a unique combination of old-style Eskimo chief and modern statesman, died in a freak accident in Seattle. My guess? Twenty years from now Alaskans will still be talking about what they were doing when they heard the news.

I was chopping firewood, one of the less frequently mentioned requirements of a mission priest. I'm able to do this even though I sat through no firewood-chopping class in seminary and attended no convocations on kindling splitting. It's true that my parishioners chipped in to buy me a used oil furnace but my cabin still—also—has a woodstove. To be able to use it, I have to venture out on crisp autumn days like this one, and "make" wood, as old timers say.

Before long, thanks to the exercise, I'd set aside my bulky wool sweater, finding myself warmed from within. Wearing khaki slacks, a pair of wedge-soled Red Wing boots, and my black clerical shirt, I lacked only the stiff white priest's collar to complete my work uniform.

Andy asks me somewhat routinely, why I'm doin' work in my dress-up Sunday clothes instead of work clothes.

"These *are* my work clothes," I tell him each time.

I had just tapped the wedge into place, heavy maul poised to strike, when Molly Joseph, with one-year-old Henry, bound to her front by a sash, burst around the corner sobbing, searching for me. I'd been expecting her, but not in tears. We had a date to go across the street to what is locally known as the mission barrel, a half-round, metal Quonset hut stuffed with used clothing sent by churches in the southern U.S.—that place Alaskans call "The States."

We had been meeting and finding clothing together, mostly for Henry, since before he was born.

A glance told me something terrible had happened.

"Oh, Father," she wept, her voice catching. "They have taken Senengatuk. He is killed!"

I led her by the elbow, in through the small vestibule at the back of my cabin to my tiny kitchen and got her settled, still weeping, on one of the tippy stools at my dining table. I turned on the gas, striking a kitchen match to get water boiling for soothing tea, and switched on the small red Philco radio to get the tubes warming for news.

From Fairbanks, just about eighty miles distant, the announcer's voice faded up into the room, confirming our fear.

"Senengatuk—the hope of not just Eskimos but all Alaskans—dead in Seattle at the age of sixty-one."

Apparently Senengatuk had caught the Pan Am Clipper out of Nome the previous day. He'd been subpoenaed by a grand jury looking into allegations that someone in the Federal Bureau of Indian Affairs might have made sweetheart deals for petroleum rights in the high Arctic. These deals bypassed the Eskimo population that had lived on the land for ten thousand years.

The story in the villages was that someone with the government or with the oil companies, had tried to pay him off, offering a storybook fortune to shut up and get out of the way. Senengatuk not only refused to be bought, he tipped the whole thing to a Federal prosecutor who filed a suit on behalf of the cheated tribes.

2

It wasn't just the north coast Eskimos who were upset. Here in the interior of the Territory where I live, the Indian tribes also called foul.

Landing in Seattle, he'd been met by the Federal Marshal's Service—standard procedure they said—and transported directly to his hotel. Who knew the restaurant located immediately below his room, closed since before labor day, would develop a gas leak late that night? Detonating that Monday morning just after five, the explosion killed Senengatuk, a U.S. Marshal, the hotel's night clerk and a passing newspaper carrier for Seattle's *Post-Intelligencer*.

I remember wondering at the improbable coincidence. He lived his whole life in the high Arctic, then deliberately traveled to this very particular place—a modern city—at the precise time that would kill him. Literally a date with death.

He might have died hundreds of times in the Arctic, hunting polar bear, harpooning whales from a small, skin boat. He might have frozen to death or been torn to pieces by something he hunted that got him first. In 1925, when many in Nome had diphtheria, Peter Senengatuk was one of those who hitched up his dog team and helped relay serum from Nenana on the old Iditarod Trail. After a life that read like an adventure tale, he died in a hotel room in Seattle, reading the morning paper or brushing his teeth, just above a restaurant closed for repairs. I remember telling myself, *it seems wrong.*

I had awakened late that morning. Allowing for the one-hour time difference, I figured I awoke at almost the precise moment Senengatuk was blown to pieces. Did I sense the shift? Did the *wrongness* wake me?

I know it was about six when I rolled out to dress, say my morning prayers, and make coffee. The sun rose just after seven and when I brushed aside my red-checkered kitchen curtains to look out, saw a shimmer of frost on the ground. A skein of geese in their characteristic V, flew high overhead, winging south through a faultless sky. I heard them calling out, doubtless laughing, celebrating that they could fly and I couldn't, and I remember thinking that this would be a good day.

Evie was first to arrive, as if confirming my expectations. I heard the welcome sound of her quick knock, the door opening, the *Hello?* she called out as she came down the short hall into my kitchen. Dressed in denim girl jeans, the zipper on the hip, she wore a white blouse beneath a light yellow sweater—looking like a million bucks against her coffee-colored skin—and one of those dandy Pendleton wool jackets that feels so toasty on a lightly frosty September morn.

I put up my lips and she kissed me on the way past as I sat contemplatively over my coffee. Selecting a mug at the rack she poured steaming coffee from the pot, doctoring it the way she likes with a little canned milk and a half teaspoon of sugar.

Placing her coffee mug on the table, she settled on one of the locally famous tippy stools. They'd been made by students at the now-closed old mission school. Evie had gone there, her cousin Andy—my first friend here—and most of the Athabascan population of the small river town of Chandalar, where I serve as the Episcopal mission priest.

Adults usually manage the stools pretty well—though we'd lose one now and again—but they were guaranteed to be hazardous for kids. With the stools a part of local history, I couldn't very well take them to the dump or burn them, which would also mean I'd have to buy more.

She took a sip. "The first sip is the best," she said, and I agreed. Then she looked at me. "We need to talk."

"Okay," I said. Any kind of conversation with Evie always felt like I'd won a prize. Having her in my life continued to surprise and delight me. When I came here, to remote Chandalar, I thought the chance to feel this way had passed me by, or—more precisely—had died.

I'd been married—news that still shocks some people. "A priest, married?" But that's because they're thinking of a Roman Catholic priest. Episcopalians, along with other Christian sects, like their British cousins, the Anglicans as well as Russian and Greek Orthodox, all have priests who marry. St. Paul recommended marriage for priests!

But my wife died about two years ago. Just about the time I finished seminary, was ordained, and—as we had planned together—came north. I traveled and lived for a time in a fog of loss and grief. Anyone telling me I'd love again, I thought mad.

Somehow during my first turbulent year here, love happened. And it happened without much help from either of us, unless you count someone trying to kill both of us together, out on the frozen river. That can bring a couple together. It worked wonders for us but I don't recommend it.

Although I read the Bible, I like the way the *Desiderata*, in about twenty-six lines sums up much of human wisdom, saying among other things, that love is "perennial as the grass." We both had our reasons to not rush into anything. But then last summer—just about two months ago, though it seems longer—a couple of really bad guys threw me into the paddle wheel of a riverboat out

5

on the Yukon. I should have died but somehow I didn't. Our glimpse of lives without each other pushed us over the cliff-edge of knee-jerk holding back. So here we were, two legal adults in our mid-thirties, making a struggle out of what most people do somewhat casually and without a net in their late teens.

I looked at her and smiled. "What's up?"

She smiled back, but not full wattage. "I'm a teacher now," she said, which I knew, of course. "And this is a small town." Late in the summer, out of the blue, she was offered a teaching contract based on significant performance in just her first year in education at the University of Washington. I wasn't surprised. She's one of the smartest people I know, has read nearly everything and remembers most of it.

It also helps that Evie is Native American, the only teacher in the Chandalar public school to be anything but white. She was already here and available when the stateside teacher, who had been hired and moved up for the position, got gunned down in a local saloon. He'd been trying to bring in a little extra cash working as a bouncer.

"That's what we need to talk about? That you're a teacher? I know that. I was in the room when they hired you."

"We need to talk about me being a single teacher in a tiny town, with a *boyfriend*. The way she said the "B" word made it sound like the way people shared that you had *something* on your shoe. No one ever said, Oh, boy, you have something on your shoe!

I looked at her. "You're making this sound like it's not a good thing."

"It brings up awkward questions."

"From second and third graders?"

"And others."

"Oh," I said. "So we need to talk about this? Maybe share ideas, find a solution?"

"Not exactly." She smiled. "I've already worked out, I think, the only reasonable solution."

I smiled back. It was hard not to smile back at this face on the person I had come to love. She had dark skin, deep brown eyes, shiny black, wavy hair, and right now, a small, earnest wrinkle in the middle of her forehead, as she concentrated on whatever it was she felt she had to say.

"Okay," I said.

"I need to break up with you."

Ouch. I hadn't exactly seen that coming. "Teachers don't have boyfriends?"

"Not priests," she said, "and usually not mixed race."

"So who do they think should be your boyfriend?"

She laughed and maybe blushed a little. "Oh that's easy. Edward Two Deer."

I drew a blank. "Not Athabascan, with a name like Two Deer."

"No, Lakota Nation, from Oklahoma, I think. He *is* pretty dreamy."

"Dreamy, huh? I can be dreamy."

"Yes you can," she said, in that gushy way people reassure children.

"So why are we talking about this now?"

She pressed her lips together. "One of my third-graders asked if it was true that I'm your squaw."

"Athabascans don't say squaw," I objected. "Who says squaw?"

"Television, apparently. *The Lone Ranger.* Have you seen it?"

7

"No TV." I looked around me as though there might be one here in the tiny kitchen of my log cabin, one I'd previously missed. "I used to listen to it on the radio, though. I used to think the Lone Ranger was some kind of hero, but now he's torpedoed my love life."

She smiled a little.

"You *can* see," she said, "that us as a dating couple could be distracting to my children."

"I suppose."

"And you agree that there really isn't another solution."

"I don't," I said.

"Well tell me then."

"We could be engaged. I could give you a ring." I reached across the table to take her warm hands in mine. "Will you marry me?"

She looked at me and opened her mouth but sound took a while.

"I …yes …no. You know I can't marry you. And you can't marry me. What kind of foolish idea is that? We've been over all that. I …" Without warning, she burst into tears, stood up, emptied her coffee mug into the sink, rinsed it, and turned it upside down in the dish rack. Snagging her Pendleton, she kissed me on the forehead and went out, wiping her eyes all the while.

Before I had time to give it much thought, there came another knock, not Evie. William Stolz came in the front door and down my hall.

"I passed Evie," he said. "She seemed to be crying. Is something wrong?"

"*Something* is," I told him. "Her school kids want to know if she's my squaw, so she feels we should break up. We talked it over."

8

"And?" asked William.

I looked up at him. "I asked her to marry me."

"Oh," said William, with irony, "that would certainly simplify things. What did she say?" He poured his coffee. "She said 'yes.' Well, and then she said 'no.' Then she called it a foolish question and left in tears. So that's where we are."

"You have already had a busy morning." William seated himself, holding his mug, a blue one, in both hands. A tall man, he looked and carried himself as though merely thin. But I'd been around him enough to know he did a hundred pushups, sit-ups and chin-ups every morning and what looked like 'thin' was lean muscle, hard and resilient as spring steel. He wore silver rimless glasses, his steel gray hair combed back. He could have been anywhere from forty to sixty-five. In the year I'd known him he'd already saved my life several times.

He worked in Chandalar as a school janitor, but I had discovered him to secretly be a U.S. government agent. At least part of his job had to do with security at the nearby government base at Clear, under construction, one of a string of DEW Line first-defense RADAR stations aimed at the Soviet Union.

The 'Soviet Menace' had become our national obsession. All over the United States, school children and others endured weekly duck-and-cover drills, dropping to the floor, crawling under desks and furniture to practice curling up and waiting for the Soviet's atomic blast.

I wondered, would the Communists in the USSR always be our enemies? These RADAR stations only aimed in one direction. I'd recently seen a photo of Nikita Khrushchev, banging his fist on the podium at the United

9

Nations. But what if, as nations, we 'kissed and made up'? I asked William that question and he shrugged.

"Why, we should build *more* RADAR stations and aim them in new directions!" he said, with some enthusiasm. "These stations are not just protection. They are helping to build the economy, providing jobs, making defense contractors and their shareholders wealthy beyond imagination. War and 'rumors of war,' as it says in the Bible, are highly profitable!

"And Evie is not wrong," he added, "about local comments concerning the two of you. You would have far fewer *professional* problems if you would just sleep with her. Marry, and your career advancement as a priest ends. Married to an Indian you would never be anything but an Alaskan Bush priest."

"An Alaskan mission priest is what I want to be and what I am, beginning and end of story," I protested. "I'm only thirty-five and I've already achieved my life goal. There are no promotions, no ladders to work my way up. Being a mission priest is all I want and all I expect. The job *is* the job."

William sniffed. "I admit advancements in your world are subtle. But they exist. If you two married, there would be no call in your future to a stately cathedral, no ascension to a wealthy and challenging parish back in the States."

"I never said I wanted those things!"

William lifted his eyes from his coffee mug to meet mine. They were steel blue behind the spectacles. "It is not just about being a priest and your career. It is personal, racial."

"Racial? You're kidding."

He shook his head. "Yours is a racist nation," he said, having been born in Russia. "The idea of your white skin

10

and her brown skin together inflames people, ordinary people, in ways that almost nothing else does."

"But these are modern times," I protested. "This is 1956. We have Einstein—well, until last year—and we have Elvis, jet airliners, Teflon …we have …transistors!"

He shook me off. "Just last year a fourteen-year-old Chicago boy—Emmett Till—on a summer vacation to Mississippi, whistled at a white woman. Whistled! A group of ordinary citizens—church-goers, business people, even mothers and fathers, beat him to death, gouged out one of his eyes, shot him in the head, tied him to a piece of mill machinery, and threw his body into the Tallahatchie River. I was sent down there to help recover and transport the body back to Chicago. In the war, I scarcely saw anything so horrible."

He waggled a cautionary finger in my direction. "Even in times so modern, America is not just a racist nation, but one of the *most* racist nations, and you forget it at your peril."

He looked at his watch and I saw him mentally shift gears. "I must be away for a few days, Stateside. Can I bring you anything?"

"Coffee," I said. "Especially fresh roasted, if you can find it."

"I am only going to Seattle, not Italy or Brazil. Do not get your hopes up. Seattle is a coffee wasteland." I found myself sighing. He was right. We'd been over this before.

"Is this," I hesitated, "*business* travel? Secret stuff? Dangerous?"

He waved a hand at me. "Yes, it is business, and maybe a bit secret but certainly not dangerous. I am assigned to the Senengatuk hearings, undercover, acting the tourist and general lay-about. Something I excel at."

"But danger?" he said, tipping back his head to empty his coffee mug. "I would say not a bit of danger."

Words I'd remember later.

CHAPTER 2

People from the States sometimes ask how I fill my days here, how I keep myself occupied in a tiny river town of just three hundred fifty people. The answer is, I don't know. Days fill themselves. I move from one task to the next and rarely find myself with nothing to do.

So Molly Joseph and I—and young Henry—spent an hour or more finding clothing that would fit the boy, "for about a week," I said to her, the way he kept growing. She would sniff now and again, or wipe a tear from her cheek as we went about our business that sad day, turning over stacks of small garments, checking sizes, all the while unable to take our minds off a dead man twenty-five hundred miles away.

Snapping the padlock on the Quonset hut, I turned to watch Molly with her two bundles—one of them Henry— walk away up the dirt road, each footfall releasing a puff of fine river silt. The river once flowed here and only now flows alongside the town as a kindness. Sometimes in the spring, the river forgets and flows back through the town, up the streets, as if time had changed nothing.

By about noon the early frost melted. Soon nothing would melt. In a month or two, this street would be snow-packed and glazed—hard and slick enough for kids to ice-skate on—shouldered by four-foot snow drifts. These cottonwood trees with leaves gold minted in a slant of noonday sun, would be stark and bare. Fireweed along the road edges, bloomed out and fuzzy at the top instead of pink and buzzing with honeybees, would be a memory.

I have a refrigerator now, so don't have to try to keep moose meat from spoiling on a cool porch. I also have a small freezer, which is a little silly, since in about two months, my whole world becomes a large freezer with an average temperature of about minus thirty-five. I sliced off a bit of the moose meat for my lunchtime sandwich, putting on a fresh pot of coffee, scooping—not fresh-roast Italian—but the old standby coffee from the large 'red can that means good taste.' It was okay. Only Andy really hated it. But then he hated all coffee—and many other things—not Italian.

I missed Andy, not that I didn't see him. He had recently opened an Italian restaurant, the first in central Alaska, in Fairbanks, just about eighty miles away. The diminishing size of my chunk of moose meat, the last of last year's moose, reminded me that he and I—and William—had an approaching date to go hunting. Andy, a dead-eye sniper in Italy in the last war, made a good hunting partner. He has a reputation for bringing in a moose in years that few hunters in the valley can.

I drifted from the kitchen, after finishing my sandwich, carrying my coffee down the short hallway— it's a tiny cabin—to my study, where I fiddled with a sermon for Sunday. Autumn feels like a time of reflection for me, a little melancholy. Yom Kippur, the Jewish Day-of-Atonement, had begun on September 14, more than fitting as a sermon topic, right to me in an Alaskan sort of way. In these last days before snow falls, all the human preparations for the continuing sacrament of life must be recalled and considered.

South of here, in Kentucky and Tennessee where my people were from and where I had been mostly raised, the small speed bump of Labor Day hardly mattered, except for kids going back to school. In Sewanee, where I went to seminary, and Chattanooga, where I met Mary, the

14

hardwood trees are still green, days still in the 70s and 80s, nights still balmy. If I missed anything up here—in this moment, at least—I missed summer nights. I missed the smooth, scented honey of warm southern nights under stars, walking hand-in-hand down a glowing ribbon of still-warm pavement between fields dark and lush with late crops.

In short, absolutely nothing like being here in Alaska's wild and remote Interior.

A tapping sound, soft as bird skitter, pulled me from southern idylls, admittedly not finished with my sermon on atonement. I listened, heard it again, and climbed out of my squeaky oak office chair to answer my front door. I already knew who I'd find there. The knock, or near lack of knock, gave it away.

An Athabascan woman I had come to think of as Mrs. Big Scotty Nielson—I didn't know her given name—stood in my vestibule. Child-sized, not more than about four foot ten inches, she wore summer mukluks—moccasin high-tops—and an old-style cloth parka, the hood raised, framing a tear-tracked face.

"Come in," I said, touching her elbow, guiding her. By the look of her, I already knew why she had come.

She walked into my front room, though so lightly she may have glided. As I pushed the door closed, she came to rest directly in front of me, standing so close we could have been touching, with only molecules of air between us. Looking down at the top of her parka hood, I remember thinking this must be Molly Joseph's view of young Henry strapped to her front.

Slowly, ever so slowly, her forehead tipped to meet my chest as she began shaking with soundless sobs. Just as slowly, just as gently—like hands softly cupping a wild

15

bird or a dandelion puff—I put my arms around her, pulling her close, holding her, patting her as she cried for what seemed a very long time.

"He is taken," she said at last, her voice muffled in my shirt front, "he has gone into the woods, and now I am alone forever."

In time, I led her down the hallway to my kitchen, installed her on a stool—cautioning her about it—filled a kettle for tea and struck a match, lighting the propane burner. The ritual of soothing: something I'd done a lot of lately.

She didn't speak until I settled steaming tea on the table in front of her.

"He was very quiet when I woke, and I think I knew. But I waited for a long time to see if he was just being quiet or if ..." She sobbed, sniffed, and I handed her a Kleenex. She looked up at me. "But he had gone. And now my life is over."

"Drink your tea while it's hot," I told her, and she took a sip. "May I know your given name?"

"Adele. After my grandmother."

"And may I ask how old you are?"

"I am forty-seven, married to Big Scotty since I was a sixteen-year-old girl at the mission school. He was my whole life, my morning and my evening. How will I breathe without him? How will my heart beat? I am laughing my whole life with him. How will I ever laugh again?" She pushed her teacup away from the table edge, lowered her forehead to her arms, and sobbed. After a bit, I walked around the table to sit on the stool next to her with one arm across her shoulder, patting her. There wasn't a single other useful thing to be done.

Big Scotty had been a dashing figure in his youth—I'd seen pictures. Tall, lean and square shouldered, with an Errol Flynn mustache and lots of teeth in his smile, he'd come up here in the early days looking for gold and finding adventure.

I did the math. Mrs. Big Scotty—Adele—had been born in 1909, married Big Scotty at sixteen, so 1925. They'd been together thirty-one years, one year shy of a full two-thirds of her life. It made a pretty good love story except for the parts about him disappearing. For several years, during the thirties, he'd gone south to join the CCCs and again during the war years when he'd been involved with something for the war effort.

I'd only known him a little more than a year, his glory days well in the past and even the mustache a memory. A calendar drinker, he binged each time he received his government check, and then sick, hungover, and no longer young, he'd call for a priest and prepare to die. I'd go and sit with him, say a prayer, and we'd talk for hours about the old days when life was good and simple, and still mostly in front of him.

He'd been many things, including a gold miner and a pilot. Once—drunk—he flew his brand new biplane into the side of a barn in the Matanuska Valley, destroying the plane and not doing the barn a lot of good. Then he limped away, hitching a ride on a potato wagon back to Anchorage, to the same saloon for more.

By his telling, he'd made several fortunes and lost them. He and Adele lived in a tarpaper cabin near a wild, cattail lake, fat with trout. A considerable shot, he'd get a moose in the fall, she'd tend a garden through the brief, bright growing season, and they got by. He could be cranky, especially when he was fully involved in "dying," but I knew he'd been crazy about her. Once—on a good day—I saw him throw his arms around her, lifting her completely off the ground in a wild embrace.

Now, abruptly, it was all done. I knew about some of the feelings. My life with Mary lasted about a minute. When a good thing is done, I'm pretty sure it never feels like it lasted long enough, like carnival rides, done too soon.

When Adele settled, I left her at the kitchen table and went to make phone calls. I hadn't finished dialing the four numbers of the first call when she materialized, silent, watching, at my elbow.

"Evie," I said, when she answered. "Big Scotty has died and Mrs. Big ...Adele ...is here with me now. Can you ...?"

"I'm on my way," she said.

I also called the church sexton, Oliver Sam, who could build nearly anything out of wood, with a hammer, saw and maybe a chisel. The church bought wood for coffins, which I'd haul in a pickup load from nearby Nenana, and Oliver would store in his meat shed. He tried to stay one coffin ahead of the need, which was sometimes difficult around here.

"Yes," he said quietly, "I have one." But when I told him who had died, he said, "May be tight fit." He agreed to meet us out at Big Scotty's to measure.

"I need to go back to your house," I told Adele. "We'll bring Big Scotty down to the Quonset hut, just for a time. Evie is coming to sit with you," I said just as Evie tapped at the door and let herself in.

"Adele," she said, sweeping the small women into her large embrace, one I knew well, holding her, crying with her.

18

With the two of them settled, I had begun easing myself out the door when Adele raised her head. "We're going, too," she said, taking Evie's hand, and the three of us walked to the truck. I opened the passenger door and tried to put Adele in first, but she demurred. "You two together," she said. So Evie slid in and sat close beside me, as she often did, and Adele sat by the door.

I started the truck, giving it just the few seconds to oil up, feeling the warmth of Evie along my side, where it belonged. I turned my head to look at her, seeing her profile as she faced forward, face framed with soft, black, shiny waves. I didn't say anything but it didn't matter.

"Oh, Hardy," she said, as she often does, and reached over to quickly rub my gear-shift arm as I steered us out of the driveway and away.

When I go out to see if someone is dead, I go always hoping that it's a mistake, that they'll sit up and say, "What are you doing here? No, not dead yet," and we'd laugh about it.

So far that hadn't happened and wouldn't be happening with Big Scotty. He had moved on.

I served as a medic in France during the war, and tended more than my share of corpses. It didn't help. The presence of the irrevocably dead set off a brainstorm of thoughts and memories about their lives and my own. One death reminded me of another, and another, a chain of deaths that always led back to my own father, or now to Mary.

I wanted Mary to die, prayed for her death. Yes, previously I had prayed for her to live and walk and breathe on her own. Others in the polio epidemic had recovered, why not Mary? But it wasn't to be. So I stood close by, willing her to move on to a better place, out of sight on my horizon and into view of waiting friends and loved ones across that great divide.

Rigor mortis was well established on Big Scotty, even in the cool cabin, still cooler inside than outside in the sun. He had probably died in his sleep or briefly startled from a dream. Did he wonder, "Is this it?" Their two small beds, made up with surplus military olive-green wool blankets, stood at either side of the narrow room with about four feet between. Did he reach out to try to touch her, to whisper, "I'm going on now, come along when you can."

Oliver arrived with his tape measure. I held the tape at Big Scotty's feet for the height measurement. "Big man," said Oliver, himself not more than about five-four. Big Scotty had been nearly a foot taller.

Reeling in the tape, Oliver shook his head. "Too darn big. I gotta build a new box." He turned and took Adele's small hand in both of his. "I am so sorry. He was a good man."

In a few moments, others arrived. The 'usual suspects' plus a few, as Big Scotty had probably weighed in north of two hundred-fifty pounds. With difficulty we rolled the stiffened body enough to get a blanket under him. For better access we slid the bed out from the wall finding an array of dust bunnies, old shoes, wood shavings—Big Scotty whittled—and a mouse nest. With three of us on either side, we lifted him, squeezing out the narrow door into daylight, sliding him gently as we could into the bed of the Ford.

Adele walked just ahead as we moved him, her fingertips on Big Scotty's shoulder, making soothing sounds like a mother makes when fearing baby might wake. He didn't.

Closing the cabin door, we all climbed into the pickup, only Evie sitting up front with me as the others sat in back on the sides. Adele sat on the pickup bed, gently patting her man.

We set up a table at the Quonset hut, pine boards and sawhorses, carefully sliding the body into place, leaving the blanket for now, then went out—Adele reluctantly—and I padlocked the door.

"Can I come back and see him?" she asked, a bit anxious.

"Anytime," I offered her the key but she said no, turning slowly to accept Evie's waiting hand. The two paused briefly and Evie's eyes met mine, our morning conversation still very fresh, even in light of this new sadness.

"I love you," she said, and kissed me on the lips, both of us catching the quick glimpse of ourselves in the love and loss of Big Scotty and little Adele.

Oliver and his crew made their goodbyes, Oliver heading home to his pine boards and wood shavings. This time of year he would still be building them out in his yard, but I knew in winter he'd build these boxes in his kitchen, moving his few other furniture items to the room's edges, putting shavings and bits of wood scrap directly into his burner. He and his small cabin always smelled faintly of pitchy pine.

He'd stop on his way, to enlist others to go along to the cemetery, on a hill overlooking the river, to dig a right-sized hole. Later in the year, digging a grave would mean first building and tending a fire to thaw the ground—a long, slow process. Or it could mean the alternative, a body stored in a meat shed or in the church's Quonset hut until Breakup. Some parishioners thought bodies in the Quonset hut unsettling when they went in to find clothing, so we kept that as our last resort.

I found myself talking to them when I had to be out there in the cold, rummaging around. It seemed easier in that moment than just ignoring a person lying there. But it amplified the utter loneliness later, when they had gone.

Back in my squeaky office chair, I found myself with few cogent thoughts about atonement, but many about sadness, the end of love—if indeed love ends—and about loss, which made me think about Evie.

And then my phone rang.

Back in the south, a ringing phone usually meant a friend calling, like hearing familiar footsteps on the broad, shady front porch. Here in Chandalar, where few actually have telephones, a phone call comes in a darker package and I never reach for the shiny black handset without trepidation. Calls here, during my year-and-some had been mostly about untimely deaths. By bullet, by the bottle, by train, drowning, fire, automobile, the gruesome list went on. So I was relieved when I picked up the handset to hear Andy's voice.

"You know that guy I was sorta seeing," he said, "Richard—the maps guy with the State?"

"Sure."

"He's gone."

"He's gone? You had a falling out?"

"No falling out. Having a great time, actually. But, when he didn't answer his phone, I went over. Somebody busted in his door and trashed the place. Everything's turned upside down, and no sign of him. He's just gone."

"*Gone?*"

"Yeah," said Andy, sounding—for him—a bit testy. "That's what I keep tellin' ya."

CHAPTER 3

"I may be in trouble," was Andy's greeting when I reached Fairbanks, not hello, nice to see you, or you made good time.

Hanging up from Andy's call, I dialed Evie's number, told her briefly about Andy, packed an overnight bag, and climbed into the Ford. Fairbanks would be a bumpy two-hour drive over narrow, dusty, gravel roadbed with spotty radio reception.

Andy's revelation earlier in the year, that he was homosexual, what he called "gay," wasn't the shocker he feared, at least to me. In fact, I'd pretty much worked it out on my own. Although a territory, Alaska wasn't immune to Federal "crimes against nature" laws, a broad brush of Victorian notions that frankly, rendered a lot of heterosexual practices illegal as well, and included prison penalties.

A recent report on sex and sexuality, by a man named Kinsey, with the dubious title "sex researcher," suggested that ten percent of people in the United States and—I suppose everywhere—had been born homosexual. Every tenth person. Although I didn't exactly 'get' homosexuality, I wasn't ready to condemn those persons.

People often ask a priest, what did Jesus say about this or that, even though there is no more public document than the Bible. They could read it for themselves. What they would find is that Jesus didn't actually say much, or it wasn't well recorded. I mean, it *is* most of two thousand years ago. What we're pretty sure he *did* say is, "Love one another." After two thousand years, we're still not good at it.

I found Andy at his restaurant, being bullied by a large, red-faced man in a blue Fairbanks city cop uniform with a heavy leather belt that went, not only around his significant waist but up over one shoulder. The man, taller than Andy by most of a foot, stood too closely and talked too loudly to be involved in anything but intimidation. He stepped back when he saw the clerical collar. Most people do.

"Who are you?" demanded the cop, turning his unpleasant face in my direction.

"Father Hardy from Chandalar," said Andy. "Meet Fairbanks police chief Kellar."

"What are you doin' here?" demanded Kellar.

"My friend …my parishioner …called me. I came."

"You always come running, when your …*parishioners* …call?" He said it suggestively, with an implied sneer that made me—yes, a priest but also an amateur boxer—want to flatten his nose.

Instead I forced myself to smile at him. "Yes, and we're also friends," I said.

He didn't answer, didn't change expression, but when he returned his attention to Andy, he took a step back. Assuming a more conversational tone, still heavy with suggestion, he said, "You let us know when you hear from your …*other* …friend again."

"Right," said Andy, and no more.

Backing up, Kellar used both hands to shift the weight of his gun belt, somehow making even that look like a show of force.

"Father," he said, as he passed me, touching the short brim of his service hat.

Andy just looked at me until the door clunked shut and we heard the patrol car start up. "Want coffee?" he asked, as though he hadn't just finished an episode with a big, hostile jerk.

"Is this the good stuff?"

"Oh, yeah. Had it shipped over from a little roaster I found just outside of Florence. I only serve this to my *A* list."

"*A* list?"

"People I want to impress."

"I'm impressed already." I watched him pour boiling water over coarsely ground coffee in the bottom of a straight-sided glass coffee pot. The pot's lid had a metal rod through it, fastened to a fine-mesh screen.

"Italian gadget?"

"Yes. A lot of people call this a *French* press coffee pot, but it was patented by an Italian in the late twenties. Italians call this *caffettiera a stantuffo*," he said, in convincing-sounding Italian, "which means piston coffee-maker." He smiled. "*I* call it darn tasty."

We stood in comfortable silence by the coffee pot, as we had stood a number of times around humbler coffee makers—usually a battered aluminum perk pot on my stovetop or over a campfire.

I'd known Andy less than two years, but with rare good fortune had become friends within about the first ten minutes of knowing each other. For one thing, we both had the war, Andy as a sniper in Italy and me, a medic in France. Haunted by the faces he'd seen through his scope, he was still drinking too much in those days, and looking like it. Unshaven, shaggy hair unclipped, and clothes that looked like he slept in them—which he often had. That was all quite a bit different from today.

Today's Andy could only be called *dapper*, especially standing in his own restaurant, named after himself—

Andrea's—Italian for Andrew. He said it was what they called him *back home* in Vernazza. "From the Greek," he told me, "meaning manhood or valor, which is me all over."

With his olive skin, black hair neatly cut and oiled, sideburns precisely trimmed, and a thin Charles Boyer mustache, he looked like nothing so much as an Italian matinee idol. Not by chance.

And it didn't end there. He wore expensive-looking leather loafers with tassels, nearly yellow slacks, a white knit shirt and sky-blue cardigan.

"Who are you and what have you done with Andy?"

"What d'ya mean?"

"No flannel anywhere."

He smiled, happy in sartorial splendor.

I hated to break the mood. "Tell me about Richard."

Andy's happy look turned bleak. "Aw nuts!" He said it, quietly but with passion. "Thought we might have something going, not that it's easy around here. Cops are in every day for protection money or free protection food. Pretty much have to give it to them. My cook, Antonio, spits in anything he gives them.

They do everything but fondle the waitresses and they treat *me* like I'm a fairy. Way it's going, be a whole line of us spitting on the cop food." He laughed a little, liking the image.

"You think the cops have something to do with Richard?"

"I don't know. They act like they're in no hurry to find him but they haven't been out of my sight since he disappeared. So I think they really would like to know where he is, but for their own reasons—if that makes any sense.

26

"And they're using my interest in him to leverage me, to up the ante from just restaurant graft to hide-the-homo graft. Of course the people a homo most needs to hide from are them!"

He pushed the plunger. With the grounds trapped at the bottom of the pot under the mesh screen, Andy poured steaming, aromatic coffee into a glass mug he'd already warmed. "You're gonna like this," he promised.

I took a sip. "*Perfetto!*" I exclaimed, one of only about three Italian words I had, which made him laugh.

"Your accent is worse than mine, if that's possible. Italians make that *p* almost sound like a *b*, and then they kind of twist it." He laughed a little, but then I saw his face shift back to looking serious as he thought about his missing friend.

"Richard came in here last ..." he paused to look at a calendar, one that featured a Technicolor view of the Mediterranean, "Tuesday, and he looked worried. When I asked him, he told me 'work stuff,' and I didn't push it.

"But I thought about it later. When most people tell you they got work problems, they look tired or frustrated, but he looked ..." I waited.

"Scared," he said, finally. "Just scared."

Sitting at the bar, I couldn't help a quick glance around at the place. My first time here, just three or four months ago, this was a dusty abandoned saloon, its significant redeeming features being the bar—reportedly brought around the Horn under sail—an arresting portrait of a Victorian-looking lady with ample breasts bared—and a fully-outfitted, modern, commercial kitchen. Actually, the bar hadn't been a bar for decades, but the kitchen had been in regular use until just the last year or so.

27

Now, the bar gleamed with fresh polish, the nude—
and everything else in the place—dust free. Add fresh
paint, checked tablecloths all around, and beeswax candle
stubs stuffed into wax-dripped wine bottles on every table,
and the place shouted 'Italy.'

"You even shined up the lady." I nodded at the
portrait.

"Richard did that," he said. "Spent a couple of days
fiddling with it, cleaning the canvas, touching up the
frame, waxing and polishing. I have to admit, she looks
great."

Andy introduced Antonio, the spitting chef, when he
came in. The man laughed. "Just Tony," he said. "No,
never been to Italy," he replied when I asked. "But my ol'
Chicago mom knew her way around a meatball or two
…and those were just some of my dads," he finished, with
a comedian's flourish, after the appropriate timing beat.

As more of the staff filtered in, Andy and I, with
coffee refills, moved to a corner table at the back, Andy
choosing the seat that gave him the best view of the room.
All the while we visited, his eyes tracked preparations for
the dinner hour, with the restaurant opening soon, at five.

Without our even placing an order, plates, utensils,
napkins, and finally food began appearing at our table. I
had to admit, the place ran as smoothly and quietly, as the
legendary well-oiled machine.

"Is this chicken?" I asked him.

"Do you like it?"

"It's wonderful." And it was.

"Duck," he said.

I feigned bobbing my head and he favored me with a
pained look. "Naw, wild duck. This guy was grazing in
Creamer's Dairy field just a day or so ago. Watch out for

28

bird shot." He gave me what, for Andy, was a hard look. "Yes, I have a permit."

I didn't ask him until dessert arrived, along with more of the wonderful coffee. "What do you want to do about Richard? Leave it for the cops?"

"Those guys," he said, mildly, "couldn't find their asses with a compass. I'm thinking, we don't find him, he don't get found." He tested a bit of the torte, chewing slowly, tasting, swallowing, liking the flavor—smiling—but only until he remembered again that his friend, someone he had allowed himself to like a lot, had disappeared.

"We'll find him." I tried to say it like we actually might. People went missing in Alaska somewhat routinely. Mostly we found them floating, or when the snow melted, or when animals dug up the shallow grave. Sometimes, more rarely, they turned up in a postcard from some exotic place, or a jail, or they sobered up—the guy or girl they were with left—and they wandered home.

"You say they trashed his place?"

"Yeah."

"Can we get in?"

He dug in his yellow slacks for a brass key and held it up. "Yeah."

Richard's place turned out to be about three blocks from Andrea's. It sat on a block of small and cheaply-built, one story, oddly California-like cottages decorated with the occasional birch tree or dead car up on blocks. We took the Ford, though we could easily have walked. We were shadowed through the twilight by a uniformed officer in a marked Fairbanks police car, a two-tone 1953 Chev with the bubble light like a cherry on top and a chromed, bullet-

29

shaped siren. The cop 'tail' was as subtle as lipstick on a moose.

Richard's house fit on its block. By the look of it, about four rooms, stucco, with a flat roof—of all things—in an area known for six-foot snow accumulations. The door featured one of those little 'speak-easy' openings, with a hinged black metal cover on the inside, so the occupant could look out or talk to a visitor without opening the whole door. I knew that little metal cover would be frosted white all winter, probably frozen shut and constantly bleeding cold. It seems having a lookout hadn't helped Richard.

Letting ourselves in, Andy closed the door quietly, as though we might be in danger of waking someone. We weren't. The house sat cold, still, and empty, with a faint, not-objectionable scent of Old Spice. Living room, kitchen, bedroom, bathroom—Richard kept a clean house, cleaner than mine, without a lot of clutter. He had books, a few framed pictures, a Philco cabinet-style hi-fi, in cherry wood—an RCA-label Frank Sinatra LP on the turntable—and not a lot else in the place. A stuffed fish on a plaque, labeled Homer, Alaska 1954, hung from only one of its nails. A gun rack above the sofa still held its three guns: a pump .22, lever-action 30-30, the obligatory 12-gauge, and a pricey bamboo fly rod. Everything else in the room looked disarranged, like the house had been picked up and shaken.

I tipped up one of the photos to find myself staring at a smiling Andy. He saw me seeing it and started to say something. "It's okay," I said. One by one I went along tipping up each photo and then setting it back as I found it. Why? I don't know. Maybe just feeling we should leave the place undisturbed.

I worked my way through the living room and then into the bedroom where the drawers had all been tipped out and dumped and the mattress tossed half off. I found a few more framed pictures in there, on the dresser top and the night stand—oddly again, none of them broken, just tipped. I saw, probably a mom—who looked like Richard—a sister, Richard, and another guy wearing a mustache, maybe a brother or a close friend.

One painting on the wall was a print by Machatanz, his famous portrait of Mt. McKinley. It hung only slightly askew in a house where every other single thing had been toppled or dumped, which pulled me to it. Lifting one corner, I peered behind, expecting to find—what? I don't know.

What I did find turned out to be a small microphone on a twist of wire, drilled through the wall and then the hole sealed with some kind of putty to keep cold wind from whistling through. About the size of a fifty-cent piece and half the thickness of a pocket watch, the mic lay nicely behind the frame, picking up every word, every sound, from the bedroom.

Laying a finger across my lips, I waved to catch Andy's attention, directing his gaze behind the painting. His face went white but he didn't say anything, pressed his lips together for a moment, then looked the other way. A secret man with a secret—and in its way dangerous—life, had just found himself horribly exposed. I couldn't even begin to imagine how he felt about things he may have said or done here in this room. Things that had rippled into the world like carrier pigeons of danger or shame, outward bound, with no hope of ever calling them back.

I forced myself to speak. "Not finding anything useful. You?"

31

"Nah," he answered, speaking casually with difficulty. "Been over this before, nothin' here."

Before leaving I went to the small kitchen with its tiled counters, canisters of coffee, flour and sugar dumped, a propane range and a smallish pre-war refrigerator with the round compressor on top.

Just as I stepped into the kitchen, I saw it, oddly upright and distinct, like a coastal lighthouse on a storm-littered beach. On top of the reefer, just in front of the compressor, stood a small, blond wood figure, a knight from a chess set, one I was pretty sure I'd seen before. It stopped me cold.

"Let's get out of here," I said, and we left, locking the door, walking back to the truck in what had become darkness. If the cop still watched us, I couldn't see him and didn't want to make a big show of looking around.

When we had climbed back in the truck, slammed the doors and turned the engine over, starting it, I looked at Andy, with just enough light from a distant streetlight to see him looking at me.

"You okay?"

"No," he said. I pulled on the headlight knob but didn't put the truck in gear and we sat there, heater running, the quick warmth feeling good after the various kinds of chills from the empty house and the now subfreezing evening.

"That *was* a mic," he said.

"Yeah."

"Then I'm done here. Cops went to that much trouble, I'm out of business already and on my way to prison. Maybe it's time to go back to Italy."

"Wait a bit. I don't think that's a police mic."

"Not cops? Who then?"

32

"I don't know, exactly. There's something else going on here, but I'm not sure what. And I still don't have any idea where Richard is ..."

"But ...?"

"I think I know who he's with."

CHAPTER 4

"You think cops are harassing you because you're gay," I said to Andy.

"Yeah," he said with a couple syllables, not like 'this is true,' but like 'this is *obvious*.'

"Maybe," I said, "But I think there's something else going on, too."

We were back at the restaurant, now closed and otherwise empty, repositioned around the Italian French press. Yes, I would be awake half the night from the caffeine. We had the radio on and cranked up, just in case the restaurant had been bugged as well.

"Next up," said the announcer, "the Platter's new hit, *The Great Pretender*."

"Swell," said Andy. "My theme song."

He took a sip of the dark coffee, sliding sugar and real cream across the counter in my direction. "Sorry," he said, "out of Carnation from the can."

Lowering my voice, I asked him, "Isn't it true that the microphone at Richard's would have given them plenty of evidence that you really are gay and really are, from their position, breaking the law?"

It was the most personal question I'd ever asked him. He looked at the floor. I could only imagine how embarrassing this would be for him to talk about.

"Yeah, it's true," he said, the words squeezing out, as if against his will.

"So?" I held up my hands expectantly, "Where are they?"

"Huh?"

"They're not here arresting you. You're not in jail."

34

He looked at me, the realization dawning. "So it's *not* their mic," he said. "The cops *don't* have evidence."

"Right."

"And whoever *is* listening, is not the cops," he said with some relief, and he nearly smiled. He looked around the restaurant. "Feel like helping me turn this place over?"

We did. Thankfully there were no bugs of any kind at Andrea's—and we looked!

As we moved through the restaurant, lifting things, turning things, standing, stooping, even crawling, I became increasingly aware of the nude, high on her wall, watching me.

"Got a ladder?"

When Andy produced a stepladder, I squeezed it in behind the bar and cautiously climbed to the top, standing on a sticker that read "not a step," to be able to reach the twelve-foot tin ceiling.

I lifted a corner of the painting to peer behind and saw nothing on the wall. But something, the weight of it, made me lift the painting again and lean in to peer at its canvas back. *Bingo!*

With Andy's help, we wrestled the surprisingly heavy painting off the wall to place it nude-side down on the bar. Just for the moment, we found the back of the painting more interesting than the front.

Glued to the canvas were four, large manila envelopes, each stuffed an inch or more thick. In one, we found documents, what appeared to be oil lease contracts complete with detailed maps. In the other three we found cash. In fact, we counted forty-thousand dollars—fifty-dollar bills in bundles of twenty—with Ulysses S. Grant smiling up at us.

"Yours?" I asked.

"Must be. It's stuck to the back of my painting. No wonder Richard spent so much time fussing with this." He looked at me across the canvas and cash. "What happens if this stuff 'goes missing?'"

"Somebody will have to come and ask you for it."

"That's gonna be trouble."

I considered. "Yeah, but it should be easier to let them find us than us hunting around trying to find them. It's a big territory and one thing I know is we don't have a clue what this is really about."

"You take it," he said, and I did.

The bad part: we still didn't have a clue what had become of Richard, or why he'd hidden this stuff at Andrea's. In fact, we still had no answers and now even more questions.

Driving home the next day, the one question I kept playing back through my mind had nothing to do with money or documents. It was the part about the chess piece, something I held back from Andy.

Way last spring, I'd been cleaning in the parish hall, with help from William. We'd gotten some fresh games and puzzles from a church in the states. They arrived only slightly used, complete or with only a piece or two missing, unlike some of ours with several pieces gone. Around here a chess game in play, with all its 'stand-in' pieces—spools, stones, cabinet knobs, plastic army figurines—looked more like spillage from a junk drawer than an actual game.

So I was headed for the garbage can with half a chess set when William intercepted me.

"I will take those pieces." He reached for them. I must have looked surprised, though I knew him to be a chess nut.

36

"Spares," he said, by way of explanation. Scooping up the pieces in one hand, he dropped them into a jacket pocket and went off. I hadn't seen any of them again until yesterday, eighty miles distant.

Of course maybe this piece wasn't one of those. "A lot of them look the same," he might say, and he'd be right. Maybe I was trying to make pieces connect that really didn't. It wouldn't be the first time. At some point I stopped thinking about William, and about Andy, and went back to thinking about Evie—as I often did—until suddenly I found myself back on the riverbank at Nenana, a short ferry ride, and about twenty miles from home.

Home! When did this tiny Alaskan village become home, I wondered, and in that moment couldn't imagine being anywhere else in the world. I planned to come here with Mary. This was our dream, an Alaskan mission, but now here I was by myself. As I watched and waited, the little sternwheeler ferry, *Princess of Minto*—with a small car barge made fast alongside—came battering back across the muddy rips and swift current, rainbows shifting and playing in the sunlit spray of her bright red stern wheel. I imagined seeing it for Mary, too. She liked boats, and especially liked rainbows.

We buried Mr. Big Scotty Nielson on the hill overlooking the river. It was a chilly, overcast Tuesday in late September, with birch leaves gone to gold around us and the river shushing gently below. I turned to look out over the valley, with its two shimmering rivers and miles and miles of near-perfect flatness. From the top of this hill, on a very clear day, I'd seen Denali—Mt. McKinley, something a person didn't soon forget—shining in the sun. The first time I climbed up for a look, I couldn't actually see the mountain. To my eye, it disappeared into clouds. Then Andy pointed out I wasn't looking high enough. Most of the mountain reached well *above* the clouds. I'd been looking too low. *Is that the human condition,* I wondered on the way back down, *always looking too low, expecting too little?*

About twenty-five of the villagers made the journey to the graveside, including Andy, who'd caught a ride down from Fairbanks and would return on the train. Also along, his "tail," now in plain clothes and an unmarked car. Another '53 Chevy, pale blue with the chrome jet bird hood ornament. It was pretty obvious in a town where most people walked.

Oliver had done an excellent job on the box, even adding extra handles—ropes drilled through and knotted—to deal with Big Scotty's extra weight. Adele stood between Evie and me, mostly dry eyed, sometimes holding Evie's hand. When it was all finished, she took up the first handful of dry valley sand and let it sift through her fingers down into the grave. "Goodbye, my man," she whispered. "Goodbye."

Later, some of us gathered in my kitchen—Andy brought coffee—six being about the 'legal' limit, but eight showing up. After a bit, that number dribbled down to just four: Evie and me, Andy and Adele. Evie had just put on a fresh pot and insisted on walking a mug of it out to the 'copper' on duty.

"He seemed embarrassed," she said, "but took the coffee."

Adele cleared her throat, in that obvious way people do when they have something to say. "I have a son," she said in her small voice. "Big Scotty's son! I've written to invite him to come visit."

38

Going through Big Scotty's effects, she'd found an old letter, actually written just after the war, from another Mrs. Big Scotty, a riveter at a wartime airplane factory, postmarked Cincinnati, 1945. The woman, who signed her name Bitsy, with a little heart where the *i* dot should have been, also wrote Edna in parentheses, to avoid confusion. "I've found someone else," she wrote, "and hope to never see you again." But went on to tell him about his son, also Scotty, but nicknamed Butch. And she just wouldn't have felt right about not telling him. "So goodbye forever," the letter concluded.

Adele seemed so happy about this, after the heartbreak of losing her man, that—admirably, I thought—no one bothered to tell her she had very little chance of even catching up with her "son" after all this time, and less chance he'd trek off to Alaska to meet a woman he'd certainly never heard of.

But we toasted Adele and her new son, Butch, with our fresh, really tasty Italian roast, and all too soon the party broke up. Andy drove my Ford to deliver Adele back to her cabin, and himself to his cabin—he'd bring the pickup back by on his way to the train in the morning.

"So," said Evie, "we're alone at last. What will we do?" And then she kissed me a long time. We were standing next to my new, well, new to me, Amana refrigerator. I'd bought it used from one of last year's teachers heading south. Now I didn't have to keep my cool things on the back porch anymore, and always sniff the canned milk before adulterating—as Andy said—my coffee. As it turned out, the Amana was very nice to kiss by.

"Throwing caution to the winds I asked her, "Does this mean you've decided to be my squaw?"

39

"Oh, Hardy," she said, and kissed me again, but not as long. Then she led me by the hand into my living room and sat us together on the sofa, her arm threaded through mine. I liked that, and she looked pretty happy. We hadn't done this for a while.

"I've missed you," she said.

"It's only been a couple of days," I reminded her.

"They seemed like long ones."

"Yeah, for me, too."

"And you were gone," she said. "I came by."

"Andy called. He had a problem." I took her through the 'Andy business,' which was friend business, not priest business, so I actually could tell her about it.

The two were cousins, close, raised at the mission school. She listened to my story, not interrupting.

"This Richard relationship," she said at the end, "this sounds serious."

"As serious as it can be when you're gay," I said.

She looked at me. "Some gay people live together their whole lives, love each other, and are faithful to each other."

"Like they're married," I said. "Except they're not."

"That's sad," she said.

"Sad?" I admit I hadn't thought about it a lot. But it was sad. Many people, myself among them, thought marriage to be more than just two people deciding to be on the planet only for each other. Marriage, somehow, especially as blessed by God, made the sum of one-plus-one greater, and it was true: totally excluded gay people.

"What does Richard do," she asked, "besides being gay?"

"Maps. Andy described him as a 'land man,' for the Territory. He's the guy who plows through mountains of

40

mining claims documents, maps, and leases. He's actually a Federal employee, I guess."

"Leases? Like oil leases in the Arctic?"

"I guess." Andy hadn't told me much—maybe didn't even know much.

"That's odd."

"What's odd about it?"

"Senengatuk ...that's why he flew to Seattle, to testify about oil leases. So Richard's gone—maybe taken—and Peter Senengatuk is dead—maybe murdered?"

"You have an active imagination," I told her. I think I also told her I was sure the explosion was an accident. I'd remember that the next day when I saw the headline on the front page of the *Daily News Miner*: "Sengentuk Explosion Set?"

I didn't tell her about the painting.

CHAPTER 5

It snowed October third, just a light dusting, and the wind blew all day, making it darn chilly. It felt even chillier for Andy and me, camped out on a good-sized island sandbar downriver. We tried to hunker down out of the wind behind a big old cottonwood log, while also keeping eyes out for our moose.

We'd been talking about the Senengatuk explosion, whether it was or wasn't an accident. With the investigation still under way, sides were forming and radio and newspapers speculating.

"Aw," said Andy, "easy to think everything is some kinda evil plot, 'specially when we lose somebody we can't afford to. People always swing around to the notion that it's a conspiracy—a big plot by someone never named—to make somebody dead. And then there's another bunch of knot-heads who think a guy is not really dead at all. On some island someplace. Yeah," he concluded, "as if."

"Still no sign of Richard?" I asked him, after a quiet spell, although I was pretty sure if Richard turned up, I'd know.

"None." Andy abruptly looked glum. He had seemed more like his old self out in the wilderness with a rifle in his hands. It looked like I needed work on my conversation skills.

"You know," he said, "what troubles me is, sometimes I think maybe he got scared and took off because of *us*. We were getting sort of serious. I mean, I was starting to feel like all the other kids looked when we were in high school, and they started discovering each other, falling in love—

42

maybe having sex—going around looking sort of goofy blissful. I thought that would never happen to me. Never happen to a gay guy. Then, all of a sudden, I'm feeling like ...*that*. And it was great while it lasted. I should have known it was too good to go on." He looked over at me. "Think he left on account of me?"

"Not for a minute."

He stood up then, putting down his rifle—the sniper rifle he'd brought back from the war—and poked-up the fire. We didn't hear the shot at first, but the bullet cut a clean knife line across the sleeve of Andy's good hunting parka.

"Damn," he said, fingering the sleeve.

I would have ducked. That's me. I'm a natural ducker. But Andy grabbed his rifle, bolted a shell into the chamber and—with the gun canted skyward—fired off a round, shouting "Hey, we're over here, and we're not moose!"

I knew what he was thinking. That it was hunters out shooting at things they couldn't see. Somebody got killed that way, somewhere in the Territory every year.

But the 'hunter' theory evaporated when the next bullet passed just under his arm as the shooter adjusted for windage and came that much closer to hitting vital organs.

Andy dropped like a stone behind our log, just as I also ducked my head low, though—as it occurred to me later—if they'd been trying to hit me, they would already have put a slug through my head. I'd been sitting with my head arranged at the top of the log like a prize pumpkin set up to shoot at.

The shooter must have thought, from the way Andy fell, that he scored a clean hit. But once out of the line of fire, Andy grabbed the rifle with its big scope, and cradling it in his arms, scuttled the length of the log to sight around

43

the end. He easily drew a bead on the over-confident shooter. Clad all in camouflage, the shooter stood, panning our direction with the scope, no doubt congratulating himself on a job well done.

I watched Andy sight, breathe, and squeeze the trigger. The round shattered the scope as it knocked the rifle out of the shooter's hands, sending him on a clean dive into the underbrush.

"That's gotta hurt," muttered Andy.

"Did you shoot him," I asked, from cover.

"Nah. Seen too much of that in the war. Ruined his scope and maybe soiled his drawers, though. Unless he has another rifle, he's out of the long-shot business for today."

"Who was it? Could you tell?"

"Masked," said Andy. "Funny hunting getup for moose."

"But just right for someone hunting you!"

"Yeah, but why?" he said. "I don't know nothin', don't *have* nothin'. Why shoot at *me*?"

Though we waited and watched, we saw nothing and no more shots were fired. The shooter's rifle lay where it had fallen. When it seemed certain he'd gone and the coast was clear, we climbed into the boat and still keeping low, I pulled the starter rope. With Andy spotting through his scope from the bow, we motored cautiously across to pick up the rifle and scout for clues.

I gently nosed the long boat up onto the slope of sandy riverbank as Andy leapt out, grabbed the rifle and did a quick circuit. He came back in a couple of minutes. "Old equipment road back there," he said. "Forgot about that. Tire tracks. Shooter long gone."

He stood looking out across the river as I sat at the stern watching him, the Johnson burbling softly as I repeated his question. "But why shoot you?"

"Got no idea. None at all."

Luckily, we found a moose later that day, a big bull that came nosing out of the island willows, upwind about three hundred feet with only the slightest breeze.

"Your shot," said Andy. With my father's old deer rifle, a Winchester lever action 30-30, I managed to drop him with a clean shot to the heart, just behind a foreleg. He went right to the ground and was dead by the time we reached him.

Unluckily, it meant our campout and aimless time together in the wilderness ended almost before it began. That night, and again in the morning, we spent skinning, butchering, and carrying the huge sections to the boat, arriving back in Chandalar before the end of our second full hunting day.

"It's nice to get a moose," Andy said, nosing the boat up on the riverbank at home, "but it sure spoils the fun of going hunting."

It was our tradition—okay, we did it last year, too—to barbecue the ribs on an open fire in my back yard, inviting a big crowd in the evening, with the area's legendary mosquitoes gone for the season.

About twenty people showed up, including Evie, Adele, Oliver, Rosie, and assorted friends of Andy's. We had a really good, relaxed, smoky time, eating tasty moose ribs and standing around the fire telling old hunting stories, or as Evie said, "telling lies." Before Rosie left, she said, "I need to come talk to you."

"Tomorrow?"

"Sure," she said. Even at a cookout she stood out, with her turquoise eyeglasses sweeping up and back—reminding me of fancy car tail fins—a white silk-like scarf with sharp black dots knotted into her shiny, black hair. She had a lovely smile with lots of even white teeth and an occasional dimple. I noticed the dimple often came out when she smiled at Andy, and saw lots of it as she circled the campfire, laughing and talking, and orbiting him.

They had grown up together here, both gone to the mission school, and likely shared each other's earliest memories. But somehow she managed to miss critical information about Andy, information that would not arrive as good news.

"So, where is William?" Andy asked me later, as we cleaned up, the happy eaters gone home.

"I don't know," I confessed. "He was supposed to be headed for Seattle. Something to do with the Senengatuk hearings. When that whole thing went south I expected him back, but no sign. Oh well, I guess that's the spy game. Too bad. This was a banner year for moose ribs."

We finished putting things away and washing dishes. Evie came back after walking home with Adele and immediately set to, drying dishes to my washing, the whole thing feeling very domestic and nice.

"Okay," I said to her as we finished up, "maybe I could be *your* squaw?"

She laughed with her eyes crinkled up in a way that makes her look adorable. Her eyes followed my hands into the dishwater. "Looks like you have the skills."

"Why shoot you?" she asked Andy later, as we sat around my kitchen table with coffee. It was the question Andy and I had been asking each other all the way home. "Someone bugs Richard's house, for some reason we don't

46

know. Richard disappears for some reason we don't know. Cops follow you, why? There's one out there now. And someone shoots at you. Where was he when that was going on?" It was a good question.

Rosie arrived the next morning at ten, after the breakfast rush at the Coffee Cup. As lone waitress, she held out from six o'clock on, taking orders, flirting, scolding, small-talking, and pouring scalding coffee faster than anyone I'd ever seen while moving through a small, crowded, noisy, room mostly filled with men.

She was in her glory there.

I led her into my office and showed her the chair. She did what people often do when they sit in that chair: burst into tears. I slid the Kleenex box across my desk and waited while she pulled herself together, gradually subsiding into sniffs and hics before she looked at me and said just, "Andy."

"You're in love with him."

"How can you know that?" She gasped, eyes wide, looking at me in a way that suggested I might have gone down to the crossroads at midnight and made a pact with the devil to get the information.

"You've probably loved him your whole life," I said. She nodded, eyes still round.

"Ye-e-es."

"But that's not the problem, is it?"

Her face fell. "Someone told me something. I need to know if it's true."

"Something about Andy?"

"Yes."

"Then you need to talk to Andy," I told her, as gently as I could.

"I'm afraid to. I always knew he liked me, hoped he loved me. What if I ask him this and it makes him not like me or love me?"

"That doesn't sound like Andy."

"No," she agreed."

"But what if," she hesitated, "what if this thing, a kind of bad thing, were true, and it made me not love him. I mean, I was hoping for a life, for children. What if I …hated him for this bad thing?"

"That doesn't sound like you."

"No, I guess not." Her eyes met mine. "Do you like him?"

"He's my best friend on the planet."

She peered at me a bit suspiciously. "You mean like, just friends, right?"

"Nothing more," I assured her. She seemed to start breathing again.

"But what about this bad *thing* in the Bible? What would Jesus say?"

"He would say …he *did* say, *love your neighbor*. So the question is, can *you* love Andy even if there's nothing in it for you?"

"What do you mean?"

"Can you be his loving friend, even if he never marries you and you never have his children?"

Her eyes fell. "I …I …don't know."

As October moved along, the days took on a rhythm of getting ready for snowfall and winter. I went around and put plastic on all my cabin windows then wrapped my well and pump piping with salvaged garments from the mission barrel—items that went season to season, year to year, picked through again and again without being chosen. This

48

year's pipe wrap fell heavily to prom dresses and summer-weight sport jackets, neither of which anyone had ever come looking for, except maybe once for a funeral. Not a prom dress, a suit jacket.

I put a new sixty-watt light bulb into the wooden box that holds my propane bottles for the kitchen range. When the temperature falls to around minus thirty-five, that smidgen of heat keeps the gas flowing. Circling the cabin, I picked up and put away anything I didn't want to stop seeing and needing until spring, and tipped an old dog sled of Andy's that I used for wood or groceries up against the cabin so it wouldn't get buried or freeze hard to the ground—or both.

Andy often came home to Chandalar on weekends. Whatever social life he had in Fairbanks disappeared with Richard. With night-time temps falling to near zero, his Fairbanks copper, parked out near the fence at the corner, must have been miserable. Evie sometimes took him coffee, said his name was Stanley and that he had drawn the short straw—apparently as the new guy on the force—to get to follow Andy around.

One late-ish evening, with Andy and me about halfway through a chess game and Evie putting on a fresh pot of coffee, she gave me one of her 'deliberate' looks.

"You'd better go out and fetch Stanley in," she said. "It's too late and too cold for him to be sitting out there trying to keep warm in that car."

"I don't think he'll come," I told her, reluctant to put on my outdoor gear to invite in someone whose presence irritated me anyway.

She smiled in that annoying, knowing way. "Christian charity." She came around the table to take my face in her hands and kiss me.

"Come on," groaned Andy, "we're playin' a chess game here. I'm just about to beat him again. Get a room!"

She smiled at him, undaunted. "There's more where that came from." Seeing me reach for my jacket, "It's about zero out there. Put your parka on."

When I first came to Chandalar, I formed the bad habit of dashing across the street to the heated parish hall without putting on my parka and outdoor gear, the temperature well in minus numbers. Andy took me to task, patient but firm. "Always," he said, "always, put on all your gear even if you're just going across the street."

I told him okay, but my heart wasn't in it. That same week, one of my parishioners did put on all her gear just to go across to the neighbors. A dog sled, driven by a drunk, managed to knock her down and out, breaking her arm. She lay there unconscious, at forty below for an hour or more, long enough to be dead if she hadn't been dressed properly.

So I pulled on my winter boots, parka and mitts, took a flashlight, and walked out to the Chevy. I smelled the exhaust as I moved across the darkened yard, and soon heard the idling engine. With the car dark, I couldn't see Stanley inside, but assumed he could see me and would open the door, but he didn't. I knocked on the window, in case he'd fallen asleep, but he didn't open the door, or roll down the window, or anything. Just in case the latch hadn't already frozen in place. I tried the door. It was locked.

Finally, I flicked on the flashlight and saw what I feared: Stanley, unconscious, skin ashy gray but with bright red, blotchy cheeks. Carbon monoxide! Stanley could be dead or dying.

I tried all four doors, all locked, then—regretfully—picked up a stone and smashed the back window, reaching

50

through to pull up the lock button, open the door, turn off the engine and drag Stanley out onto the icy ground. Then I laid on the horn until I saw Andy burst out my cabin door, pulling on his parka, and I started artificial respiration on Stanley.

I'd been a medic in the European war, and then too old for service in Korea—fortunately—but I knew the drill. I checked his airway and moved his tongue, which had flipped up, then crossed his wrists over his lower chest and began to compress his chest, twelve times per minute.

I'd only accomplished about twelve when Andy jogged up, pushed me aside, and flopped on the ground next to Stanley. Also checking the airway, he tipped Stanley's head back, pinched his nostrils together, and put his mouth completely over Stanley's, blowing air into Stanley's lungs. I'd heard about this, mouth-to-mouth, the new artificial respiration, but never seen it done and certainly never wanted to have to do it. After several lungsful, he looked up at me. "Take your truck and get Maxine. Bring oxygen!"

I set off on a run to the truck, at the same time, digging in my pants pockets for the keys. Evie, her face anxious, came out my porch door. "Something's wrong," she said, seeing my face as I darted into the circle of yellow porch light.

"Carbon monoxide. Stanley. Call Maxine and tell her I'm on my way and we'll need the oxygen." I cranked the Ford into life, gave it about sixty seconds to start to circulate oil, and reversed, fast, out of my driveway. Maxine, the public health nurse lived only three blocks away, but it was too cold for her to ride her bicycle—and too slow—plus difficult or impossible to carry even a small steel bottle of oxygen.

51

In the minute or two it took me to get there, she'd thrown on her mukluks and parka and grabbed her kit, plus the oxygen bottle and a mask. She burst out of the door and down the several steps as I pulled in. "Do we need the stretcher," she called out. "It's just in the porch there."

Collecting the mostly canvas stretcher, I threw it into the pickup bed and quickly retraced the path to home, pulling up in front of the cop car, bathing the scene in blue-white headlights. Evie was now spelling Andy with the mouth-to-mouth, him standing by coaching.

"Heartbeat?" Maxine shouted, rushing up with the oxygen.

"Yes," said Andy, and weak breathing. Unconscious."

We watched as she slipped the mask onto Stanley, valving the tank on, and calling out to me for the stretcher. We got Stanley and his oxygen bottle aboard and with Andy and me doing the lifting, carried him into my house, into my warm living room, Evie moving the truck and Maxine hurrying ahead to open doors.

Depositing Stanley, I went directly to my office, flipping on the light, grabbed the heavy, shiny black telephone handset, and dialed zero.

"Operator," said a distant, tinny voice.

"This is an emergency," I told her. I gave her the Army's Ladd Field medical evacuation number from memory.

"One moment please," she said, and I heard a series of clicks and small echoes that always sounded to me like doors to long hallways opening, as though I could actually hear the physical distance. I heard a distant ringing, then the voice, "Ladd Field."

With the helicopter on the way, I had one more number to dial. "Chief Kellar," I said, when he answered, groggy and out of sorts. He sounded like he'd been sleeping, drinking, or both. I was not a bit sorry to interrupt him.

"This is Father Hardy in Chandalar." Even at distance I could feel him click up to 'business' mode, immediately alert.

"Yes, what is it?"

I told him about his officer, the situation and the helicopter. He listened hard, repeating back "check," after each of the details. "I'll meet the chopper," he said finally, "and thanks."

The line went dead and not quite silent as he hung up, leaving an odd pattern of chattery static and faint high-pitched whine to hear as I still stood, phone to my ear. I felt a tiny electric current of—not fear, exactly—but certainly recognition, and hairs stood up along the back of my neck. I'm *not* paranoid, but I watch movies and read my spy novels.

At least I read enough to be pretty sure about a tapped telephone line when I hear one, with someone listening.

CHAPTER 6

"Tapped your phone!" said Andy, incredulous, "the *church* phone? Who would do something like that?"

"The same ones who bugged your place, I imagine."

"Someone who wants to know what you know," Evie added.

"It's all about Richard," Andy said, taking a sip of his now-cold coffee. He looked up hopefully. "Anybody want more?"

We were sitting in the kitchen with the little red Philco turned up to 'blare,' just in case someone had also bugged the house, Patti Page singing *Allegheny Moon*.

"It's nearly midnight." Evie, yawned, stretching her arms out from the shoulders, twisting them, making fists, "And it's a school night." She got up and pulled on her wool jacket, knotting a scarf under her chin. "I'm worried about you two." She snapped off the radio just as Gene Vincent started up with *Be-Bop-A-Lula*.

"Be careful." She kissed each of us and went out, boots scuffling the frozen gravel in my driveway. She lived about two blocks away, in a cozy little cabin off the road. Nothing was very far away in Chandalar.

Andy switched the radio back on, which—tubes still warm—came back quickly. "This phone thing, if you're right and it is tapped, means I've either pissed off somebody over at the government, or somebody with a heck of a lot of money ..."

"Or both." I finished his thought.

"Or both." He looked around the kitchen, then stood and reached for his jacket, which clunked heavily against the chair as he lifted it.

"Gun?"

"Just a small one," he said.

"Want to stay here instead of being a target all the way home? I've got a great couch."

I didn't think he would. But he hesitated, thought about it, then said, "Yeah, probably makes sense. And then I can just walk over to the train, easy, in the morning."

We took turns in the bathroom, brushing teeth and such, and I wished him a good night. He'd already climbed onto the couch, wrapping himself in a blanket.

"Yeah," he said, and then, "wish we knew where to find William."

So where is William? I wondered in the morning, sitting over coffee after Andy had gone for the train. I thought of calling our mutual friend, Frank Jacobs, U.S. marshal in Fairbanks. If anyone knew William's whereabouts, it would be him. But to do it, I'd have to use my 'infected' telephone. No sense letting anybody else know I was looking for him, just in case. I had one other emergency number to call for him, one I'd never tried. *Is this the time*, I wondered? *Is this really an emergency?*

Still walking around with that question, and before I could start my priestly agenda for the day, I had a decidedly unpriestly chore to accomplish: hunting for planted microphones. It took me most of two hours to go over every square inch of the living portion of my cabin—I left out the pump room/laundry—too noisy and not likely to be the scene of much conversation. But I searched every other surface, including the bathroom, laughing a little at the thought of how a listener's tape log of bathroom audio might read: brushes, spits, farts, flushes.

I found one mic which I believed was meant to be obvious, and another behind my office desk, that I might never have found if I hadn't found the first one and been inspired to look harder. It made me angry that things people told me here, that were supposed to be between them and their priest—and their God—now also included whoever this was, listening, feeling powerful. I found myself resolving to do everything I could to mess with that sense of power, though just now I couldn't imagine how I possibly could.

I own a pistol, a snub-nosed Colt .38 Special, what Colt calls their Detective Special. Mine had some miles on it, probably manufactured in the late '20s or early '30s. It had been an inadvertent gift from a sometimes parishioner who tried to shoot himself in my office, missing, leaving a hole in my roof that leaked when it thawed or rained until I finally climbed up to the rooftop to patch it. Although I never imagined a priest carrying a pistol, it had come in handy, actually saving my life.

There were a number of times I thought of carrying it, but didn't, because I think a gun changes things. The more you carry it, the more likely you are to need it. Don't carry it and another solution may present itself. Of course if you show up at what turns out to be a gunfight, without your gun ...

Now I picked it up, held it in my hand, pulled back the hammer and spun the cylinder counting five live rounds, appreciating the weight of it, and feeling very tempted to drop it into my jacket pocket or tuck it into my belt. There's something about knowing you're being watched and listened to, privacy invaded, that makes carrying one of these feel almost comforting. But at the end of my contemplative moment, I put it back in its hiding place on the bookshelf in my study, tucking it behind a set of the works of Shakespeare, hearing one of his lines as I did: "By the pricking of my thumbs, something wicked this way comes."

I hoped not.

Headlines the next morning confirmed the Senengatuk blast as deliberate. No wonder the investigation took so long. According to the newspaper account, FBI investigators literally sifted the rubble of much of that part of the building to finally find fragments of a kerosene lantern that shouldn't have been there. It wasn't a sophisticated device with a timer or a fuse, just a lit lamp and a twisted-open propane valve. Crude *and* effective.

The article went on to recount Senengatuk's lengthy career as a Territorial and Eskimo leader, possible governor, and a man among men who had gone out of his way to not make enemies, to remain on good terms with everybody. Even the people who flatly didn't agree with him liked him and mourned him. So no wonder the article ended with the line, "The authorities have no suspects."

I spent the morning with a meat saw borrowed from the general store, cutting up and paper-wrapping our moose. With temperatures at or below freezing since the hunting trip, the moose sections had kept well in my meat shed. Now I filled my deep freeze, Andy's and Evie's, and distributed the rest of the moose to Adele and others who had no one to do their hunting. We might get out again, get another moose, but in the meantime we all had just enough to make it through 'til spring.

After lunch I got a call from a woman I knew slightly, Judy Morgan, whose husband worked as night radio operator for the CAA.

"He's late," she said. "He went out early for ducks at the gravel pits, and said he'd be back hours ago. I'm sorry, I didn't know who else to call. I'm pretty sure his truck broke down again."

"No problem," I told her. I knew the truck, a 1943 Chevy pickup, with its vertical toothy grill painted, not chromed, made for the military during the war years and then sold for surplus. Ken Morgan's truck was best known for being spotted broken down here and there around town, since he insisted on being his own mechanic, and clearly wasn't one.

I drove out north of town, just about a half mile from the river, on the rough little one-lane road built to haul out gravel. It was a road to drive cautiously, threading willy-nilly between small and often steep-sided, water-filled pits, where, for decades, gravel had been taken for the railroad and various road-building projects.

In the summer, the people in town swam here, those relative few who did swim. Kids, mostly. Although the gravel pits were far safer than the swirling brown and deadly river, people still drowned here and I'd already been present for two different "draggings," towing a grappling hook on a rope around the pit until it snagged a body. What's worse, both times it had been children. So this was a hard road to drive and not think dark thoughts.

All the way out, ducks and geese landed and took off, finishing up resting and feeding on their way south. Long skeins of them threaded overhead, gold-washed in the lowering angle of the sun, their farewells echoing back through cold clear air.

Trees were small here, and brush disinterested, so the Morgan truck stood up on the landscape, easy to find—but no frustrated driver standing by. It didn't seem to be broken down. The ample toolbox in the truck bed lay unopened, undisturbed, no tools out and no sign of mechanical problems.

I also saw no signs of hunting. No ducks, fish, packs, gun, rods—no canoe—his preferred duck hunting method, and no immediate sign of him walking along the pond rim or paddling, and no sound of shots, in fact none heard on the drive out.

"What's wrong here," I asked the truck, which didn't answer. "Ken!" I shouted, and again, "Ken!" And listened. No answer. No friendly, "Over here!" In fact, no human sound at all.

So I began to walk the three closest ponds, the biggest ones. The farther I walked, the worse I felt, the surer I became about what I would find.

Sure enough, in the third lake I found the overturned green canvas canoe, one end floating high and the other sunk. A red felt hunter's hat bobbed gently, breeze-pushed against a thin skim of shore ice. I called again, without much hope or heart for it, and headed back for my truck, back to town, back to Judy Morgan.

"People keep dying," I said to my empty cab. But the Ford didn't answer, and driving back, the sky had a hard look I'd missed on the way out. *I don't know if I can keep doing this*, I thought, but knew I would. Knew I had to. It's the job.

She answered the door cheerfully, had been baking cookies, and the wonderful homey scent of them washed over me as she opened the door. She took me by the elbow, pulling me in, quickly glancing at the yard for signs of Ken or his truck. If she found it odd to see me without him, she didn't let on.

"These are just out of the oven." She handed me three of them on a small plate, pouring coffee, indicating my place at a red-seated chromed chair, by a matching chrome-rimmed table top of something that looked like shiny gray-marble.

"He's had such good luck hunting this year," she said. And then, each time I opened my mouth to speak, went on to tell me something about Ken, about hunting, about other years good or bad, a desperate monologue, as I finally began to eat my cookies and drink the coffee—definitely from the red can.

Hers was the closest I'd seen to a stateside kitchen in Chandalar, all shiny plastics and bright color highlights, mostly red. She even had an automatic dishwasher, the first I'd ever seen built right in to the kitchen counter next to the sink. I marveled that Federal employees took such luxuries for granted while the people they worked for, at least around here, sometimes still pumped their water with a pitcher pump by hand, and did their business in an outdoor privy or a honey bucket.

When she finally stopped talking, the silence felt thunderous. We looked at each other as though across a vast distance. She put her left hand on a chair back, supporting herself, her right hand to her cheek, her eyes finally meeting mine.

"He's *not* coming home. That's what you've come to tell me, isn't it?" I nodded. She took her apron, awash with bright red roses, folded it up to hold it to her face, and then like a squall blowing in, began to cry. She cried softly at first, just the murmur, like falling water, then harder, the

60

torrent of loss, broken promises, broken dreams, fear, and loneliness, undammed, pouring out.

"Judy," I said, when I could, "I'm so sorry." She walked up to me then, and I put my arms around her as she began to cry again in earnest, into the roses of the apron, and there wasn't a single other thing I could do for her.

In time we said a prayer together, and she gave me the telephone number for one of the other CAA wives, which I dialed, and explained into the handset. She'd be right there, she said, and was.

Back in town, I rousted Oliver and a few of the others, and we took a skiff, along with ropes and grappling hooks back out to the gravel pit. I picked up the hat and helped the others to land the canoe, pour the water out of it and right it. We found the 12-gauge still in it, wedged under the center seat, still fully loaded, no shots fired, no sign of dead ducks or geese. On about the third toss, I heard a shout. They'd snagged something large and heavy that turned out to be Ken. Together we hauled him into the shallows with the rope, and then several of us waded out, wetting ourselves to the thighs, to get hands on him and bear him to shore.

He was almost too much for the four of us. With his heavy wool jacket, now water soaked, and hip-boots, water-filled—no life jacket—there could be no mystery about how and why he died.

As we set him down on the sandy shore and straightened, Oliver looked at me. "This didn't have to happen. Does God make this happen?"

I could feel myself making a face, a face shrug. "You think God told him to *not* wear his lifejacket," I asked. "You think God *insisted* he go out in a tippy canoe in these big boots?"

"Naw."

When I got home, I called Evie. "Can you come over?"

"Something's wrong!" she said, hearing it in my voice. "Is it Andy?"

"It's ...um ... I'll tell you when you get here, but no, Andy's fine."

We split a small moose steak, something I usually devour single-handedly. We also had potatoes and frozen peas, grown in my garden.

"You going to eat that," asked Evie, eyeing the rest of my steak. I had to admit not much appetite.

As we ate, I told her about the afternoon, about Ken, and about Judy with the cookies, the dishwasher, and now the broken heart. And I told her, honestly, about the long dark time I seemed to be caught out in the middle of, with only death and sorrow like sign posts along the way. I remember telling her I didn't know if I could make it to the other side.

"You will," she said, softly. "I know you will."

Afterwards we sat on the sofa together, very close, sometimes holding hands, talking until late, unable to not see the overlay of the Morgan's tragedy on our own lives, and already anticipate—however distant—our own final leave-taking and loss.

CHAPTER 7

On Saturday morning I met Evie for breakfast at the Coffee Cup Café. It formed an oasis of warmth, light, and good smells, abuzz with chatter and human contact on an otherwise frosty, blue-gray day that looked like snow. We slid into two of the three empty seats over at the side, under the dusty and humongous moose head.

Rosie wore her pink waitress uniform this morning, cotton long underwear pulled up almost out of sight beneath her knee-length skirt hem, revealing dark, firm, smooth calves above bobby sox and saddle shoes. She had on the white-framed glasses, another of the Detroit tail-fin pairs she owned, sweeping back to a kind of teardrop point at the sides of her eyes. Very fashionable.

Although Rosie waitressed at the Coffee Cup—which she actually owned—she gave over the rest of her life to fashion and style. She subscribed to *Life* and *Look*, probably *Photoplay*, and anything else that gave her hints about clothing, makeup and the good life out in the 'real world.' When Andy began his Italian transformation, she studied Italian! She sent for Arthur Murray dance maps and perfected her Samba. And even at this great distance from the States and from all things civilized, she put considerable effort into always being "in the know."

Once I found her studying an article titled, "Eight Signs You Might Be Headed for Divorce."

"You're not married," I pointed out.

"Never hurts to study ahead."

Evie and I pulled off our jackets and got them hanging on chair backs just as—coffee pot in hand and menus clamped with an elbow to her side—Rosie smoothly 'hipped' her way over to us, between the crowded tables.

"Hi, you two." She flashed a smile, one I thought might be just a bit sad around the edges.

"Hey, Rosie," said Evie, looking around at the crowd. "You need help in here!"

Rosie followed Evie's gaze, raising her eyebrows. "No place to put help," she popped her gum. "We'd be crashing into each other, getting less done. But thanks!"

Rosie's dark eyes met mine. "Out of the hash," she smiled sympathetically, knowing I'd be disappointed. Then she spun away, already headed off in another direction. She was right. Just hearing about the moose-meat hash made my mouth water.

We ordered, then sat companionably listening to Fairbanks station KFAR on Rosie's new Crosley. Pat Boone sang *Tutti-Frutti*, having successful appropriated another of the Negro—or sometimes called "colored," songs of rocker Little Richard, pushing it to number twelve on the Hit Parade—compared to number 17 for Little Richard—according to the DJ.

Winter wool socks, he continued, had arrived at the Northern Commercial Company, all sizes in stock, and were now fifty cents off when you buy two pair. The number three Beaver Traps, were in, also a bargain. "NCCO, for all your trapping needs," promised the smooth-voiced announcer.

"Got to get me some of those." Evie looked up as Rosie pushed heavy plates in front of us, set down the Heinz ketchup bottle with a thunk, and hurried away.

"Socks or beaver traps?" I called after her.

"Oh, the beaver traps, definitely," she smiled over her shoulder.

We began eating our eggs and bacon as Dean Martin came on singing, *Memories are Made of This*. I looked at Evie across the table, near and dear, and realized Dean was right. Memories of small moments—like this one—became treasured snapshots in time.

She looked up, saw me seeing her and smiled. "Eat your breakfast. You can stare at me later."

"They came to get Stanley, the copper's car," I told her. She looked at me, expectantly.

"And ..."

"It wouldn't start."

She took a bite, chewed, thought. "It was running when you turned it off."

"Yep."

"There's more, isn't there? You're not telling me something." She took a sip of coffee and made a little face.

"I'm not telling you about the rag someone stuffed in the tailpipe."

"Ah ha!" she said, with feeling. "So, not an accident." She smeared a toast half with bright red high-bush cranberry jelly, took a bite and chewed. "Why would someone here want to kill a policeman? Does that make sense?"

"Not to me. Not yet."

She put a warm, quick hand over mine. "But you'll figure it out, won't you?"

Rosie came and topped off our coffees, then sped away. "You know Rosie used to have a terrible crush on Andy," Evie said.

"At the mission school?"

"Yeah. When we were in fourth or fifth grade, maybe nine or ten years old, he took on the big-brother job. She even called him 'brother' for a while. The Deaconess made her stop. I don't think she's ever gotten completely over that first crush."

Over the clatter of the breakfast crowd, I heard the door's dingy bell. I didn't pay much attention until someone edged through the crowd into my field of vision, searching for the last empty seat in the place, at our table.

"May I join you?" I looked up.

"Alice," I said, rising to pull out a chair. "Sure, sit down."

She hung her jacket on the back of the chair, and sat. At once the table seemed crowded. It wasn't her, she was tiny. It was the presence of the top curve of her breasts, clearly exposed and difficult to not look at. All of a sudden I didn't know what to do with my eyes.

To be honest, I had never been this close to this much of a pair of breasts I wasn't married to. Well, once. And I'd never even seen a pair this exposed in public. Okay, sure, it *is* 1956, where have I been hiding?

I was in the war of course, and saw plenty of pinups and blue magazines. I was still in college, although already past thirty, when the new men's magazine, "Playboy," debuted in '53 with a photo spread on the actress and sexpot, Marilyn Monroe. I confess I might have examined that magazine carefully. But otherwise, this much exposed breast hadn't been part of my life until this very moment. The fourteen-year-old, still living in my body just wanted to stare at them. "It's nice to see you again," I said, instantly regretting my word choice, my eyes fixed on hers.

She smiled graciously, and I knew in that instant that she knew exactly what kind of effect she could have in this little town, and she liked it. She liked being in charge.

She had been a teacher's wife when we met, already feeling helpless and betrayed. She had not wanted to come here and was not happy to be stuck here. And then her husband, who had insisted she come, got himself shot while moonlighting as a bouncer at one of the local saloons. I had been there that night, helping the nurse with first aid, trying to keep him alive on the saloon floor—and we did. He made it to Fairbanks and lived several days.

Although we offered her money to get back to the states, to go home, she stayed. That night she said, "Looks like now I get to make my own decisions." Her first had been to get herself hired as barmaid in that saloon. She was very popular there, and now I saw why.

I'd forgotten how tiny she was, not five feet tall, and slight framed, so that her voluptuousness surprised me. Blond, with hazel eyes, now with makeup and lipstick on, I could see why she'd be a draw at the Bide-A-While. I heard they built a step, running the length of the back of the bar, to lift her to where she could serve the beer—and be more visible.

Evie looked at her carefully, deliberately, at her face and at her breasts. It was a long, slow look, partly while Alice studied the well-worn, one-page menu. Alice met her eyes and the two smiled at each other. They seemed friendly but I'd long since given up assuming I knew what women were really thinking.

"Out of the hash," I told her. She nodded. "*That's* too bad."

Another few seconds of studying and, decision made, she set down the menu and turned to me. "I never got to thank you *properly* for keeping Brad alive."

The way she said it made the prospect of "properly" thanking me seem like it might be a whole world of—x-rated—possibilities. I let it go.

"I'm sorry we weren't able to do more."

"He was *not* going to live." She sighed. "He *insisted* on doing things. On coming here, on taking the bouncer job so he could afford a *better* hunting rifle—he already had two! In a way," she concluded, "he *insisted* on being shot to death and leaving me here alone—which turns out to be okay. I'm *okay* alone, or mostly alone." She looked at us both in her deliberate way. "It *suits* me."

It turned out she was a quick eater, being served her food after ours, but finishing before we did. She shook loose a Tareyton and lit it, after offering each of us one from the pack. She drew deeply and sighed a silvery ribbon from each nostril, tipping her head back to watch it rise, spreading at the ceiling. The move made her neck long and the expanse of it, with the exposed cleavage, even more difficult to not stare at. As women went around here, she was very pale.

We talked about the weather, about Evie's teaching—Evie had been hired to teach as her husband's replacement—and I remember some speculation about first serious snow. On a day like this, it would be hard to find someone to argue that snow wouldn't come soon.

When she finished her cigarette and stubbed it out in the glass ashtray, breakfast was over. "Thanks for sharing your table." She rose, reaching for her coat but then hesitated. She stepped toward me, bending, taking my hand on the tabletop in both of hers. She leaned as if to kiss me on the cheek—well, she did kiss me—providing me and much of the restaurant a full and spectacular view. I think I felt the room tilt and oxygen get thin as some

68

twenty-five men collectively gulped air. We don't see much skin around here, especially in the winter. Most women piled on more covering, not less. She whispered two words in my ear, then straightened, slid into her parka, zipped it, and turned to go. Smiling and greeting, she made her way to the cash register, parting the breakfast crowd like Moses at the Red Sea. Most of the room turned mid chew, or mid syllable just to watch her pay and go out. It was like that in a town with so few women. They always watched Evie leave, too, and she, fully dressed.

We walked back the several blocks to the rectory, hand in hand. "You did good back there," she said.

"I'm good with a fork," I told her, not sure what she was talking about.

"Yes you are," she agreed, "one of the impressive eaters, but I'm talking about the breasts. You did good not staring at them and maybe swallowing your tongue, like some men might."

"Thanks, I think. It seemed important to keep eye contact. I don't get how such a tiny woman can have such prominent breasts."

"It happens, but a lot of that is the push-'em-up bra she's wearing. Lifts 'em up, shoves 'em together, and stops traffic. I think I still have one. I'll wear it some time. Only thing I can't figure ..." She hesitated.

"What?"

"It seemed like she came in there for a reason, besides breakfast, like it was all for show, but I don't know why. I mean, well, it *was* all for show of course, but I just can't figure out what it was all about."

"She whispered something in my ear," I said, "but that's not all." I showed Evie the object in my mitted hand.

It was the yellow-wood chess piece, a bishop, that Alice Young had placed in my hand while distracting the room.

"It's about this."

CHAPTER 8

Evie stood in the middle of my study, holding a chess piece in each hand, the one from Richard's place and the one from Mrs. Young. "They look like brothers." "I think they are," I told her. "From the same set." "Nah." Evie examined them again. "With one in Fairbanks and one in Chandalar?"

I opened my mouth, but suddenly felt exposed standing there talking about possibly important stuff. I admit I glanced at my phone and at the place I knew the microphone still lay hidden behind my desk. I took her by the hand.

"Let's get some coffee."

"We just *had* coffee! I'm coffeed-out."

But she allowed herself to be led down the short hallway to the kitchen. I turned on the Philco and fussed with running water and the coffee pot while the tubes warmed and Perry Como's voice, singing *Hot Diggity*, expanded to fill the room.

When she looked at me like I'd lost my mind, I thought it might be time to remind her about the microphones.

"Oh-h-h." Her voice lowered and she glanced around the room as if she might spot more.

She stood the chess pieces side by side on the countertop and bent to squint at them at eye level.

"A knight and a bishop," she said. "We actually do know a bishop, but if there's a knight around Chandalar …except for you, of course," she flirted, fluttering her eyelashes.

"The thing is," I said, "I'm pretty sure I've seen these pieces before. Right here, as a matter of fact."

"*Here* here?" she turned, gesturing around the kitchen.

"Across the street at the parish hall. I was cleaning out games, I think in July or so, throwing away the remains of a chess set, and William wanted them. Of the original sixteen pieces, there were only about seven left. I was about to drop them into the trash when he asked for them and scooped them into a pocket. He said something about spare pieces always coming in handy."

We stared at the two figures for a long minute, as if waiting for them to speak. Fats Domino came on singing *Blueberry Hill*, and Evie hummed along.

"I like this song."

Still, the chess pieces refused to tell us anything.

"She said something to me ..."

"Who?"

"Alice," I said. "Or at least I thought she did. I couldn't quite make it out and it seemed like it was supposed to be a secret, so I didn't want to ask her to repeat it. Two words."

Evie looked at me, her very brown eyes seeming impossibly large. I wondered how she did that.

"Something like 'come with me to the casbah?'" she murmured seductively.

"I think I would have been able to make that out. No, two words, but they just don't make any sense."

"A name, maybe?"

"It sounded like nasal dee or maybe hazel dee or hazel bee. Do we know anyone named Hazel Bee?"

She gave me a scornful look. "Nasal dee! Sounds like a sinus condition. I keep forgetting you're new around here. *Hazel B* is an old river boat, parked at Nenana about a half mile back from where it joins the Tanana. It's sheltered there, protected from the Tanana breakup.

"Silly me," she went on, "thinking an attractive, half-dressed woman was brazenly nuzzling my man in a public place, and it turns out she was delivering an important secret message!"

"My man," I repeated with a grin. "Has a nice sound." She smiled and gave me a pat on the chest. "Let's stay focused." She turned her attention again to the chess pieces. "So *Hazel B* is a message from William! He can't call—the phone is tapped. He can't come here because your place is bugged—and probably watched."

"That's why they needed to get rid of Stanley!" I said. "They couldn't risk him watching, seeing *them* watching."

"Or worse," she added. "Remember, they were *shooting* at Andy." Her eyes narrowed. "We're going out there, aren't we?"

"You bet we are, cupcake," I said, trying for a Humphrey Bogart tone.

"Cupcake?"

"Well ..."

"I can be cupcake," she said, with more eye fluttering. "As long as I'm going with you."

With the mission priest at Nenana off to the states on furlough, it fell to me to fill in with services at St. Mark's on alternate Sundays. Also to keep his pipes from freezing and his plants watered.

Nenana being the larger town, Father Gunn, lived in a stateside-type two-story house sheathed bright white with those new asbestos shingles that don't burn or stain, never need painting, and blind you on a sunny day in snow. Also, in a region of six-foot snowfalls, inexplicably, this was another house built with a perfectly flat roof! I could imagine Father Gunn up there, midwinter with a snow shovel, trying to keep his roof from caving in.

"Doesn't fit much." Evie eyed the boxy white eyesore, plopped down hard by a turn-of-the-century log church building.

"It's better inside," I told her.

This far into October, the sun set at about four, with full dark about an hour later, just about the time we parked in the manse driveway and let ourselves in.

"Roomy," said Evie, "but not cozy like your place."

"I wouldn't trade," I said. We went around watering houseplants and closing curtains, finally turning on kitchen and dining room lights. It turned out Father Gunn had a television. We snapped it on and pushed the rabbit ears around until we could just about make out a snowy, black-and-white image of what must have been local TV from Fairbanks. "What is that?" I asked.

"Curling," said Evie. "Sort of like ice bowling."

We watched one man bowl a large, round heavy-looking thing, sliding it down the ice while another with a broom swept frantically in front of it.

"Sweeping creates a little glaze of water that makes the weight slide farther," she explained.

"People watch this?"

"There's nothing else on."

Plants watered, we went out the back door, noiselessly pulling the door to, sneaking away through a small wood. We looped the tiny main street business district—mostly a post office, general store and two bars—emerging in a narrow rail yard, headed for the Nenana River.

Nenana had been a railroad boomtown in the twenties, with a population of some five thousand. There was a hospital here then, vast railroad maintenance sheds, street

74

lights, even a water system. But when the railroad moved north, the town 'went south,' dropping to a population of several hundred within the next ten years or so, where it remains.

Most of the boomtown progress has been wiped clean by time. The abandoned warehouses and railroad garages were burned by drunks or vandals, or collapsed under the snow load, or were simply scavenged for homes, sheds and privies. Once, walking out in the woods beyond town, I found a circa 1920s fire hydrant, standing tall and narrow, as they did in that day, long lost in a willow thicket.

Streetlights had also been abandoned out on this side of town. We mostly felt our way down narrow sandy streets, frozen hard underfoot, until we met the railroad tracks. There we turned west to walk along between rails silvered by a rising full moon, above the clouds, high in a leaden sky. As we walked, a gentle sift of the season's first snow tickled our noses.

We didn't say much, sometimes held hands, stumbled a good bit, and looked around often for someone following, but saw no sign.

After about fifteen minutes of steady walking, a right turn at the North Nenana rail crossing, brought us—in about five more minutes—to the riverbank and gentle murmur of moving water. This would all be frozen hard and silent in another two weeks or so. We could make out the hulking cluster of riverboat shapes in the darkness, including several paddle-wheelers, one of them the *Hazel B.*

Here and there on the boats, small, dim squares of yellow window light cast a glow on snow flurries. Beside me, I heard Evie sniffing the air. "Wood smoke," she whispered.

"I'm sure there's a watchman," I whispered back. I'd brought the .38, and even now had it in my hand, in my coat pocket.

"You got my message," said a soft voice, just over my left shoulder, startling me so badly I darn near clenched and shot a hole in my leg!

"William!" Evie threw her arms around him. I put out my hand but he hugged me, too, seeming—here in darkness—more ebullient, less the austere government-agent Russian.

He led us down a path by the riverbank to the last boat and across a short gangplank. From what I could tell in darkness, *Hazel B* was shorter and less tall than the others, likely carrying freight on the main deck with just the pilothouse and space for a small crew above in front. We followed William down a side deck, then up a narrow, steep stairway to an unlit door.

Somehow in darkness he found the lock with his key and turned it, opening the solid door into an unlit space about the size of a phone booth, with an inside, lightproof wall formed by hanging canvas. Pushing through the canvas overlap we emerged into a stuffy, interior room with another solid door on the opposite side but no windows. There wasn't much, a tiny pot-bellied iron wood stove—flat-topped for cooking—two bunks, a small wooden table with two chairs, and the Alaska staple, wood Blazo fuel boxes stacked with basic food and supplies.

"We're home," said William, and that's when I noticed the figure at one side, wrapped in a surplus army blanket, close by a small light bulb, reading.

Crossing to shake his hand I said, "Richard, we've been worried about you."

He unfolded himself from an uncomfortable-looking chair, unwrapped himself from the blanket and pulled off his frameless reading glasses. Taller and thinner than I'd imagined, he looked more the worried, introverted scholar than the smiling boyfriend of portraits I'd seen.

He shook my hand. "Have you seen Andy? Is he okay?"

"He's fine," I assured him. At least I hoped he was.

He reached to shake hands with Evie, too, but she wasn't having any of it, wrapping him in her arms and pulling him close. I had to admit, if anybody ever did look like they needed a hug, it was this guy.

I looked at William. "Alice?"

He shrugged. "We have," he hesitated, "shall we say, an arrangement. I knew she could contact you and believed you'd remember the chess piece. And here you are!"

"But …what's going on?"

"Well," he began, "you heard about Senengatuk?"

"Sure."

"It is about that," he said, turning to the perk pot on his stove top. "Coffee from the red can?" he asked, reaching—then freezing—as a small but insistent buzzer began to sound. "We have company," he said with an intent look. "Were you followed?"

"Not so we could tell."

He shot his wrist from his sweater sleeve to glance at his wristwatch. "Probably not the watchman." Another buzz sounded. "More than one," said William, still casual, thoughtful, listening.

"What's making that buzz?"

"An electric eye. I will explain later."

I looked toward Evie. What had we gotten ourselves into? Our eyes met as if sharing the thought. She said nothing, but pressed her lips together.

This tiny room had gone, in one buzz, from a cozy hideaway to a rat trap, with us as the rats! And why had I dragged Evie along? What was I thinking? Simple answer: almost nothing. I felt stupid, stupid, stupid!

"Can we get out?"

"Oh certainly," said William, smiling a little, lamplight glinting on his frameless lenses. "Our only real danger here is fire."

As if on cue, I smelled—first gasoline—then wood smoke, and heard a sudden, voracious crackling.

CHAPTER 9

"We go!" said William. He turned to Richard. "Don *all* your cold-weather gear, omit nothing. Now!"

He looked at me. "You have your .38." Not a question. I nodded. "You may need it. Protect yourself and Evie, I will cover Richard."

With Richard dressed, William indicated the door we hadn't come in. "I am turning out the light." His voice sounded calm, matter-of-fact. "We will go out this door and to the main deck. There is a boat alongside. We will *not* go toward the shore. If we stay together, we have little danger. This will be *the piece of cake*." Although he'd lived in America since the war, William still had trouble with idioms.

Outside the door, instead of pitch darkness, we found a short passage adequately lit with red light bulbs, and fire glow—the actual fire still out of sight on the shore side— already beginning to illuminate the open deck beyond.

"To the companionway!" William started out into the open, glancing my way. "Stairs," he added. He gave me a long look. "Pistol out!"

I started to say something about not *really* being shot at. As if in answer, the first of what would become a spray of bullets from an automatic weapon began to blast splinters at us, as someone out there really began shooting. Worse, they fired tracers, something I hadn't seen since the war. The lit slugs revealed even more of the deck, while allowing the shooter extra light to know what he was or wasn't hitting, and to adjust accordingly. Seeking to discourage escape, but having no idea exactly where we were, the shooter sprayed the deck randomly, as if playing. "Nuts!" said William, with feeling.

Easing along in the lee of the upper cabin wall, William reached the corner and paused to pull a pistol out of each of his parka pockets—the military, semi-automatic .45 Colts he favored. Risking a peek, pinpointing the shooter's location at the tracer apex, William stepped from cover to quickly fire two-handed, five or six shots from each—thunderous—and smoky in the still air. The tracer source jerked up and to one side, as if hit or startled. The movement caused lit slugs to arc away like light strings on a carnival midway, as the shooter dodged and ducked and then fell silent.

It was as good as we would get. In the sudden silence, the four of us bolted across the small, flat, open deck and down the stairs. I think I actually held my breath until we dropped back into shelter and relative safety behind the main cabin.

"Stand by this line," William directed, indicating the rope holding the boat fast. He helped first Richard, then Evie into the boat, a flat-bottomed Tanana River freight boat powered by a good-sized outboard. Even in semi-darkness, William wasted no motions. And he seemed calm, almost matter-of-fact about all this, while I could easily have jumped out of my skin.

He squeezed the primer bulb several times, choked the carburetor and the engine started on the first pull, burbling softly.

"Cast off!" he directed. I did, and managed to step into the boat without falling into the river, just as William powered up the engine and we swept, in a smooth arc, out and upstream into the river current. Then he made a U-turn, sliding with the current toward the confluence with the larger Tanana River, just a half mile or so downstream. By then, much of the top of the *Hazel B* burned brightly, the old dry wood crackling and popping, flames lighting a swirl of muddy river and much of the row of riverboats.

"They torched her," I heard Evie say. "She's seen so many years on the river—and now this. It's just wrong!" I patted.

We heard more automatic gunfire and saw more tracers, but none aimed in our direction. Then it all stopped abruptly as, in the distance, the Nenana fire siren started up. Luckily, the much newer *Yukon*, moored hard by the burning boat, had been built all-steel. Within about ten minutes, the first of the volunteer fire department would turn up with a pump trailer hauled by a pickup truck. They'd throw the intake into the river, and work to keep the other boats from burning. The shooters, whoever they were, would be long gone by then.

"Goodbye *Hazel B*," said William, as if reading my thoughts.

Crouching, I moved back in the boat nearer William. "Can you tell us anything?"

"Only what you have probably already guessed," said William, raising his voice. "They did not want Senengatuk to speak, and you see what has happened to him. They do not want Richard to speak either, and are prepared to go to great lengths to assure that he does not."

When we reached the wider Tanana, William turned the boat upstream, back toward town. "I must leave you here," he said, "and we will keep going. I had hoped we could talk." He looked at me, his face all but invisible in darkness. "Trust no one."

"Alice?"

"A little. But keep your wits about you."

"Where will you go?"

"Better you do not know." He leaned in. "Get to your truck, get yourself and Evie back to Chandalar as quickly as possible. You understand?"

"Perfectly."

At Nenana, William cut the throttle, tipping the outboard so we could slide smoothly, almost silently up on the sandy shore. Stepping out onto the dry, I gave the lightened boat a sturdy shove back out into the quick current, heard the boat restart and quickly accelerate upstream, under the huge railroad bridge and away. We were left alone on the riverbank as the sound receded, wondering—in the fresh stillness—what had just happened, aware again of snowflakes.

We caught hands, walking quickly along the river freight dock, skirting bright halos of the occasional streetlight or warehouse light. Ultimately, we crossed the tracks within a couple of hundred feet of the church and the pickup truck, actually breaking into a jog across the churchyard.

The pickup wasn't locked. No one ever locked anything here, and truthfully, I'd left the key in. The engine roared to life as I shifted into reverse in almost the same motion, flooring it out of the driveway, only turning on the lights as we rounded the corner, heading for Chandalar and the illusion of safety.

Evie slid across the seat to sit tight next to me. She levered the heater control to "HI" and clicked the fan to "hurricane." It was only when I began to warm up that I realized I'd been shivering.

"I'm freezing!" said Evie. "Shaking."

"The adrenalin helps."

"They followed us out there?"

"Must have."

"They were shooting at us! With a machine gun!"

"Yeah …like France, all over. With tracers!"

"Trying to scare us, right?"

I looked in the mirrors. I was going about fifty, as fast—faster—than any sensible person would go out here, on a stretch of highway called the Flats. It was well named. Highway builders had filled in ten absolutely flat miles of swamp and muskeg with rock and gravel to make the Chandalar road. Whoever had been shooting at us, could be following us out here without lights. It would seem easy, shadowing our taillights, but only because they weren't from around here and didn't know about moose on the highway.

"I think they're finished trying to *frighten* us." She looked at me, dash lights showing the worry on her face as she spoke. "Now they want us *dead*."

We slept together that night, as we had a time or two before. Not *made love* together. That adventure still lay in front of us, not that we hadn't both thought of it. Well, I know I had.

But we did lie down together, mostly dressed, my .38 close on the night table. Sleeping together felt like the right thing after being shot at together. We drifted off, joined beneath my motley of quilts and war-surplus wool blankets, waking up in each other's arms. Pulling her closer, I smelled the soft perfume of her hair and skin, and a faint scent of flowers. *We could stay here, just like this,* I thought.

"This is nice," she said, without opening her eyes, as if hearing my thoughts.

But in just a few more minutes, I twisted my neck around for a look at my Westclox windup: 6:35.

Turning back, I felt Evie nuzzle my neck, kissing me gently. "I love you," she said.

"I love you." There was a time I wondered if I would ever say those words again, and mean them. And now they came out easily, joyfully.

"But why do they want to kill *us*?" she asked.

"Because," I said, realizing, "they can't take a chance we know whatever it is Richard knows." It was then I realized who else they would be thinking that about. "I've got to warn Andy!" I struggled out from under the weight of blankets and from her embrace.

"You can't call him," she said.

"Not from here."

I left Evie making coffee, with a Remington pump-action 12-gauge for company. I went out the back door into about three inches of fresh snow, my .38 in my hand. Even the raw racket of the diesel power plant across the street seemed softened by snow. Furtively I jogged the block or so in darkness around cabins and through vacant lots, following the kids' summer trails, which I knew by heart, to the railroad depot and the town's only public pay phone.

Is this one tapped, too? What were the chances every phone in town had been tapped? Since there were only about twenty-five phones, total, it was at least possible.

"Collect call for Mr. Andy Silas," I told the operator, "from Father Hardy."

"One moment, please," she said in that odd operator tone, like she was holding her nose. The connection took

84

maybe thirty seconds, a progression of mysterious relay clicks and tones.

"Huh?" answered Andy, way off, clearly awakened by the phone.

"Collect call for Mr. Andy Silas," said the operator, "from Mr. Father Hardy."

"Who?" She repeated it.

"Oh," he said, "him. Sure, I'll take the call."

"Go ahead," said the operator.

"Andy!"

"This better be good. I was in the middle of a dream about being on a beach on the Mediterranean."

"We saw Richard, in good shape, with you-know-who."

"You saw him?" I could hear Andy, snap awake. "With I-know-who? But I don't know who, do I?"

"I think you do. But here's the deal. They were firing at us with automatic weapons. We had to run for our lives."

"Richard and I-know-who were firing at you?"

"No. The other guys, they were firing."

"You're not making a lot of sense. Where are you? I'll be on the road in fifteen minutes."

"Bad idea," I said. And then I took a chance.

"Remember that guy, Albert, you used to talk about from the mission school?"

"Sure."

"Richard was with him."

"But," said Andy, knowing full well what had happened to Albert, who always went in the opposite direction he was supposed to.

"Richard was with Albert on the *Hazel B*," I said again.

"Okay."

"And when the shooting started, we all jumped into a smaller boat. Once we got to the Tanana, Albert headed upriver to drop Evie and me, and then the two of them turned around and headed downriver."

"Downriver," repeated Andy.

"Yes, I told Albert to head downriver. Got it?"

"But I ..."

"Andy!"

"Yeah?"

"Get out of there. Quickly. Now!"

"Right," he said, "I get ya." For the next few weeks I'd play those last words back in my head countless times, because he hung up—and more. He flat disappeared.

CHAPTER 10

Evie and I stayed together mostly at my place and mostly stayed in, although I did walk her home in the evenings so she could sleep in her own bed. And yes, so that anyone—everyone—could see that she slept in her own place. The rest of the time, when I wasn't involved in the Sunday service and Sunday school, we spent together. She graded papers, and I read and frittered. It felt very settled and domestic. And I liked it.

Every now and again, one or the other of us would look out at the drifting snowflakes and call the other to look, too. And we'd wrap our arms around one another, sigh and just watch snow. Everything about it would have been perfect except for the nagging details of having been shot at, and of our missing friends.

We were up to about a foot of snow. The temperature had eased down to below zero—where it would likely stay until April. And although the sun didn't rise fully until almost eleven, we enjoyed a serviceable Arctic twilight from about 9:30 on.

By then, no one had shot at either Evie or me in more than two weeks, the tap seemed to be off my phone, and—to my astonishment—the next time I checked my office microphone bugs, they had disappeared, or possibly been replaced by better-hidden ones. We were still careful about what we said to each other.

Rosie Jimmy came to see me after her Coffee Cup shift, bright and early on the first Monday in November. It had snowed again over that weekend.

"I don't love Andy," said Rosie, climbing out of her cold-weather gear and settling herself in my "customer" chair. "He's a sinner," she announced.

"Well, he might be," I said. "What else is he?"

"Huh?"

"What else is Andy to you? What else has he been in your life?"

"Well, I ..." She looked at me. "What do you mean?"

"Is he your friend?"

"Yes."

"Protector?"

"Sometimes."

"A really good guy who would give you the shirt off his back?"

"Well, sure. But he's still a sinner. He's doing this bad thing we can't talk about."

"But is he your neighbor?"

She shook her head. "He lives in Fairbanks."

"Still your neighbor, in a Biblical sense." She looked confused. "What did Jesus say about your neighbor?"

She sighed. "He said to love your neighbor. That's what I been *trying* to do! Now I find out he can't love me back."

"Jesus didn't say there'd be a payoff, at least not on earth. He just said love your neighbor. That's Rule Number One."

"But ..." she said, "isn't he sinning?"

"I don't know. Maybe. But aren't a lot of us sinning a lot of the time? I mean, technically? If Jesus said to love the ones who aren't sinning, I'm not sure I could figure out who that was. Could you? I think we're supposed to love each other anyway."

"So ...Rule Number One," Rosie said softly.

"Yep."

She got up and reached for her parka. "I don't know if I can do that," she said sadly, and went out.

With Evie teaching, I had to drink my morning coffee by myself, which gave me time—again—to wonder what had become of Andy. His restaurant ran itself. The several times I called, Anthony told me everything was fine. Cops were still coming in, the help were still taking turns spitting in the cop food, and no one had heard anything from Andy.

Since Anthony could order food and sign checks, there wasn't any reason things couldn't go on for quite a while without Andy, but with William, Richard, and Andy all absent and unaccounted for, I couldn't quite settle down. And I found that, even just walking about in my cabin, I felt uneasy without the weight of the .38 in my pocket. *Love your neighbor but carry a .38!*

A scratching at my front door bumped my pulse rate up a tick, until I recognized Adele's birdlike knock.

"He is coming," she said, when I opened the door, and I beckoned her in.

"Who is coming?" Just for an instant I wondered, *Did we jump to Easter?*

"My son is coming. Coming to visit, maybe even coming to stay. She unfolded a letter, written in pencil in a careful schoolboy hand, on a piece of lined newsprint tablet. 'Dear Mom,' it began. The letter had been posted from Mansfield, Ohio. The son, Butch, would be picking up a few things for travel, leaving in a couple of days, most likely hitchhiking.

"How did you find him?"

"I wrote back to his other mother, Bitsy." She smiled at me, joyfully, "I have a son! Now I will never be alone."

I opened my mouth to say something cautionary. But isn't that what always happens to the joyful? Someone wants to make sure they know their joy won't last. As though we don't all really know that already, deep in our cores.

So I let her leave with joy intact. She went out my door, into cold and darkness, with her heart filled to overflowing and a smile spread from ear to ear. I remembered the Wordsworth line: "Surprised by joy, impatient as the wind," and through the morning, found myself humming for no particular reason except possibly the contagion of joy.

The sun set just after three. Evie had gone back to her place to prepare herself emotionally and otherwise for another week of teaching. I heard a sound from my front vestibule, boots stomping off snow, then an unmistakable knock, not at all birdlike, rattling the door, and a man's voice, hard as stones, calling out, "Open up, I know you're in there!"

With my gun in my right pants pocket, my hand on it—and a good deal of trepidation—I swung the door open.

He put his boot in the door first, so I couldn't react and try to shut him out, then he bulled through, arms up to catch the expected slammed door and be able to push through anyway. Of course I didn't try to slam the door, in fact I swung the door wide, and I took my gun hand out of my pocket.

Although there was just the one of him, Fairbanks police chief Kellar had a way of making a room seem small. Some of it was attitude. The shouting helped, too. I

90

had difficulty getting him to shift aside so that I could get the door closed.

"I'm here privately," he said.

"Would you like coffee?"

"You tried to murder one of my officers."

"My friends and I saved your officer. If we hadn't found him, hadn't administered artificial respiration, he'd be dead."

"I suppose you deny stuffing the car's tailpipe."

"Stuffed!? Absolutely, I deny it!"

He got closer and, if possible, louder.

"I can't arrest you, but I *can* kick the shit out of you. And don't think I care about the white collar." He began pulling weapons out of his parka pockets, a pair of brass knuckles, a snub-nosed revolver and a leather sap. Then he crouched to remove a smaller pistol from a holster at his ankle.

"So you're here to fight me?" I asked, though the answer seemed obvious as he pulled off his parka and heavy mitts and swung my door back open, beckoning me outside. A wind-driven burst of snow and cold air surged in.

"Outside," he demanded.

"I think we should talk about this," I said.

"Outside now!"

"It's below zero out there."

"I'm not going to tell you again."

I took the pistol out of my pocket and he froze. I could imagine his thoughts racing. He had just voluntarily stripped himself of all his weapons, piling them on the small sofa I kept for waiting parishioners. He jerked his hands up.

I looked at him, looked at the gun, looked back at him. I had his attention. Talking to him now seemed a possibility but I have to believe policemen would be sensitive about being held—and talked to—at gunpoint. So I walked across the room and put down the .38 on a side table.

By now, with the door standing wide, the temperature of the inside of my front room was about the same as my yard. Maybe irrationally, I was thinking about all the firewood I had cut and split, now being wasted with the door open, so I made an 'after you,' gesture toward the yard and he put down his hands and started outside. I thought briefly of slamming the door and locking it, in fact the notion almost made me laugh, but I resisted.

"I'm going to hurt you," he said, not shouting now, standing in the snow next to my Ford. To my surprise, there were three more coppers out there, smoking and leaning on my truck.

"Don't worry about them," said the chief. And to the men he said, "Stay out of this, I can handle it."

"Yes, sir," they replied in a rough chorus.

"You realize you're about to assault me and that I'm going to press charges," I said.

He snorted. "To who?"

"Marshall Jacobs will listen." He paused, but only for a second.

"The Law won't save you." He pulled his ham-like fists up in front of him. He looked like an old photograph of John L. Sullivan, nicknamed the Boston Strong Boy in his day, which was a long time ago. "Wait a minute," he said, "I gotta pee." And he trudged off across the churchyard to "wring out the mop," as my Kentucky father used to say.

One of the coppers just behind me, muttered, "This is when I tell people to go down quick and stay down. If you do manage to hit him, and make a mark, he'll finish the fight by arresting you for assault. We have to testify for him or lose our jobs."

I watched the Chief walk back, zipping himself up, putting his leather gloves back on. "Hit me," he demanded, resuming his position, then lashed out with a right-hand jab that came rumbling in like a slow freight and might as well have had a whistle blaring to announce its arrival.

I met Mary when I was amateur boxing in the South, mostly around Chattanooga, in what were called Smokers—private-clubs, mostly for amateur boxing—held in places like the American Legion. They were well-advertised and well-attended, with a good prize purse. So yes, I boxed my way through seminary.

Flat on my back—one of few times—chimes ringing, I looked up through a haze of cigar smoke and the fight lights, to see a blond angel, fanning in my direction with her fight card. She spoke to me, and I swear I heard her voice clearly amid the cheers, catcalls and general shouting. "Get up," she said. It seemed like a blessing then and still does.

I started my shuffle in the snow, not too smoothly, and stepped aside as the large fist drifted by. Then I reached out and tapped him on the point of his nose with a gloved forefinger. His head jerked back like I'd actually slugged him.

He was too big for this game, too fat, too slow, held his hands too low. He also had the unfortunate habit of telegraphing his big hits by dropping his guard. He threw a roundhouse right, which I stepped inside of, and tapped him again, three times, once on the nose, once on the chest and once in the gut.

He tried a knee to the groin, but looked down first, so I had no trouble turning away from that, and was also able to avoid, by tucking and turning, a stiff arm that should have backed me up to the truck where he could use his weight and size to trap me for the 'kill.'

Already panting, he threw a clumsy left, missing. I could tell his arms were getting too heavy to hold that high—not high enough if I'd actually been hitting him—and his footwork, what there was of it, became erratic. After what couldn't be any more than three minutes of this, he looked ready to collapse, and would probably puke if he kept it up.

"Okay," I said, "I've had enough of this. You beat me fair and square." I half turned to the other police. "I give up. I'm throwing in the towel. You've got to break this up!"

They looked at each other. They weren't a quick bunch, but the three of them together were able to figure out it was time for this to end. As a group they stepped between the chief and me.

"Okay, Chief," one of them said. "That's enough. You got him. He surrenders."

The Chief looked exhausted and sweaty. "Well, okay then." He dropped his fists to stand slack-shouldered, staring at me.

"You're under arrest for assault," he said.

"Uh, Chief," said the one who had warned me. "Uh, he isn't."

The chief flared, or maybe sputtered. There wasn't much left. "He assaulted me, you saw it."

The cop stepped closer to him. "You got no bruises. The guy never laid a glove on you. And we can't testify if you got no bruise."

"Well, give me a bruise then," ordered the chief. "You hit me."

The cop stepped back—out of range—I thought. "No can do, sir," he said. Wisely, I thought. He opened the back door of the patrol car. "Let's get out of here, sir. Let's go home."

"Well," said the chief, "okay." He looked at me. "You got off lucky today," he warned. "You won't again."

"Yessir," I said. And that was it.

One of the cops came in with me to get the chief's stuff. "I'm Bob," he said. "You box, don't you?"

"Does it show?"

"And you had him."

I shrugged. "Probably."

"Did you know that Stanley is his son?"

"Had no idea."

"That's most of what this is about," he said.

"Makes more sense. How is Stanley?"

"Fine, but he's leaving the job, leaving Fairbanks. That's the rest of what this is about. He said you people were nice to him. Said he was tired of being on the wrong side. And there's more. The chief's older son, Harold—Hal—is in the hospital, all busted up, the chief says, because of you."

I must have looked as surprised as I felt. "That's crazy."

"Guess he's been working private—don't know what on—but about two weeks ago, tailing you, running without lights, his car hit a moose."

I admit I laughed. I couldn't help laughing, and the cop laughed too.

"Gosh," I said, "that's too bad."

CHAPTER 11

On Friday night, Evie and I went to see Cecil B. DeMille's circus extravaganza, *The Greatest Show on Earth*, at the Pioneers of Alaska Hall, Igloo #23. The Pioneers are a fraternal organization, like the Moose or Elks, so the hall is not a theater. We sit on metal folding chairs on a flat floor. The movies are no longer new, shown on a 16-millimeter projector that dates to before the war and probably before the Flood. Yes, *that* flood. The boy who runs the cranky projector comes early to build a raging fire in the fifty-five-gallon drum woodstove. So the audience progresses from freezing to sweating, usually in just one reel. Sometimes we scorch our faces while simultaneously freezing our backsides. The place gets comfortable just about the time the movie ends, with the fire burned down and the room finally warmed.

We watched Japan surrender again in the newsreel. We see that about every third movie, and the audience still hisses the losers. The first time Evie ever took my hand was there in the Igloo, which now seems like about a thousand years ago. But since we're no longer news, at least not *new* news, we hold hands openly, like a real couple at a real movie and we generally have a good time. I've seen so few movies in my life that I still expect them to be in black and white. I miss black and white. Life seemed simpler then.

We walked home the long way, down snowy roads instead of back trails and shortcuts. With streets already packed hard, strolling was easy and pleasant with Evie on my arm, under the occasional streetlight and gentle sift of falling snow. We were out late, by Chandalar standards—

after ten o'clock—and the town felt hushed, sleepy, and ours.

I'd left my porch light on, the rest of the cabin dark— unlocked, of course. As I pushed open the door and reached for the light switch, I smelled a wrong but welcome smell. Fresh coffee. "Andy?" I said cautiously, hopefully, into the darkened house.

"Just come in normal," he said from the darkness, almost at my elbow. "I already closed all the curtains." So I flipped on the light and Evie rushed to throw her arms around him.

"Where have you *been*?" she demanded, in her pushy-cousin way.

"Doin' what I should have done in the first place, realizing Richard was probably with William, probably right here close, and finding him.

"Good clue, by the way," said Andy, sipping his coffee when we'd settled at the kitchen table.

"What clue?" asked Evie.

Andy nodded in my direction. "This one, on the phone, told me Richard was with Albert and they went downstream."

"Albert!? He's dead. He took a wrong turn and drove …"

"Right," said Andy. "So on the phone, Hardy tells me that Richard's with Albert and headed downstream."

"So you went upstream."

"And got lucky. It snowed that night. The rest was just tracking."

"Surprised you were able to track William," I said.

"He's good, but I been livin' and trackin' here my whole life."

"And how was Richard," asked Evie.

98

Andy might have blushed, and he looked down at the table top just for a beat before answering. "He's good. Looks thin. I was just glad to know where he was and that he's okay …and that him being gone doesn't have anything to do with me."

"So what did you find out?" I asked.

"Nothing! Not a darn thing. That old Rusky wouldn't let him tell me anything. Said it only made it more dangerous for everybody." Andy smiled and shook his head. "Said now they'd have to find a new hideout, and made me promise not to track 'em again. I did promise. Told 'em if I could find them, anybody could."

"Ha!" I said.

The next morning, Saturday, was like old times with the three of us drinking Andy's coffee around my kitchen table. After that we walked him to the depot then looped back past the Post Office, stopping to work the combination on my mailbox and check my mail, something I could easily forget to do for as long as a week.

There among the 'window' mail and the letters addressed to 'occupant,' I noticed one handwritten address, sent via air from Seattle, with six cents postage in the form of two blue Booker T. Washington Centennial stamps.

"Handwriting?" Evie, glanced from the mail in her hand to the mail in mine. "You got a real letter? Who from?"

"From a dead man."

CHAPTER 12

"If you are reading this, I am dead," Peter Senengatuk wrote, probably just hours before being blown to smithereens. He hadn't mailed it then. The postmark indicated the letter had been mailed just five days ago from Seattle. My guess? That he handed it to someone he trusted, probably his attorney.

We read the letter together, walking the snowy road home. Evie's arm wrapped tightly through mine as we both squinted to read the handwriting in the dazzle of sunshine reflected off a million diamonds on the surface of new snow. We were reading a letter from the grave.

"We have never met," the letter began, "but I hear good things of you. My very good friend, Captain Simon Nicholai told me how you helped him on the Yukon, to right an old wrong, and suggested I contact you. He will vouch for me."

"Vouch for him!?" I exclaimed. "As though anyone in Alaska would need to."

Senengatuk wrote:

I hope to re-read this letter some years from now, and chuckle that I felt the need to openly admit my fears to a stranger. But I must caution you. If I am dead, by reading this, you and yours are endangered.

I suspect, but can't prove, that oil leases in the Alaska Naval Reserve Range are being manipulated. There is some trickery in the process of selecting leaseholders—limiting Native access, participation, and remuneration.

Be especially cautious with the Lakota, Edward Two Deer. If I am dead, it is likely he has killed me."

He signed the letter with his full name and the date: Peter Senengatuk, September 23, 1956.

"No!" said Evie, with feeling. "That's not possible." She let go of my arm and stopped in the middle of the road to face me, clearly upset. "He's wrong."

Abruptly I felt like I'd walked too far out on ice that I now heard cracking. "He may be wrong about Two Deer, but he's not wrong about being dead, which makes it at least worth considering."

"I ..." she said, "I can't." And she spun and walked off the other way, toward her own place instead of mine.

"And the day was going so well," I said, watching the back of her parka grow distant until I turned for home.

I heard my phone ringing, from halfway across the yard. I didn't hurry. I imagined it might stop before I got to it, and even as I picked up the handset, expected it to stop. But it didn't. It was Andy on the line, from Fairbanks. And my glum expectation was correct: not good news.

"Got a call from Kellar," he told me. "They're coming at three to arrest me for being a fag." His word.

"They made an appointment to arrest you?"

"It's nuts. I think they're hopin' I'll take off."

"You aren't going to, are you?"

"No point."

"I'm on my way."

"You sure?"

"Wouldn't miss it." I hung up about five seconds before someone knocked on my door. I hoped it was Evie, hoped she had gotten over whatever that was. But it wasn't.

Rosie Jimmy stepped in, her usually smiling face set hard in a frown. "I've decided."

"Come in." I held the door wide. It took me a few seconds to shift over from Andy being arrested to whatever Rosie might have decided. "Um," I asked, "what are we talking about?"

She gave me an impatient look. "About Andy. About loving Andy when he is doing …bad things. So I've decided I can't love him and I can't care about him."

"Is that what Jesus would do?"

"Jesus never dreamed of having Andy's children," she said. "What he's doing is bad and I want to see him punished. I think God does, too."

We looked at each other for a long moment. The room felt very quiet. "You're in luck, then. Andy just called, seconds before you got here. The police in Fairbanks are arresting him this afternoon at three for no greater crime than being in love with the wrong person. He'll be publicly embarrassed, probably lose his restaurant, probably go to jail and stay there for a while, maybe as long as five years. He could get *less* jail time for accidentally killing someone. Is that what you really want?"

She said yes, but didn't sound convinced.

"Now you'll have to excuse me. I need to drive to Fairbanks and be there with my friend when the police arrive. I want to be a witness to make sure he's treated properly and I don't want him to have to go through this thing by himself. It's been hard and lonely enough for him. So I need to go, okay?"

"Sure, okay." She went out looking stricken, closing the door softly behind her. It took only a few minutes to pull things together, enough for overnight if it came to that.

With the Tanana now frozen solid, I had no more waiting for the sternwheeler ferry to batter me over. Just beyond the city docks, the natural river bank ramped easily down to a double-lane, plowed ice road—not bare ice but packed snow over an ice base of two or three feet. Although it sometimes gave me the willies to drive where we had been boating, I knew that two or three feet of ice would be plenty good for a half-ton Ford and me.

I made good time on the Fairbanks road. It was actually smoother than summer gravel and potholes, and dust free of course. Snow isn't slick below zero so it was an easy, comfortable drive at forty-five to fifty miles an hour. I had the road almost completely to myself, with nothing to occupy my time but watching for moose and trying to figure out this thing that somehow involved Senengatuk, Richard, and Andy, and as if that wasn't enough, had now expanded to include Edward Two Deer, Evie, and me.

I found myself passing the Fairbanks city limits sign before I came out of that cloud, nothing decided, no epiphanies, nothing resolved. A few more minutes had me angle-parking in front of Andrea's, closed this time of day. I looked at my watch. It was about ten minutes to three. No sign of cops yet. I tried the door—discovered it unlocked—let myself in.

I found Andy sitting by himself in the dim room, no lights on, drinking a cup of the Italian roast. "I made extra." He did a head bob in the direction of the French press on the sideboard.

I adulterated mine with a bit of sugar and a drizzle of canned milk, two things Andy could not personally abide, and carried my glass mug to join him at the table. In the

103

silence we could hear the clock ticking down the moments of his freedom and of this part of his life.

"I dreamed of this." He looked around at the long polished bar, the tables with their red-checked oilcloth covers, even the reclining nude above the bar. "Richard loves that painting. Spent about two weeks on it. Went out to the University to find out how to clean it. He even patched the bullet hole. Kinda hated to see that go. 'Course then he hid stuff behind it." He took a sip of his coffee. "Now, looks like it's all over. Can't run it from jail."

"Don't give up on it yet. You'll most likely be out on bail by morning."

He smiled ruefully. "Damage done."

A squeak of brakes and doors slamming announced the arrival of the cops. We both stood. Andy had dressed for his arrest, looking positively cosmopolitan, but way too bright and cheery for Fairbanks, with his Boyer mustache neatly trimmed, hair Brylcreemed, canary-yellow slacks, white knit shirt and the sky-blue cardigan. Actually, the only clothes he owned that weren't khaki pants and flannel shirts.

The door banged open and Kellar bulled in, followed by Larry, Curly and Bob, the three leaning on my truck in Nenana.

"You," Kellar said, stopping abruptly when he saw me. I forced a smile at him.

"Chief."

"Wouldn't think you'd need me talkin' to you twice," he said.

"I'm here." I felt the anger rising. "Talk to me again if you'd like."

I felt Andy's hand on my shoulder. "Stay out of this, Hardy."

Kellar opened his overcoat to let his right hand rest on the wooden grip of a large sidearm. "Hope you're not gonna be trouble."

"He's not." Andy gently pushed me aside.

"I know he's not," said Kellar with a smirk. The smirk was what did it, and I admit I was headed in his direction when the door swung open, and for me at least, everything else stopped.

Into the place strode the most outrageously glamorous woman I had ever seen in real life. She looked enough like Italian bombshell Gina Lollobrigida that I'm sure my jaw dropped. Andy's did! It must have been the looks on our faces. I saw Kellar take a quick glance over his shoulder, then back, then a wide double-take as he and the stooges turned their backs on us completely to watch this woman move.

She wore an off-the-shoulders, white, satiny kind of dress patterned with bright red, quarter-sized dots. The red of her high-heeled shoes matched perfectly, and she moved like she'd been oiled, with absolutely confident long strides, hips swaying provocatively. Her low-cut dress accentuated the olive appearance of her skin, and what I now knew to be her push-'em-up bra lifted and displayed a pair of breasts that shimmered, and shimmied and shook with each footstep, as though they might have a life of their own.

As she passed the cops, who made no move to stop her, she tossed one of the trailing ends of a white silk scarf over one spectacular bare shoulder, and it hit Kellar in the face. He didn't even blink.

Reaching Andy without breaking stride, she handed me her white, swept-wing glasses as she swept him into her arms and planted her wide, wonderful, perfect red lips on his, nearly dipping him with the intensity of passion in a kiss that went on and on.

I noticed him helping, too, so much that when the kiss did finally end, he was dipping her. When the two broke, they looked up at us as if to say, "Are you still here?" Andy was wearing almost as much of her lipstick as she was. While she produced a tiny hanky from her bodice, to wipe the red from his lips, I looked around at the coppers. Their jaws hung slack. They were stunned.

"I'm back," she told Andy, clasping his shoulders, kissing him on both cheeks, gazing deeply into his eyes. In a passionate half whisper, she said, "*Dove e il bagno, mi amore.*"

"*Grazie, grazie,*" murmured Andy, with effort. Then she went in for yet another long, passionate lip-lock, which is when Andy reached behind her to cup a round, firm buttock in each hand, pulling her tightly against him and nearly off the floor. The cops turned as one and left. When the two came up for air, it was just the three of us.

She gave him one more light kiss on the cheek, whispered, "I will always love you," and turned to take her glasses from me.

"Cops gone?" she asked, needlessly. She sniffed the air and headed for the counter. "Anybody else need coffee," she called, returning with the pot to smoothly top us off, becoming Rosie again.

"It was a *really* good kiss," Andy told me later.

CHAPTER 13

Alaska's Territorial governors have always been appointed by sitting U.S. presidents, with little input—or none—from the people actually living here. Yes, it's a poor system, and one of the big reasons people think Alaska may become one of these United States, sooner than later.

Myself, I couldn't imagine Alaska a state. Too big, too wild, too fractious. Still, there were those who thought it could happen and should happen, and we were listening to one of them over breakfast as we dug into one of Andy's really good cheesy omelets.

"It is oil," the radio voice declared. "Tapping Arctic oil reserves on the North Slope of the Brooks Range will set Alaska free!" The speaker was Edward Two Deer, generally thought to be looking for nomination by President Eisenhower as first Native governor of the territory. Beyond that, who knew? President, maybe. That would be something—a Native president, about as likely as a Negro or a woman president!

But first things first. "A Native governor," I mused aloud. "What would that be like?"

"Hah," said Andy, "as if."

"Does it bother you that he's not an Alaska Native?" I asked.

"Not a lot."

"Evie thinks he's pretty special." I tried to sound casual but Andy looked at me a long beat, opened his mouth, then closed it.

"Alaska Natives," said Two Deer, "need to manage their own resources. These are the 1950s, modern times."

"Hear, hear!" Andy toasted with his coffee mug. "Red Power!"

"Red Power?"

"Indian self-determination." He took a breath. "Want to know what Evie—and a lot of others—think is sexy about this guy? Not the braids, not the stereotyped Indian nose. Just this: Red Power."

Two Deer didn't sound Native. He did sound like he'd been to school. His voice had a reedy quality, a bit nasal, and just a trace of an accent, southwestern, like Texas or Oklahoma.

"I seen him," said Andy, "on the street. He's Lakota Nation, from the Dakotas, North or South, I forget. Looks nearly white at a distance. Cowboy boots, cowboy hat, *expensive* suit, looks like they built it on him. But then he's got this big Indian nose, like an eagle, with one long braid most of the way down his back. Went to Harvard or some darn place."

The radio interview ended and a bouncy jingle about Jello pudding came on, the happy chorus singing 'yum, yum, yu … as Andy clicked the radio off mid-yum.

❖

The night before, Rosie kissed me as she said goodbye, headed back to Chandalar to be up for her morning shift at the Coffee Cup. She kissed Andy, too—pausing after each kiss to wipe off lipstick—and the two held each other tenderly for a long time before he slid his parka over her bare shoulders and the two walked out to her pre-warmed Oldsmobile. He'd started it for her, heater on high, just as she began to rustle around pulling her things together.

"What did she say to you," I asked when he came back in. "In Italian. I didn't know she could speak the language!"

He smiled and looked a little dreamy. "Perfect, wasn't it?"

"No kidding. Especially since we're not having this conversation through bars."

"She said, 'Which way to the bathroom, my love?' One of the only phrases she knows."

I remember we'd finished the coffee, and bantered a bit with Anthony when he came in to do his kitchen prep for dinner. Then the two of us had been talking about Richard, and about whatever it was he had that someone wanted, when two men wearing stateside hats and overcoats came through the door.

Andy looked up. "We're not open yet."

"Oh, yeah you are," said the one in front, the taller of the two. They stopped, took off their hats and overcoats, hung them on chairs, pulling leather blackjacks from the pockets. Seeing the saps, Andy's eyes met mine and we both stood.

"We want the documents your buddy Richard took," said the other one. "Give them to us real nice, and we're outta here. Nobody has to bleed."

The two looked like brothers, probably Indian but not from around here. They wore their black hair cut shorter on the sides, had brown eyes, lean, stringy bodies in cheap, badly-cut suits, and both wore western boots and bolo ties. Their sun-branded faces had lines and eye crinkles burned into the skin, and their flat, hard voices twanged.

They stopped, about five feet in front of us, setting themselves in a spread stance, clearly ready to fight.

The one in back stood completely still, slope-shouldered. His bare, square wrists stuck out beyond his shirt cuffs, his blackjack hanging from his right hand.

The other, the talker in front, gently socked his sap with his right hand into his left. I'd seen this tough-guy act before, not so long ago. It was supposed to look menacing and we were supposed to be afraid and to want to tell them everything we knew. It worked. I was pretty sure we both were at least nervous. I thought of the money and documents we'd hidden, but didn't feel like sharing.

"We don't know nothin'," said Andy. "Don't know nothin' now, won't know nothin' after you pound on us ...or try." He slipped out of his cardigan.

The front guy, sighed elaborately, did an eyebrow raise of false resignation and stepped toward us, roughly shoving over one of the neatly-set tables with a loud floor scrape and crash of silverware and breaking glass.

I stepped in front of Andy, so the first guy pulled his arm back to hit me with the sap. I left-jabbed him direct to the nose—feeling and hearing it snap—driving his head back, driving *him* back nearly into his partner, releasing a gusher of blood down his front. It had to hurt. It certainly hurt my fist.

"You broke my node," he wailed, and bent nearly double, eyes watering, holding his nose in both hands. "I just got healed up from the last time." His buddy handed him one of Andy's starched white napkins to staunch the bleeding.

"Occupational hazard," I told him.

The three of us stood there, nobody saying anything, just watching him bleed and coddle his nose. I had begun to think they might just take the bleeding nose and leave us alone when he straightened, stuck his hand into his

110

jacket pocket and pulled out a snub-nosed revolver—a .38 like the one I owned and wasn't carrying. He aimed it at me, the live round in every chamber giving off a coppery glint.

"One more dime," he said, his voice muffled and clotted by blood and the napkin. The room became very still. All we heard was the ticking regulator clock and the cocking snap of the twin hammers on Anthony's sawed-off shotgun.

The table scrape and crash had brought him, unseen, from the kitchen, to the 12-gauge behind the bar. The four of us turned together to see him now, training the short, deadly weapon at our visitors.

"Put the gun on the floor, easy, and leave now," he said quietly. The 12-gauge looked comfortable in his hands. "Do *anything* and I'll spray you all over that back wall. You'll have more than a nose bleeding."

The thugs exchanged a glance, and the one with the gun slowly dipped it to the floor. When he straightened, they both reached for their overcoats and hats and began backing to the door.

"We'll be back," said the bloody one, and they went out.

Friday afternoon from about four on, I found myself listening for Evie's footsteps in my front vestibule, her quick knock before letting herself in. Movie night this week featured one of her favorites, the manly Rock Hudson in a 1953 oater called, *The Lawless Breed*. Hudson was all the rage. Rosie, who studied everything Hollywood, had informed me that *Modern Screen* magazine declared Hudson the best actor of 1956. Only weeks earlier we'd seen his first film, *Fighter Squadron*, from 1948, which reportedly took him nearly forty takes to deliver his one line. He'd come a long way.

But six forty-five rolled around, and Evie didn't. *Were we supposed to meet at the show?* I wondered, but knew we weren't. I admit I didn't want to show up at the Pioneers' Hall without her. Yes, people would ask, and would wonder, and talk. So I sat down to lose myself in a book, but couldn't. At about eight I dialed her number but she didn't answer, and again at nine, and then I gave it up, turning in listlessly at about ten and not drifting off to sleep for a long time. *Had I lost her? Over this?*

Saturday she didn't come for early coffee, nor for breakfast. I decided to have lunch at the Coffee Cup. Sure enough, Rosie glanced around behind me as I came in the door, raising her eyebrows. I tried to look nonchalant but sensed she saw through me. I ordered the hamburger with fries for $1.50 and the Coke for another fifteen cents.

"Comin' right up," said Rosie, patting me on the shoulder, something she didn't usually do.

Was that a pity pat? And I couldn't help but think of just a day or so earlier when she kissed me on the cheek and drove away after saving Andy's bacon. The Italian bombshell had been replaced by the hard-working waitress in the pink uniform, with "Rosie," stitched in red above her now-well-concealed left breast. She wore her hair pulled back in a simple ponytail, with the teal-colored glasses, a yellow stub of pencil behind her ear, and a pair of high-top caribou mukluks to round out the ensemble.

"Hey Rosie," called a voice, "where's my lunch?"

"It's cookin'," she called back over her shoulder, patted me again, and whirled away.

Sunday came, with the service at eleven, but Evie didn't. No one asked me about her, but I sensed them wondering. Or maybe it was all just me. I felt like we might be having a fight, or at least a lover's quarrel, except that we weren't technically lovers. *Did we have our first fight and I missed it?*

Back when I was married, in seminary full time, Mary would say, "You can be so obtuse!" *Is this me, still being obtuse?* It certainly wasn't my intention.

Evie still wasn't answering her phone so Sunday afternoon at about two, with the sun heading low, I walked the couple of snowy blocks to her house, just to make sure she was alright. I found a note on cardboard, thumb-tacked to her door. Gone to Fairbanks, it read. Back Wednesday. So she had not only skipped out on me, but skipped out on her teaching as well. By now thoroughly dejected I trudged home, still not sure exactly what had happened.

On Wednesday early, alerted by 'bird scratchings' at my door, I opened it with my face still half shaving-creamed to find Adele in my vestibule quivering with excitement. In her beaded mitt she clutched a Western Union telegram. "He is arriving on the train today," she said, eyes round with anticipation.

"When did the telegram arrive?"

"Yesterday, but I didn't open the mail until this morning."

So the telegram had likely arrived in Chandalar two or three days ago from Seattle, then mailed overnight to Adele, who waited to open it. So much for speedy service. To be fair, if Adele had a phone, the Western Union agent would have tried to call her.

I settled Adele at the kitchen table with a mug of coffee—half canned milk—while I finished shaving. By the time I joined her, offered her breakfast, and started flipping eggs, it was still only about 8:30. The train from

Fairbanks wouldn't arrive until 10:10 …unless it hit a moose.

"His favorite breakfast is scrambled eggs," Adele told me, and his favorite color is blue." Turns out, Adele had written again to Edna—AKA Bitsy—to exchange "mom" information. She also learned that her "new son" Butch had been serving "a nickel" at the Mansfield Correctional Institution in Ohio. She informed me "a nickel" was prison lingo. He'd actually been put away for two-to-five years, but had gotten time off for good behavior—and a promise to leave the state of Ohio. She had no idea what he was in for, except that, according to Bitsy, he'd been falsely accused.

I'd already begun to imagine the talk I'd have with this guy, the 'jailbird.' Adele had become very dear to me, and I felt protective. The only reasons I could imagine for a guy like Butch to come this far, to a "mother" he'd not only never known but never even heard of, weren't good ones.

The depot is a five-minute walk from my cabin, but Adele insisted on heading out at 9:30. It turned out the train had been delayed, not by a moose, just late getting away from Fairbanks, so it wouldn't be arriving until 10:30. We waited on the platform at about minus twenty degrees, until I convinced Adele we wouldn't miss its arrival in the waiting room.

It was there I noticed a several-day-old *Daily News Miner* headline, "Political Action Committee Summit," with guest speakers including "Native activist" Edward Two Deer, and was able to guess what had become of Evie. I was still pondering what a "Native activist" might possibly be when we heard the distant train whistle and we hurried out to stand in the snow and the cold again.

Between the first distant whistle and the dark blue-and-gold train thundering, clattering, and hissing into the station, about twenty-five people appeared out of almost nowhere. Some had cases and were traveling. But most just turned out so they wouldn't be missing anything. Meeting the train was as important as listening to a favorite show on the radio. This way, they'd know who was in town, who was out of town—and in some cases, who they were out of town with—and have plenty to talk about over coffee or a beer.

As the train squeaked and squealed to a full stop, the brakeman swung down gracefully to place the stepstool and offer a smile and a hand to ladies and children. When I was a boy, I thought brakeman must be the greatest job in the world. It still looked pretty good.

About a dozen people got off, men, women and children. Spotting Butch was no problem. I'm about five-seven and Butch was most of a foot taller. He wore a too-small stateside overcoat, with plenty of wrist sticking out of the sleeves, rubber overshoes, and an almost completely useless black felt porkpie hat, the one with the flat crown and the brim turned up all around. For a man his size, especially with his huge, broad shoulders, it looked like he had a mushroom on the top of his head.

Butch took the hat off when he saw us, exposing his nearly- shaved head, large ears, and odd gray skin tone. He carried an honest-to-God carpetbag—a bit threadbare—that had to be left over from the previous century. It had probably gone south with northern opportunists after the War Between the States.

He shook my hand, making it disappear in his great paw, the skin calloused and as work-hardened as crab shell. Then he looked down at Adele and his gunmetal eyes softened. Right there in front of God and everybody he dropped to his knees in the snow, arms wide, gathering her to him, holding her close.

"Mama," he whispered, "Mama, I'm home."

CHAPTER 14

Evie came back excited. The impassioned speeches, by the first viable Native governor for Eisenhower to appoint, the fast track to statehood and full U.S. citizenship, had her blood at full boil. It was clear in her telling, with flushed cheeks and flashing eyes, that handsome, passionate, brilliant Edward Two Deer had been the lightning bolt of the event.

"It was historic!" She clapped her hands. "History happening in the room, and I was there!"

The retelling happened in my kitchen, over coffee, with Evie so excited that I might *not* have been there. It's an odd feeling to see someone you love become totally fascinated with someone else.

She had come in the door with her usual quick knock, hugged and kissed me, and poured coffee into the 1953 Anchorage Fur Rendezvous mug. Everything seemed the same, except it didn't. So I didn't have the chance to tell her about Rosie saving the day or about the arrival of Butch Nielson, which now didn't seem nearly so compelling as her news. The last thing she said before she went out the door was, "In twenty years, when Alaska's been a state for quite a while, when we get to vote for president, and Native corporations manage and profit from our oil and minerals, I can tell my school kids—or my own kids,"—here she got a bit flustered—"that I was there!" She went out triumphantly and closed the door.

So the next few days I threw myself into doing what I do. I split kindling, worked on my sermon, and helped people sort through used clothing and baby goods in the icy Quonset hut. Admittedly not much like plotting the future of the Territory.

I visited the sick, praying over them and anointing them with holy oil, as it says in the New Testament. Putting a bit of the oil on my thumb, I draw the sign of the cross on their foreheads. It's olive oil, blessed at the altar, carried easily in my parka pocket in a small food-coloring bottle. I like that priests and others in the Church have been performing this blessing for at least two thousand years. I like seeing myself as a link in that chain.

On Thursday, I helped a parishioner complete his overdue income tax returns for 1953 through 1955. He didn't owe anything, had never had more than odd jobs, and made most of his living trapping rabbit and beaver. But we both felt good to have him caught up.

On Friday morning, a bit after nine o'clock, I was at my typewriter, and had just taken a sip of lukewarm coffee when someone knocked. It was a serious knock, not a bird scratch or a cop-boomy knock. You can tell a lot about people by how they knock. This one had a firm, precise, commanding quality. So I wasn't much surprised when I opened the door to find the 'great man' himself, Edward Two Deer.

"Father," he said, stepping in, removing an expensive Stetson that didn't attempt to cover his ears. I couldn't help a quick glance at the thermometer. I could make it out through the layer of frost on the inside of my window: minus twenty-two degrees. Warm enough for earmuffs.

"Come in," I said, but he had.

I took his hat and waited while he shucked his heavy wool coat—not a parka but a long, dark, stateside topcoat. He wore a blue suit with dark cowboy boots, a white shirt and yellow-and-blue striped tie. His long black hair was arranged in a thick braid down to the middle of his back.

Depositing his hat and coat on my visitor sofa, I faced him. "Mr. Two Deer," I said, and he smiled. I supposed it *would* feel good to have people know who you are.

"Call me Edward," he said, extending a cool hand, soft to the touch. He hadn't been rough-necking in any oil fields lately.

I led him into my office and got him settled in the guest chair. He didn't burst into tears as so many of my visitors do. I supposed that was a good thing.

"May I smoke?" I nodded and he fished a pack of Lucky Strikes out of an inner pocket, selected one and torched it with a silver Zippo. He drew deep lungsful of smoke and then exhaled, watching the silvery streams drift to the ceiling.

I'd been in the counseling game long enough to know that smokers go through all their little rituals to buy time. They do it to control a situation. The party doesn't start until they finish up with the smoke stuff and are ready to start. I waited, the clock ticking, tiny dust motes dancing in shafts of morning light.

He examined me, and the room, and himself reflected in window panes. He seemed pleased with what he saw. With all that accomplished, he turned his head to smile at me sincerely and say, "I need your help."

I doubted he did. But just the same I said, "That's why I'm here." He chose that moment to notice, or pretend to notice, Evie's five-by-seven picture on my side shelf.

"I know her," he said. "I met her in Fairbanks just this past week. Evie …uh …Williams," he said, in a way that felt false. "She's from Nenana!"

119

"Chandalar," I corrected. I didn't know what else to say so didn't say anything, just tried to look pleasant.

"Look, I'll be honest."

For some reason I couldn't put my finger on, I doubted that, too.

"I want to be Alaska's next appointed governor, and when statehood comes—and it will, soon—I want to be the first 'duly elected' governor, not some white man."

I felt my eyebrows raise.

"Not," he said, back paddling, "that there would be anything wrong with an Alaskan *white* governor. But this has been our land—well, native Alaskan Indian and Eskimo land—for ten thousand years. We should have a say in how it's managed."

"I agree completely."

"So you'll support me?"

"I don't know anything about you."

"I'm Native."

"The whole town is Native. Much of the Territory is. Evie would make an excellent governor."

"A woman? Not likely. Who thinks being governor is woman's work?"

"Wyoming, in 1925," I told him, the only one I happened to know, from a report I'd written for high school history class.

"So you don't feel you can support my candidacy?"

"I don't know you," I said again.

"I'm like you. A regular guy trying to do a good job and get ahead, move up. Be honest. I'll bet you daydream about being Bishop, or Dean at a big cathedral. I'm the same. I want more."

I didn't tell him I didn't care about those things. I didn't want more. *Am I supposed to?* People keep telling

120

me it's what I should want. Well, Evie had told me and now this guy. Hardly a quorum. "I'm just a mission priest. I don't have a lot of clout. None at the territorial level. I'm not sure what you think I could do to make a difference."

Something flickered in his eyes—green eyes, I noted. He leaned forward.

"You can start by telling me where to find Richard Owens."

I'm sure I looked confused.

"Owens?"

"Richard Owens." He sat up straighter, took another big lungful of smoke and stubbed out his Lucky in my guest ashtray. "You remember," he said casually, as if commenting on the weather, "your buddy's fag boyfriend. It'll go better for Richard if I can find him before the oil company does. I think you already saw them at work, out on the riverboat. That didn't go so well."

"I *can't* help you," I said. "I truly have no idea where to find Richard. But I *am* curious why he's so important to your campaign."

He didn't answer, at least with words, but stood abruptly. The we're-close-friends veneer stripped away and I could see muscles working in his jaw. When he spoke his voice sounded quietly menacing.

"You better find him. Or things could go badly for you," he let his eyes drift to Evie's picture, "or your friends."

"Leave Evie out of this," I said, following him back to his coat and hat, anger rising.

His eyes locked to mine as he shoved his silly cowboy hat down on his head.

"It's on you." He shrugged himself into his overcoat and left.

CHAPTER 15

"You didn't tell her that Two Deer threatened you …and her? You left that out?"

"I didn't think she'd believe it. She'd decide I'm only saying it because she likes him—that I'm jealous."

"Well, sure you are," said Andy. "I would be. She's your girl. Or seemed like it until this guy showed up. Maybe I should talk to her."

"You must be kidding."

"Yeah, well, maybe I shouldn't," he said, coming to his senses.

Andy showed up on Monday's train, about lunchtime, packing a bundle that turned out to be a large Thanksgiving goose.

"No birdshot," he assured me. "Bagged it with a .22. Needs to thaw, though."

The sun came up about ten o'clock, brilliant in a cathedral-like arch of cloudless blue. It would set a little after three. Thursday would be Thanksgiving, the twenty-second. By the solstice next month, the sun wouldn't rise fully until eleven, setting just a bit after two-thirty, so about three hours and forty-five minutes of daylight. It was my least favorite time of year.

He also brought a loaf of Italian bread that Anthony baked up, crusty and delicious when warmed for a few minutes in the oven. We built sandwiches out of lean, dark slices of meat from our moose, mine with good old mayo and Andy's with olive oil. "Brings out the bread," he told me. And he brought along a fresh bag of the good coffee.

"Where do you keep getting this stuff?"

He grinned. "That's a trade secret." But then went on to tell me that a Catholic monk he'd met in Vernazza shipped it to him monthly in return for Andy's generous and on-going support of Italian war orphans. "I do what I can," he said, striving to look modest.

We had Fairbanks radio on. Tennessee Ernie Ford sang *Sixteen Tons*, taking us up to the news at noon. We got to hear a jingle from Parliament cigarettes about their recessed filter, "…a quarter inch to prevent dreaded filter feedback. Someday all filters will be made this way!"

"Uh huh," said Andy.

In the news, the British and French were irritating Egypt with plans to remove war-sunken ships from the Suez Canal. More locally, in Fairbanks, a break-in had been reported at the Federal offices of the Naval Reserve Range, the place Richard worked, back when anybody could find him. And we got to hear 'Native activist' Edward Two Deer speculate about it.

"Maybe it's a break-in," he said. "And maybe it's one more way to block the progress of the distribution of oil lands to Native corporations. When I'm governor …" I snapped off the Philco, mid syllable.

Andy took a bite of his sandwich and chewed thoughtfully. "He might be right."

"He threatened Evie," I said. "He's not right."

"Even a broken watch gets to be right twice a day," said Andy. "And you gotta admit, a break-in there now, is a large coincidence."

"It is," I agreed.

We had six for Thanksgiving. Evie and me, Andy, Rosie, and Adele and Butch. It seemed like more than six with big Butch in my tiny kitchen, all of us balanced on the tippy stools. We felt stuffed-in like sardines. Everything smelled, looked and tasted wonderful, and we all agreed that this Thanksgiving together would be the first of many.

Evie smiled and helped cook, but didn't say much. Andy did most of the cooking, with Rosie helping, and both cheerful. The two of them were cute together. They would have made a good couple.

Adele and Butch just looked happy. Neither of them said much or ever stopped smiling. I said grace and then added, "I'm grateful for all of you." And on Andy's behalf I said, "and I'm grateful that people we care about are safe."

"Amen," said Andy.

"Have to say, I'm grateful for Rosie," said Andy. "Otherwise," I'd be enjoying Thanksgiving from jail."

"I'm grateful," Rosie said, with a glance toward Andy, "for this goose." And we all laughed.

"I'm grateful for my son," said Adele.

"Grateful for my ...mom," said Butch.

"I'm grateful we could all be here together," said Evie. "Now let's eat, I'm starving."

Andy, Evie, and I did the cleanup. The others had gone and the kitchen seemed calm and quiet—and much larger. Inevitably, the conversation turned to statehood, to the recent political summit, and to Edward Two Deer.

"I just admire him so much," sighed Evie. "That he's Native with a real education, and that he's willing to do something that gives back to our people."

"And good-lookin'," said Andy. "Don't forget that."

Evie actually blushed. I dried a dish and kept my mouth shut. I knew how dangerous Evie could be with a kitchen knife.

"Okay," she said, "yes, he is good looking, and all those other things." She reached out to take my hand. "But I'm not …"

We all heard a dull thud at the door. We looked at each other. "Somebody forgot somethin'?" suggested Andy. We listened. If it were a knock, we didn't hear any more.

"I'll get it," I said.

It turned out we had one more guest, late and bloody. William collapsed in my icy vestibule. I dragged him into the warm living room by his parka, slamming the door and calling out to the others.

"It's William! He's hurt!"

Together we peeled him out of his cold-weather gear, right there on my front room floor, not wanting to move him again until we knew the extent of his injuries. The only bleeding turned out to be from a head wound. He was conscious, watching us, not saying anything.

"Should I call Maxine?" Evie asked.

"Not yet," I said. "Looks like the bleeding has stopped. Let's let her have Thanksgiving, if we can."

"Who did this to you?" I asked William. It took him a long time to answer.

"Not sure."

"Where's Richard?" asked Andy. Again we watched William considering the question for a long time. I'd seen this before, in France during the war. "Looks like he has a concussion."

"Serious?" asked Andy.

"I don't know." But, then I did know. We all knew.

"Who's Richard?" asked William.

CHAPTER 16

We called Maxine and she arrived in minutes with her bag, a little out of breath. She lived a couple of blocks over but knew all the short cuts, and—I suspected—harbored a sweet spot for William. She had a lifelong love-hate relationship with her impossibly curly, sandy-colored hair and so typically kept it tied down tight with a bandana. Today's was green.

"Yep," she said, "concussion. Somebody whacked him hard from behind. He probably never saw it coming. Can we get him off the floor?"

Together the four of us pulled William to his feet and walked him into my bedroom, stretching him out on my creaky bed.

"Got an ice bag?" I shook my head. "Ice cubes?" Didn't have any of those, either.

"Get me two or three snowballs in a dish towel?" I did, and she helped William roll to his side so she could position ice on the wound. She went down on one knee to make eye contact with the patient. "Do you know my name?"

William considered the question. "Mickey Mouse?"

"Funny," she said. "Everybody's a joker. No, really."

"You are Maxine," said William, in a less drifty way, and if you are curious, I am William Stolz, born in the Soviet Union, April 6, 1911. I was precocious from an early age, and ..."

"That's plenty." Maxine cut him off. "I think I liked you better when I was Mickey Mouse." She leaned over and patted him on the cheek. "Glad you're back," she said. "Keep that ice in place."

"I'm goin' out there," said Andy, after Maxine had gone.

"Out where?"

"Out where ever. I can backtrack William and ..."

"I'm going, too." I started pulling on my cold weather gear—parka, heavy mitts, high mukluks—including my 'cold-weather' .38 revolver and box of cartridges. We left William in Evie's capable hands while Andy and I slipped out the back door. We paused only to adjust to darkness before navigating the stand of willow and birch extending from my cabin across the undeveloped city block to the street behind.

It wasn't cold, just a bit above zero, with a light breeze. The moonless sky arced above, deeply black and brilliantly clear in the cold dry air. Layer upon layer of blue-white pinpricks of stars and a few planets extended— forever, by the look of it. A dog barked nearby. Distantly, a wolf howled. As my eyes adjusted, a snowy owl with at least a four-foot wing span, overflew us on a long glide.

We saw no one, heard no one, and made it all the way out to Andy's cabin at the far end of town proper—about six blocks—without revealing ourselves beneath a street light.

Easing into the cabin through the unlocked door, Andy managed to feel his way to a match and light a candle, shielding it from the windows. Andy typically kept all his long guns on a wooden gun rack in his cramped living room. "It's gone!" I said, glancing at the rack, seeing the top set of hooks empty.

"Not far." Andy knelt, pulled a braided oval rug aside, and opened his folding knife to pry up several floorboards. "Never bet somethin' you can't afford to lose," he said, drawing the sniper rifle out of its hidey-hole, swaddled in heavy canvas around soft flannel. From a metal ammunition box he pulled several handfuls of the five-round stripper clips, distributing them in his various parka pockets. He also pulled a case, about thirty inches long, six inches wide with curved sides and a strap for wearing over the shoulder.

"What's that?"

"Sniper toy," he said. "Show you later.

With equipment selected, he folded and stowed the bags back in their vault and re-placed the floorboards and the rug. From a Blazo-box shelf he grabbed a penlight, clicking it on and off against his hand to check the batteries. "Ready to move out, sir!" he whispered in mock military as he pinched out the candle flame.

Leaving the city streets, we struck out on a well-used trail, not surprisingly the perfect width of a dog sled. The trail led us slightly south and east, upriver, generally in the direction of the abandoned old mission school, just about a mile distant.

Starlight on snow lit the faint gray ribbon of trail. The foot or so of snow assured that nothing joined or left the trail without being spotted. Every couple of minutes Andy would stop, crouch, flick on the light—low—then move on.

"What are you seeing?" I whispered.

He turned to look at me in the darkness, only the faint pinpricks of his eyes visible from the depth of his parka hood.

"Did you notice William's boots?"

"No."

"You never studied," he said, shaking his head.

"Hey! I'm a priest, not a detective," I protested, still whispering.

"Redwings. New. Pretty distinctive sole print. Kind of checkered." He crouched again to chance the light, pointing to the boot pattern. "And this," he said. At the end of his pointing mitt was a round hole about the diameter of a quarter. "Not too steady here," he said. "You can see the wobble. Picked up some kind of stick to lean on. Easier to see than the boot print, sometimes."

"You're good."

"Aaaw," he said, with false modesty. "You're right. Been trackin' my whole life. That, and shootin'. Gotta do *something* well." He flicked off the light and we started again. Then he stopped.

"Thing I'm not seeing is any sign that Richard, or anybody else also came this way. I just guessed—well, knowin' William—and knowin' where he was the last time I tracked him, that we'd find these tracks here. There's a fork up here about half a mile. I'm bettin' we go left."

Another ten minutes of steady walking brought us to the fork. A quick check with the penlight told Andy what he needed to know and we did take the jog off to the left, heading toward the river and the old mission.

I'd been out here before but never at night. If ever a place felt haunted, even in daylight, it was this one. Most of the Natives in this part of the valley had lived here or gone to school here: Andy and Evie, Rosie, and their friends Jerry and Frankie—now both dead. It was Jerry who tried to kill Evie and me, taking us out on river ice, stripping us to our long-johns to watch us freeze out there. Until Andy put a bullet cleanly through Jerry's marksmanship metal, the one he wore on a zipper pull at the top of his chest.

I still thought about that shot. The three of us, Evie, Jerry and me out on the river, just about the middle, a place

Jerry chose so he could see Andy tracking us. He had Andy's long gun—the one Andy carried now—a German-made Mauser from the war. Andy shot its former sniper owner in Italy to claim it, a Karabiner 98 with the long barrel and Zeiss scope. To mount the scope low, Andy told me, the bolt had been reworked to turn down more than the standard infantry model of this gun, which also had a shorter barrel.

Jerry never heard the shot that killed him. I'm not sure I heard it either. Just a kind of *zip*, and down he went. With my father's old deer rifle, a Winchester lever action—admittedly some kind of special load—Andy put Jerry down on the ice and dead from most of a quarter of a mile. Most shooters would tell you the shot couldn't be made. Evie and I are here to talk about it only because he did make it.

But the trail circled the mission and headed for the river. It led us down the river bank and out onto glare ice. After walking on snow, the ice felt as smooth and solid—and easy walking—as a concrete sidewalk, so we made better time.

"You know where we're going?" I asked.

"I think so."

The Tanana here stretched about a half mile across. Some places, not so far up or downriver, it could go as wide as a mile. A left turn on the far side would take us along a low hill to railroad tracks and the road to Fairbanks. Instead, we turned right following only a pair of deep footprints through snow, sometimes drifted to our thighs.

"Keep in the tracks," Andy cautioned, something I was doing, just because it was easier than breaking my own trail through the snow.

We followed a snowy lane, about twenty feet wide, cutting a swath through a wooded area of small trees and around a wide smooth bend out of sight.

"Is this a road?" I asked, though I knew no other roads ran out here to connect. But then I felt ties, under my feet. "Railroad," I said, answering my own question. But I'd walked the tracks out here before, knowing there were no switches or spurs.

"Old railroad," said Andy. "Rails are gone here but they left the ties." He stopped and turned, speaking low. "Before they built the Nenana bridge, tracks ran down to the river edge and then across the ice during winter. I seen old pictures of small steam engines out on the ice in the middle of the river. There were a couple of places they tried it. This is the oldest of them. Nowadays it's just a dead end spur with one old rail car. I'm betting that's where they holed up." He paused, turned to go, then turned back. "No talking from here. Good chance this is a trap."

"And we're walking into it?"

"What's our choice?"

He had a point. I saw him flip back his parka hood, for better listening, and I did the same, hearing nothing more than the faint crunching of snow beneath our mukluks.

Around the bend, a bulldozed pile of rubble and downed trees blocked the roadbed, making this look like the end of the line. But still following the footprints, we picked our way around the worst of it, then over the top, where we found, not just ties but steel rails still in place under the snow. After another quarter of a mile, as the right-of-way narrowed with trees and brush closing in, we came to a clearing.

Sure enough, out in the middle—dim by starlight— stood a single rail car—an old-fashioned passenger coach

132

dating back to the mid-twenties. The car, with wheels still on, had been sided with vertical wood and I could make out the round brake wheels on the roof at either end of a raised brakeman's catwalk. The line of windows, like dark eyes, had been plywooded. The footprints we'd been following led to the far platform, and there we climbed three sturdy steel steps.

The door had been closed firmly but not locked. Standing to one side, Andy turned the oblong knob and pushed the door wide. A weak rectangle of flickery lantern light played on the platform and guardrail. Andy's eyes met mine and his eyebrows raised. Then he stepped first into the doorway, paused and went in. I followed. No one inside shot us.

"Left the lamp on," Andy said, taking in the long narrow room—about half the car length—still warm. It had been set up as an efficiency apartment in the wilderness. Along the divider wall stood several tall bottles of propane. "Smokeless fire," said Andy, indicating the bottles. There was even an apartment-sized propane range and refrigerator.

Two sets of bunk beds lined the wall, and a small compartment held a flush toilet, sink and the tiniest shower I'd ever seen, all testifying to the availability of running water and some kind of septic system.

Most amazing of all: the telephone. I picked up the handset, thinking it might connect directly to something, but no. I got a standard-sounding dial tone. If it hadn't been somewhere between two and three a.m., I'd have called home.

"Who even has a hideout like this," I asked. It was rhetorical. We both knew: Federal Government.

A bloodstain on the gray linoleum floor, a small puddle about the size of a drink coaster, and an extra-long flashlight with a blood smear and bit of hair stuck on, told the story. Somehow, someone got in here, whacked William and took Richard. But except for the blood, there was no other sign of an attack.

A pair of coffee cups sat half full on a Formica table top and two paperback books lay open, face down. One of them was a Nabokov novel. No trouble guessing whose that was.

The other had a picture of a large black bird on the cover. I turned it right side up to read *The Maltese Falcon*, hard-boiled crime fiction by Dashiell Hammett. I'd read some Hammett and liked it, liked Sam Spade, the hard-bitten character from the twenties and thirties. Someone had penciled initials on the inside cover, then erased them—mostly. I stuck the book in my pocket.

"This is just weird," said Andy, voicing both our thoughts.

"Um," I said, not sure how to proceed.

"Go ahead. Say it."

"There's no sign of a struggle or that Richard was forced out of here against his will."

"Yeah?"

"And we know someone walloped William."

Andy nodded. "Yep."

"So the best guess is …" I didn't want to say it.

"Richard hit him," said Andy. "And took off. But …why?"

CHAPTER 17

The first bullet hit so close, a spray of splinters and wood particles hit my face, stinging. We had just blown out the kerosene lantern and eased out the door onto the platform. I threw up my arm for protection, at the same time ducking and falling away from the shot, down the far-side steps into a snowdrift. I ended up behind a set of the huge—bulletproof—steel wheels, my heart thudding.

"You hit?" hissed Andy, with something like panic in his tone.

"Splinters," I said, gingerly stroking my raw-feeling cheek. "I'm okay."

"Shoulda known this would be an ambush."

"We did know," I reminded him. "We still had to come out here."

"Yeah." He worked the bolt on the Mauser and popped the covers loose on the Zeiss scope. Then he opened the curve-sided case he'd been carrying, pulled out one long tube and two short ones, threading the short pieces onto either end so they stuck out at right angles.

"What is that thing?" I asked.

"Periscope. Feel like running it?"

"In the dark?"

"It's got pretty good mirrors. Take a look."

He was right. Instead of darkness, I could easily see a monochrome woodland with every object distinct and three human targets crouched behind small willow trees that didn't nearly give them cover.

"Three guys with rifles," I told him.

"See any scopes?"

"None."

"Well, that's good," said Andy. "Now, figure this railcar is a line on the clock from nine to three, right across the face. You just look out there, pick one of 'em and tell me what time they're at, like at twelve or one or whatever. I've got a couple of pretty good sight-lines through these wheels."

"Can we *not* kill them?"

"Gonna be their call. They might not give us a choice. Got your .38 handy?"

"Right here."

"Got bullets?"

"You wanted bullets, too?"

He huffed, impatiently. "Gimme a time."

"Twelve oh five,"

"Okay, now ask yourself if twelve oh four or twelve oh six would be better."

"Well, six, maybe."

"Here goes," he breathed.

The rifle fired, the noise like a hammer to my left eardrum, leaving it ringing. The bullet cleanly split the small tree the target had been standing behind, half of it slowly folding to the ground. At the same time, a hoarse cry of pain, almost lost in the rifle report, signaled a hit. I could see him clearly through my scope.

Instead of falling over or hunkering down, the man leapt up, dropping his rifle, both hands clutching his behind.

"That's gotta hurt," I said.

"Where'd I get him?"

"Gluteus maximus," I told him. "Looks like a clean shot to the left buttock."

"How'd I hit him in the *butt*?"

136

"It was sticking out."

As I watched, the man's two friends ducked over to him and one picked up the fallen rifle, shouldering it next to his own. Then each got under one of his arms and limped him away through the sparse brush. I watched them until they dropped out of sight down a grade.

"Okay, they're gone." Andy rolled over to lean against one of the massive train wheels, replacing the spent shell and snapping the scope covers shut.

Distantly, we heard a snowmobile start up, the sound echoing. They'd probably parked it down below on river ice.

Andy exhaled audibly. "Wish it was always like that, one good shot and they leave. Trouble is, we still don't know as much as we didn't know when we got here."

❖

We walked home the long way, just in case. It would be too easy to just set up an ambush somewhere along the path we'd come, and wait for us to walk back into it. We found William still asleep in my bed and Evie asleep on the couch, the house gone cool. She had covered herself with one blanket but looked all curled up to keep warm so I covered her with another and kissed her cheek. She made what I took to be appreciative sounds, without waking, and I left her to her dreams.

While coffee perked, the two of us sitting at my kitchen table, we went back over what we knew. Only— as Andy said earlier—it felt more like what we didn't know.

First, we knew there was a lot of money, and an envelope full of oil leases, probably rich ones, at stake. We knew Richard had something to do with it. And we knew that someone thought *we* had something to do with it, which was why they kept shooting at us.

"So here's a question," said Andy. "If it really was Richard who bashed William, why now? They been hiding out for weeks."

"I keep thinking about that telephone," I said. "What if Richard called somebody? What if he found out something, maybe something that rattled him?"

Andy sniffed and took a sip of his coffee. "Didn't call *me*."

"No, he called somebody who told him something alarming enough that he needed to break out. He needed to get away and deal with it."

"Good luck figuring that out."

A distant toilet flush told me someone was up, and seconds later, Evie wobbled her way into the kitchen, patting Andy fondly on the top of his head, making a beeline for coffee. A slow awakener, she had an adorable cuddly quality first thing. Setting down her coffee mug she came to stand behind me, hugging my neck and bending to kiss me and rub her cheek against mine. Fortunately, not the sore one. It was a pretty good way to start the day.

In another minute or so, William came shuffling down the hallway, gingerly balancing what had to be an aching head at the top of his neck.

"Give me coffee or shoot me," he said.

"Sit," said Evie, indicating a tippy stool as she rose to fetch his coffee. "Clear, just the way you like it." She set the unadulterated beverage down in front of him, no cream, no sugar. The way the coffee god intended, as William had been known to say. He managed a sip of it without bending his neck much or tipping his head.

For a long moment, we all sat in companionable silence, taking solace in each other and the hot drink. Of course Andy and I had been up all night, so that made it easy to not have much to say. William had his brain rattled around in his skull. Only Evie had gotten most of a night's sleep in a warm place.

"As long as I have you all here," she said, "my ... men. I have news." She gave me a quick side glance. "And I hope you'll be happy for me." Something about the glance warned me.

"I have two weeks off coming up, and I've been asked—invited—to stay in Fairbanks at the Denali Lodge, and work for the Edward Two Deer political campaign committee. As it was described to me, I'll be researching and helping to speech write, as well as making policy decisions—and coffee. Now," she turned to face me. "Tell me you're happy for me."

"I ..." I said, but then couldn't come up with the rest of it. To make matters worse, Andy chimed in almost immediately.

"Sounds like a great opportunity."

Even worse than that, William added, "I am happy for you, my dear."

"Yes," I said, but at the same time conscious my head was shaking no. Her eyes narrowed and one side of her mouth tucked into at least half a frown. She stood, no longer looking cuddly.

"It *is* a great opportunity," I finally managed. But it was too little, too late. This had been one of life's tests that I managed to fail outright.

She stood by my side looking down at me. "I love you," she said, "but I think it's time to make changes in my life. The idea of a Native American governor thrills

139

me. Statehood thrills me, especially since it seems I get to participate. And," she hesitated, now not so sure. "I need the opportunity to explore a mature, honest relationship with a dynamic, intelligent, honest, man of my own race. I need to at least consider a life with someone who can truly know me as Indian.

"I need to feel like I'm moving ahead, not wonder if I'm being held back. I'm sorry." Kissing me on the forehead she turned, walked down the hall, out the front door—closing it firmly—and apparently out of my life.

One time, when I was about twelve and just starting to box, I got gut-punched. I nearly threw up. In one stroke I felt both sick and injured, and in that one same heartbeat, hopeless. Exactly the way I felt now.

I suppose Andy and William said something consoling. And I suppose they washed out their mugs and hung them on the rack. I'm sure they said goodbye. But I missed all that. The next time I looked up, the sun had risen, finding me alone at my kitchen table with a cold coffee mug in my hands, shaken—rattled—by the perfect storm of Evie moving out of my life and the devastation left in her wake.

The blizzard seemed appropriate. Within twenty-four hours the temperature dropped to the mid-minus thirties. The wind came up. "Hurricane gusts," the radio said. I built up the fire in the woodstove and sat close to it, holding a book. I would have said I was reading, but I still don't know what it was about. It was just something to hold while my thoughts, plans, hopes, and dreams whirled, shook, and tumbled.

In the end, I felt cold, trapped—very much alone—and about half buried, with snow drifts four and five feet

140

high, even obscuring the lower halves of many of my weather-side windows.

When it all blew over, I knew I had to dig myself out.

CHAPTER 18

Because I didn't get to sleep until nearly three, tossing and turning, I didn't wake up or get up until after nine. I felt pummeled.

I made coffee, made breakfast, and sat by myself, chewing food I couldn't taste, listening to radio stories I couldn't seem to follow.

One story that caught my ear, a rumor that my old team, the Brooklyn Dodgers, planned to trade Jackie Robinson to the Giants! As if that could happen. Trading Robinson, especially to the Giants, seemed about as likely as the Dodgers ever leaving Brooklyn. The world would end first.

I did get to hear Frank Sinatra singing his new hit, *Hey! Jealous Lover.* Appropriate.

And I got to hear a dandy quote from political rising star, Edward Two Deer, about his run to influence Eisenhower to name him governor. "We're putting together a campaign," he told the news, "gathering the best of the best here in Alaska, to begin making decisions that affect Alaska right here in Alaska, not all the way over in Washington, D.C."

Grudgingly, I agreed. I also agreed about the "best of the best." I thought fleetingly of calling Evie, or writing her a note to congratulate her and to say I support the effort. I knew she'd be pleasant if I did somehow manage to connect, but probably not too interested. I couldn't get over feeling like old news.

In the meantime, I had my own real problems to attend to. Like, nearly sixty feet of driveway with three and four feet of drifted snow, a snowed-in pickup truck, and most likely, an even bigger mountain of plowed snow at the street. I heard myself sighing. Deep in my heart I knew I'd be shoveling for days.

So the sun had risen by the time I wrenched open my outer porch door, pausing to admire the door panel impression formed in the snow to about waist height. I now knew to keep the snow shovel inside the porch, instead of, as with last winter's first big snow, having to wade to my shed to fetch it.

It was a perfect day for snow shoveling, the sun rising just a bit off due south in a freshly washed blue bowl of flawless sky.

Focused as I was on my own digging, it took me a while to notice someone digging from the street end of the driveway. From the far side of a six-foot glacial mound, I saw full shovels of snow flying at two or three times the rate I tossed mine. It wasn't unusual for parishioners to show up to help, but as I went down my list of likely helpers, Oliver, for example, I couldn't imagine any who could throw snow like a machine. Until finally I saw the top of his hatless, closely shaved head shining in the sun. Butch!

By the time I'd shoveled out the little jog from the porch to the driveway, he'd mostly cleared the snowplow pile. And by the time I reached the front of the truck, parked near the porch, he'd come halfway up the driveway.

By now I'd peeled out of my full parka and heavy mitts, wearing double gloves and a heavy jacket—it was still twenty below out.

Butch wore standard leather work gloves, blue denim work pants and a heavy sweater over a flannel shirt. As he worked, rivulets of sweat ran down his face, fell to the sweater—red with some kind of Christmas ornament design—and froze.

As he worked, he effused. How he liked Alaska, his new home—his freedom—the sunny weather, having a new mom, even the blizzard. He'd never seen anything quite like it and he told me how he'd rigged a lamp to shine outside and spent hours at the window, watching the snow fall, listening to the wind blow.

In about ninety minutes, we cleared the driveway and cleaned all the stacked snow off the truck, Butch even jumped up to shovel out the pickup bed.

When it was all done, I invited him in for coffee. "Nah," he said, looking around at the snow like it was bounty. "Thanks, but I got plenty of snow left to shovel around town. I should make the most of it."

"Let me pay you."

"Aw, you don't ..."

"I do." I fished in my pants pocket for bills. Even though we'd finished in less than two hours, it looked to me like a five or six-hour job, so I gave him six and threw in a dollar tip for good measure. He smiled radiantly, like I'd given him gold.

"This is nearly a full-day's wage!" And it's my third driveway! I've made nearly half a week's pay just this morning. Thank you!" And he grabbed my hand in his huge paw, shaking it enthusiastically.

A bright flash—a burst of sunlight off moving chrome—diverted us as a new Chrysler pulled into our freshly shoveled driveway. We didn't see many cars around here the same year they were manufactured. I'd admired this one in magazine ads, the Imperial model with the split grill, painted in black with white tail fins.

Sunshine blindingly reflected off the windshield kept its occupants a mystery.

It happened quickly. The driver door swung wide and a man in stateside clothing stepped out, leaving the engine running and the door open. He kept his head down, sun in his eyes, I assumed. So all I saw was the top of his gray fedora with a bit of red feather sewn into the hat band. With his black overcoat open, he advanced quickly. At the last minute, he reached into his coat front and too late, I saw him raise his head to look at me, exposing the adhesive tape pasted across the nose I'd re-broken for him just last week at the restaurant.

He was a lefty, grabbing my shoulder with his right hand, at the same time pulling the snub-nosed pistol from a shoulder holster. With his eyes fixed on mine, he jabbed hard into my ribs, painfully, with the pistol barrel, and I saw his eyes set and jaw muscle tense as people do when the gun is about to fire.

And he did fire, three times. Except that by then, to the surprise of both of us, the barrel aimed skyward. Cat quick, Butch had grabbed his wrist, yanking the arm up hard, stretching this guy all the way up on his tiptoes in the time it took to blink.

After the third shot, Butch reached up with his other hand to rip the gun out of the man's grasp. Then Butch easily lifted the man by the wrist and one leg, pitching him, maybe ten feet, into deep snow.

Gun in hand, Butch charged around to the Chrysler's passenger door, yanking it wide, finding the car empty, which was fortunate. A second man could have shot us through the gleaming windshield.

He did all this while I did nothing, standing in one place rubbing my sore ribs.

As the gunman picked himself up, wallowing in the snow, brushing it out of his collar and sleeves, retrieving his hat, Butch kept the pistol trained on him. So that when he finally made it back to the shoveled driveway, he raised his hands.

"What do you wanna do with him?" Butch asked, his voice different, lower, colder, with an overtone of …well, danger.

"Let's let him go," I said. Butch blinked.

"He tried to kill you."

"Yeah."

"Don't you want to …do something with him?"

I looked at him, looked into his eyes, which had grown troubled, maybe even haunted. I began to understand what prison in Ohio may have been about.

"Not my job. He's not worth shooting. Trouble would be over for him and just beginning for us. Most days there's no law around here any closer than Fairbanks. If we call them and throw him into the meat shed, we have to worry about him freezing to death. Let's check him and the car for more guns, and send him on his way."

I didn't mention that I'd be calling the marshal the instant the new Chrysler left the driveway. With two roads possible, one north and one south, it was a good bet he'd be stopped by the highway patrol before he got anywhere.

We found a rifle with a scope in the trunk, kept it, and sent him on his way.

"It's different up here," said Butch, thoughtfully, after the man had gone.

"Only if we make it different. A whole lot of people come to Alaska to get away from what bothered them in the states—and they bring it with them."

146

"I get it." Shaking my hand, he went off looking happy again, nearly giddy about the great good fortune of all this snow.

❖

"Tried to shoot you!?" exclaimed Andy on the phone. "For what?" I called him from the depot phone again and had to wait to answer until a roaring snowplow passed.

"Hard to believe he'd want to shoot me just for breaking his nose. It didn't look like I was the first one."

"Maybe he shot the other guys, too," said Andy.

"Maybe we should put that stuff back behind the picture," I suggested. "Remember, it was just after we peeled it off the painting and hid it, that people started shooting at us."

"I thought they were just tryin' to scare us."

"It worked! My ribs are still store from the jab with that pistol. I don't think you can call 'point blank' *trying* to kill us. If it weren't for Butch, I'd be dead."

"But why kill us?"

"Because whatever it is they think we know is a matter of life and death to someone ...or a ton of money!"

❖

Christmas came and went without Evie. On Christmas Day, Andy arrived on the train, and five of us gathered in the evening to celebrate Christmas with small gifts and an absolutely delicious moose roast, prepared by the Rosie and Andy Team. Adele and Butch came, still pretty much aglow with one another. Except once, in a quiet moment, I watched him take her hand. She held it briefly and then looked up to see me seeing. I smiled at her and looked away, but noticed how quickly she let go, gently pushing his hand away.

147

I invited William, but he had another commitment, I suspected with Alice Young. I couldn't help but imagine a completely different kind of Christmas celebration for the two of them.

We exchanged gifts, including a packet of Italian coffee for each of us, from Andy. I got Butch a brand new pair of leather work gloves. After seeing him at work, I knew the pair he had wouldn't last him long. And I got a few skeins of deep green knitting yarn for Adele, delighting her. I'd been here nearly two years and so far everything she knit was red. I didn't know if that was because she liked red or it was all she had.

Rosie had sent away for a bottle of aftershave for me. "It's the new Elizabeth Arden scent. Sandalwood. The most popular scent for men in America for 1956," she assured me. I thanked her and she put out a cheek to be kissed. I kissed it and she presented the other one. "That's how they do it in Italy," a tidbit gleaned from a recent issue of *Life* magazine.

Sandalwood, more popular than Old Spice? Hard to believe. She dabbed a bit on a fingertip and applied it below each of my ears. Then she inhaled rapturously. She got some for Andy, too, but he declined wearing it just now.

"Room's too small," he said, ever practical.

So we feasted on moose meat, high-bush cranberry sauce, potatoes from the garden, Rosie's moose-meat gravy—a masterpiece—canned peas, and canned peaches with a bit of vanilla ice cream. And coffee, of course. It was all wonderful. Or as wonderful as it could be without Evie.

After the Christmas dinner crowd straggled away, I sat on my sofa and finished the last dregs of good coffee, replaying my conversation with Two Deer. At the time I'd been worried about him snatching Evie, dragging her away, threatening her, hiding her. Okay, a little dramatic, but with people shooting at us, not completely out of the question.

Now—and partly my fault—he didn't have to snatch her. She put herself on the train and went straight to him and away from me. I had imagined myself protecting her. But there was not a lot of protecting going on now. "Nuts!" I said to the empty room, and again, "Nuts!" A dark sort of empty feeling—one I used to know well but hadn't felt for a while—began to envelope me, like a cold, gray fog moving on shore, surrounding me, cutting off the twinkle of distant lights and warmth.

Soon, I swallowed the last of my coffee, and feeling very much like a sad dragon from some old story, scraped my sorry claws into the bathroom to brush my teeth and drag myself to bed.

Tomorrow will be better, I told myself, but without a lot of confidence.

It was a long week until the New Year. Andy went back to Fairbanks, planning a big restaurant New Year's Eve party, and he invited me to go along. The way I felt I couldn't even imagine spending an evening like that with noisy, drinking, happy revelers.

So I did what I do. I visited and anointed the sick, worked on my sermon, shoveled snow, wrote letters to churches in the South 48—who sent us things—and generally moped.

My phone rang just about suppertime on New Year's Eve, and my heart sort of jumped. *Evie?*

"It's Rosie. I just want to give you a little bit of warning that you're my date tonight for the New Year's dance at the Civic Center. You do know there's a dance, right?"

"Uh," I said, trying to remember whether I knew that or not.

"No matter," she said. "Shave, comb your hair, use a little bit of that Sandalwood, and I'll walk over and collect you about nine."

"But, Rosie," I said.

"And I'm not calling you Father tonight, not on a date. I'm calling you Hardy. Get used to it. Nine." She hung up.

Last New Year's, at the Civic Center Dance, I kissed Evie at midnight for the very first time. I hadn't expected to. I don't even remember expecting to dance with her, but we did dance and it was very nice. And then at midnight, when everyone kissed everyone, I kissed her and she kissed me. "And now she's in Fairbanks and I'm here talking to myself." And I tossed aside the October *Saturday Evening Post* I'd been reading—the one with smiling President Eisenhower on the cover—crawled off the sofa and went to clean up.

So there I was, "saucered and blowed," as they say in the South, at nine o'clock when Rosie came to "collect" me.

She stepped in quickly when I answered her knock, paused to fiddle with the knot in my tie, and take a long, appreciative breath of my Sandalwood.

"Mmmm, you smell really good …Hardy." She said it deliberately, as if trying my name. She moved her hands to my shoulders and ducked slightly to enhance eye contact.

"You really need to get out," she said. "This is supposed to be fun. You can cheer up if you decide to. Did I mention there's no firing squad?"

150

I smiled.

"That's better," she said.

She took my hand as we walked over, or more precisely, her heavy mitt took mine, and just before we went in, she paused and turned to face me. "You're my date and I'm yours. For the next two hours we're going to dance and smile and look like we're having fun. And maybe we will. Andy's off doing what he does and Evie is off doing what she does, and we're here. Together. So come on ...and remember to smile!"

"You're right," I said, because I knew she was. And I did smile and we went in.

The Civic Center is a big gymnasium really, the center of the town where meetings are held, the town Christmas party, holiday bazaars, public school P.E. classes, Native potlatches, and town dances.

People toss their parkas on a section of folded-out bleacher, take off hard-sole shoes and dance in socks or mukluks on the gleaming floor. At one side, Cub Scouts were selling hot dogs and Cokes, and there was free coffee and a supply of boughten cookies from the general store. I hadn't had an Oreo since I came here last year.

Teenagers managed the music. They had a fat-spindled 45 rpm phonograph plugged into the house P.A., cranked up so loud I imagined a trumpet solo might bring down the walls, like Jericho. But there were no trumpets here, just jangling guitars. We danced to mostly last year's hits. I recognized *Shake Rattle and Roll* and *Rock Around the Clock*, by Bill Haley and His Comets, *Earth Angel*, by the Crewcuts, a couple of this year's Elvis hits, *Heartbreak Hotel* and *Don't Be Cruel*, and Chuck Berry singing *Maybeline*.

151

I danced a lot, though mostly just the slow dances, and mostly with older ladies and younger girls—those less likely to have come with a partner, or with a partner who would actually dance. I'm not much of a jitterbugger, so had to be coaxed out for a couple of faster dances with Rosie, who is really good. She reminded me she sent away for floor diagrams of where her feet were supposed to go, and then actually practiced.

At some point, I lost track of time and stopped looking at the big gym clock with its protective wire face mask, and gave myself over to the fun of it. Before I knew it, I heard fumbling sounds from the microphone, and a young voice say, "This is the last dance," and I discovered the evening at an end.

I heard the scratch of the needle settling, then the piano intro to a slow one. A shy elementary school girl, with absolutely no one else to ask, had come over to me as the absolute dregs at the bottom of her dancing barrel. I had already resigned myself when Rosie mercifully showed up and aimed her at one lone boy her own age, hiding by the bleachers. She hurried off with a grateful look as Rosie opened her arms and I opened mine and we began to hold each other in a warm comfortable, friendly way and dance.

"Forever my darling, my love will be true,
Always and forever, I'll love just you."

I knew the song, *Pledging My Love*, by a Texas singer, the late Johnny Ace. For me, the song had as many layers as an onion, of sadness and loss. Ace shot himself on Christmas night two years ago—1954—on a break backstage, for no reason but alcohol and stupidity. He was playing with a pistol and one of his band mates said, "Quit waving that gun around, man."

The story goes that Ace smiled at him, said, "It's not loaded, see," aimed it at his own head and pulled the trigger. Merry Christmas. Just try to live long enough to forget a sight like that!

It's the last song Mary and I danced to, shortly before polio set in and, in short order, she couldn't dance, then couldn't walk or stand, and then couldn't breathe or live.

"Sad song," I murmured to Rosie. "It plays to a lot of sad memories in my head."

"*Pledging My Love*," she said, "doesn't have to be sad. You just need a happy memory to go with it. And then we heard, "...three, two, one ...Happy New Year!" and all the dancers started kissing their partners. I looked at Rosie and she looked at me, and then we kissed each other, warmly, comfortably—as 1957 slipped in around us.

They were both right, Andy and Rosie. It was a very good kiss, and it made a warm happier memory. After I dropped Rosie at her place, I admit I walked home humming.

CHAPTER 19

"Caught your shooter." On Monday, Marshal Frank Jacobs settled himself into the guest chair in my office, balancing his steaming mug of undoctored coffee while trying—one handed—to twist his service holster to a comfortable spot for sitting.

The marshal appeared at my door about noon, about an hour after sunrise, having piloted himself in his government Cessna, down from Fairbanks. He declined lunch. "Need to talk." He always spoke like he'd be billed for the words, though now that I'd known him a while, he might relax and string together as many as six or seven.

He had come into my kitchen to stand near the coffee pot, about five foot eight, cutting a snappy figure in official olive drab and leather. Clean shaven but neatly mustached, his steely blue eyes looked out at the world from behind military-issue, amber-framed spectacles, probably not missing much.

We poured coffee and I led him down the hall to my office.

"So who is he?" I asked when we'd gotten settled.

He gave me a glum look. "Nobody. Well, claimed to be Bill Holden from Arizona—Nogales. Turns out he's really Lonnie Morgan, strong arm for oil interests in Arizona. He's working for somebody here but nobody knows who."

"And we can't ask him?"

"By the time we heard back from Arizona, a stateside lawyer had claimed him, paid the bail, and they both disappeared. We'll catch up with the lawyer but we've seen the last of your shooter. And no, he wouldn't have

154

told us anything. A guy like that doesn't work long if he talks."

We both sipped.

"What are you into?" he asked, clearly concerned. "He would have killed you. End of story. Yours, anyway!"

"I don't know," I said, meaning it this time. I had told him that at other times, when other lives at stake made deceiving a policeman feel like the least of my sins. But this time I really had no clue.

"It might have something to do with a friend of Andy's who disappeared."

"Oh yeah, government guy. I saw the flyer. Andy know something about that?"

I shook my head. "He's mystified."

"Heard you beat up Kellar," said the marshal, smiling for just a beat, changing topics, "in front of witnesses."

I managed a face shrug. "Never laid a glove on him."

He laughed, short and sharp—more like a bark—then grew serious. "He's big and fat, old, stupid, and dangerous. Kellar's been running Fairbanks a long time. It's not safe there for you, or Andy. I'm serious. The last guy Kellar beat up still drools."

With the new year underway, I had been hoping to see Evie, hoping the two weeks away might have softened her resolve to try life without me. Apparently it hadn't. I had a couple of small Christmas gifts I'd bought for her and still intended to give her. For now, I put them in a box on the small guest sofa in my front room, figuring I'd see her sometime.

I had imagined she'd get back from Fairbanks on the train yesterday afternoon, and maybe stop by on her way home, excited to tell me how it went, but she didn't. I stayed up until ten to give her plenty of opportunity, with a book in my hands—with no idea what I was trying to read—listening for a knock that didn't come, until I couldn't keep my eyes open any longer. Finally, I crawled into bed and dreamed everything about her: her smile, her walk, her voice, the scent of her hair, her laugh.

"Get over it," I said to myself in my dream. I knew I would but I didn't want to.

Monday's highlight was the marshal's visit, shedding light on almost nothing.

Tuesday I spent much of the day in the frigid Quonset hut, helping parishioners sift through for suitable clothing or to pick out baby supplies. It didn't help that several of our contributing churches were southern, one in Miami and one in Chattanooga.

I had written, suggesting to them several times, gently, that we had no need here for seersucker, especially Bermuda shorts and blazers, but seersucker kept arriving.

Wednesday, I had a vestry meeting in the afternoon, and sat in on a choir practice in the evening. One of the school teachers, Mrs. McMillan, played piano and organ, and had agreed to take on the choir, which numbered about five, which is sometimes three and sometimes eight. One of them, Oliver, is a hearty singer and complete monotone, but that seemed to inspire others to sing louder in a mostly vain attempt to cover him up.

Again, I fell into bed exhausted.

❖

The siren woke me at three a.m. I was on my feet, dressed and running out the door, still pulling on my parka and mitts, before I fully awakened.

Though still a couple of blocks away, the crackling roar of the thing in the clear cold night air terrified me.

Jogging along, my mind's eye filled with the scene from the last night fire, a row of three small pine boxes Oliver built in his kitchen to house the scorched remains of children who died in their beds. Pressing my knitted muffler over my nose and mouth, I ran.

Finding the fire was easy. I could see the glow from my front porch. Closer, it snapped, spit hot embers and roared, already so hot that even at minus thirty-something, yard snow melted.

We were all there: Oliver, Maxine, and Rosie. Evie jogged up just as I arrived.

"Are they out?" I asked.

Oliver shook his head. "Not all. Rosemary's still inside."

"The little one?" I asked, though I knew. He nodded. "Where?"

"Living room just inside the front door. Back of that room, kids' bedroom is a door on the left. But ..."

I didn't listen to the 'but,' and I didn't think about it a lot. You can't. I just turned and ran.

"Hardy!" I could hear the panic in Evie's voice. It matched the way I felt, myself.

This is the stupidest thing I've ever done. The knowledge didn't help.

At the front door, my face felt like it might melt. A rolling tongue of flame licked out as if to taste me. I dropped flat, feeling it pass above, turned my face to the relative coolness of the floor, caught a breath and slithered on my belly like a snake.

I'd visited here before briefly, knew it to be a small cabin and roughly remembered the layout. But now, inching across the floor, even the living room felt stadium-sized. Close-up I saw toys, boots, a braided rug, dust

157

bunnies—soon to be tinder, bursting into flame—and all the while the roaring moan just above me, like I'd fallen under a freight train.

Finally, I made it to the other side, found the open door and started in. I remember thinking, *Where's the bed?* Turned out there were four beds. I knew she'd be in the last one, no matter what I did, so I crawled from one to the next, to the next, to the next. Wrong, she wasn't in any of them.

Something—a movement—made me look under the bed. The flickering light revealed my moosehide mitt scorching, smoking, probably not too far from bursting into flame.

But beyond that, a small dark-eyed girl in Howdy Doody PJs, crying in the flickering darkness and smoke, clutching a wooly bear, coughing, tears streaming from her eyes and her nose running. I reached up to grab a wool blanket from the bed and beckoned to her. Clearly terrified, she shook her head, *No!*

"Your mom sent me," I shouted to her, coughing, pressing my nose back to the floor to try for a less-smoky breath "She's waiting for you in the yard. We need to go."

She looked at me, looked at the fire. I could only imagine her thoughts. She nodded an okay.

I got her by the elbow, pulled her out and wrapped her in the blanket. Off to my left, something crashed. I thought about going out the window, but a look toward the ceiling told me that standing meant putting my head into a rolling river of flame. I opted to crawl, trying to shield my face in the small wooly bundle I scooted along ahead of me.

I made it into the living room, made it to the rag rug, back across the boots, coughing hard. I could no longer press my face hard enough to the floor to get a decent breath and I could feel myself losing momentum. The beadwork on my mitts popped as threads and beads melted, moosehide blackening, charring, and beaver ruffs searing away. I knew I couldn't be far from the door. I remember seeing William's face appear from the haze, suddenly close to mine at floor level. And then nothing.

My cough woke me. Or the pounding on my chest. Or the shouting. Or the snow they used to scour my clothing to stop the smoldering. The cough started near my belt buckle and then just kept coming until I'd pushed out all the bad air but couldn't quite get to the part where my body pulled in the good air.

So I hung there, spasmed, for a long, long, slightly panicky time, until finally my body relaxed and I started to suck in clear, cold air—soothing as cool water on all my parched parts.

"Rosemary?" I croaked. "William?"

"All good," said Evie, bending over me, putting her cool cheek on mine, which felt seared and nearly glowing.

Someone—Maxine—pushed the plastic face cup over my mouth and nose, valving on cool oxygen that made the world look and sound suddenly much clearer and brighter. At the same time, she began to smear something salve-y on my forehead and cheeks. Someone called to Evie. "I'll be back," she said to me and got up, moving out of my view.

Maxine put her freckly face next to mine. "You saved her. But that was the dumbest thing I've ever seen in a whole life of seeing dumb things. *Never* do that again, do you understand me?"

"Yes, boss," I muttered in my mask. I certainly never wanted to do it again. She kissed my sore, forehead and went away.

From where I lay, glowing ash and embers rose from a fire already dying, toward stars in the night sky. I couldn't tell where the embers ended and stars began. I felt like the embers were going home and just for a moment, I wanted to go, too.

I felt comfortable there, lying on snow, suspended on the perfect fulcrum between fire and ice. I knew in a few moments someone would want me to get up and I'd have to. I knew I'd have first and second-degree burns on my face and legs, at least—the parts of me not so protected by my parka and snow gear. And then things would start to hurt and go on hurting for the next few weeks.

Evie and William came over. "Ready?" asked William.

"As ever," I said, sounding mostly normal.

"Hands hurt?" asked Evie.

"No."

So they took me by what was left of my mitts and hauled me to my feet, holding on to me for just an extra beat to make sure I stayed standing. I did.

"Want me to walk him home?" asked William.

"No!" said Evie, maybe a bit sharply. "I've got him." And she did have me. Though I knew, when this moment passed, the next one would be awkward.

So we walked back down the snow-packed street to my cabin, her arm tucked through mine. "Promise me," she murmured, "you'll never do that again."

"I ..."

She gave my arm a squeeze. "Oh, Hardy."

CHAPTER 20

I got a call to go to Minto to visit a probably-dying man and his family, administer last rites, and then hold a community church service in the rustic log church there. Bishop Bentley, in his day, Bishop Rowe, and most of my predecessors at Nenana or Chandalar would have gone out by dogsled. It's a skill I don't have yet. Oliver offered to mush me out there, but in the end, the Bishop sent a Cessna and I was there in relative comfort in about a half hour, instead of seated on hard, frozen sled slats for half a day.

I'd been there in summer, by riverboat, but this was my first winter trip. Sightseeing didn't take long. All of Minto was fifteen or twenty log cabins, a church, and a tiny store with a post office.

I planned to stay overnight at the log rectory there, which was even smaller than mine. Somebody had built up a fire in the iron woodstove, orange firelight flickering through the isinglass. I took a bundle of food but didn't eat most of it. The town turned out for a potluck, producing plenty of food, plus leftovers, some of which I ate for both dinner and breakfast.

It had been several weeks since the fire. My scorched parts had mostly healed and my frizzled eyebrows started to fill back in. I hadn't seen Evie at all since she walked me home that early morning. She didn't linger. Of course she had to be up for her second and third graders in just a couple of hours. She hugged me and kissed me on the cheek when she left, maybe a bit awkward. "I love you," she said, and turned to go.

"I love you," I said, mostly to her back as she eased out the cabin door, pulling it gently closed behind her as, it seemed, she closed the door to that part of our lives.

When I got back from Minto, landing on river ice and walking the half mile or so, I found my house ransacked. I left it unlocked, of course. Someone had been in, gone through everything I owned—including all the church records in my office—and dumped everything. Yes, depressing.

They weren't robbers. Anything I had of value—like guns and even a bit of money—were still in place. On the assumption I was being watched, I didn't hurry next door to check the church. I had a stash, in a hard-to-find hollow behind the altar that has come in handy for me several times, as now, filled with oil lease documents and a pile of cash.

There was a time I'd have called Evie. "I'll be right there," she would say, and come help set things right. And honestly, if I did call her now, I'm almost certain she'd come. But it didn't seem like the right thing anymore, so I put down my travel pack and started the process of picking up, reinserting and filling drawers and restocking closets and cabinets. Later I'd call Andy and fill him in. Chances were at least fair the same thing had happened at his house.

On the next Saturday, I took myself for lunch at the Coffee Cup. A sign in the frosty window advertised the two-dollar moose meat, potato-and-gravy lunch special, which probably meant the train had hit and killed another moose. When that happened, they just tied the unfortunate creature to the snowplow and continued on. It would be frozen solid by the time they got here. Sometimes they had to use a backhoe to peel the carcass off the front of the locomotive.

162

Rosie greeted me as I came in the door, in the middle of one of her coffee rounds. She was wearing the white glasses with the pink waitress outfit and high-topped caribou mukluks. As had become her habit, she chanced a quick glance for Evie behind me, just in case.

"One," she said, and I nodded. There were several empty seats available. I chose to sit under the huge dusty moose head, today the less-smoky side of the not-very-large café.

She waved the menu at me but I declined. "Moose special," I told her.

"You won't be sorry," she assured me.

The radio played Guy Mitchell's hit, *Singing the Blues*, which seemed appropriate to my mood. A jingle for Jello followed, the chorus concluding with "yum-yum-yum!" and then the news. "Humphrey Bogart has died at the age of fifty-six." I was sorry to hear that. He seemed so rugged, so durable, from *Casablanca* to *The Maltese Falcon*. I would miss him.

Just then Rosie arrived with the special. I toasted her with my coffee cup. "Here's lookin' at you, kid."

"Sad," she agreed, then we heard the doorbell tinkle and she turned her head to greet with her usual, "Sit anywhere," but there was some slight eye-widening that made me turn to look, too.

Evie came through the door followed by Edward Two Deer. She hesitated when she saw me, then came on to greet, kissing me on the cheek. Stepping aside, she made the introduction, "Edward Two Deer, Father Hardy."

"Edward," I said. He nodded.

"Father Hardy." He extended his hand, which I shook, but I didn't want to.

163

"We've met," I said to Evie, who looked surprised. So he hadn't mentioned it, either.

"We're talking politics," she said, "so we'll grab a spot over here and let you enjoy your moose meat in peace." I smiled, and they withdrew to the smoky side of the room, which I admit, pleased me. I knew well how Evie went on about cigarette smoke. "It should be against the law to smoke where people are eating," she always said. And I always thought, "Fat chance." But stranger things could happen, like rocketing a man to the moon.

The two found their table and pulled off their parkas, hanging them over the backs of the chairs. Just as they sat, Evie flashed a glance my way, and I felt Rosie's hand on my shoulder as she bent in a slightly intimate way to look into my eyes, smile warmly, lower her voice, and ask if I wanted more coffee.

I saw Evie's smile tighten and her gaze drop.

"You're trouble," I said to Rosie. "You did that on purpose."

"Yep!" Popping her gum, she raced away.

Hours later, I heard the quick knock, the door opening, and Evie's voice, "Hello?"

From the kitchen I called out, "Back here." Something about her brisk walk through the front room and down the hallway warned me. Sure enough, she wasn't smiling.

"Edward told me you threatened him—told him to stay away from me."

I opened my mouth to answer but nothing came out.

"You. Are. Not. In. Charge. Of. My. Life." She said, emphasizing each word with an index-finger jab to the center of my chest.

She intended to tap out "Do you understand?" Probably a tap for each syllable, but I managed to back out of range.

"I …didn't say that."

"Then what did you say?"

"Very little. It was his meeting. He came to see me, and did most of the talking."

"So, you *didn't* tell him to stay away from me?"

"No! Well, not exactly."

She had been loud, quite loud for Evie, but now she pressed her lips together and the silence had weight.

"Then one of you is lying," she said, much more quietly. "I have a hard time believing it's you, but Edward warned me you might say anything to get me back."

She drew a deep breath. "If you do have anything to say, I'm listening."

I weighed the chances of her believing anything I might tell her in this moment. Without much confidence I decided to give it a shot.

"Two Deer came to see me," I said, "and wanted me to tell him where Richard is."

"Richard who?"

"Richard Owens, Andy's …friend."

"That's crazy," she said.

I made an involuntary face shrug. "And when I told him I didn't know where to find Richard, and couldn't help him, he said I had better, or else. And he—pointedly—let me see him looking at your photo, and yes, I did tell him to leave you out of this."

Evie stood shaking her head. "Incredible." She stepped closer, reminding me of fighters I'd known, setting up for the short jab. "Did you think we broke up before?"

"The thought occurred."

"Well, we didn't," she said, and drew another big breath.

"But we are now?"

"Yeah. Kiss whoever you want, wherever you want, whenever!" She turned, but slowly, and walked down the hall and out the front door, again closing it softly.

I admit to being a bit stunned about how the conversation veered from threats by Edward Two Deer to kissing Rosie at the New Year's dance. Looking back now, the kissing thing seemed a little silly.

But it all made one thing perfectly clear. Word gets around in a small town.

CHAPTER 21

On Monday, answering the firm, but polite, knock on my front door revealed big Butch with his porkpie hat in his hands. He looked down at me. "Can we talk?" he asked, almost shyly.

"Sure." And I led him into my office to the chair. It wasn't a good fit, with him all knees and elbows sticking out at odd angles. I watched him get settled and try to find a way to sit comfortably. There wasn't going to be a way.

He'd changed in the roughly two months I'd known him. I saw him everywhere, shoveling, pulling, lifting, carrying. He'd do any job for a couple of dollars—or trade for a frozen salmon or chunk of moose meat. He was strong as two men and clearly just liked to work.

I suspected he also liked his freedom. He arrived in Chandalar, head still shaven and gray complexioned from prison. Now he had real color in his skin, though he still kept his hair only about a quarter of an inch long. He never wore enough clothing, as far as I was concerned, even at twenty or thirty below. And he always smiled.

Except that today, awkwardly folded into my guest chair staring at the floor, clutching his porkpie like a talisman, he didn't smile.

"I got a big problem," he said finally. Then he looked at me, eyes glistening.

"Okay."

"You know my step-mom." he said, not really a question.

"Adele."

"Yeah."

"She's your big problem? I don't get it."

"I love her."

"And what's the problem with that?" I asked, though by now I knew.

"I love her," he said.

"But not as your step-mom."

"Yeah," he said. "She's like the part that's been missing from my whole life. She sings hymns in this little bitty voice when she irons. She pets me and pats me—hugs me for no reason! I know I'm not supposed to feel this way."

"Well, actually …" I said.

❖

"Butch left town?" Andy nearly shouted, aghast. He'd come down on the train for a couple of days.

"Yep," I said. It was all I could say. "I took him to the train."

"Oh, poor Adele. First Big Scotty and now Butch. How's she doing?"

"She says she had two perfect months with him here and wouldn't trade them for anything. But I know she's sad."

Andy twisted up his mouth in sympathy, then changed the subject.

"Seen Evie much?"

I told him about seeing her with Two Deer at the Coffee Cup and her subsequent visit. He made a sympathetic face.

"I see her in Fairbanks pretty regular. Can't tell if she's goin' out with this guy or just, you know, doing politics."

The newspapers had Edward Two Deer trying to get a personal meeting with Eisenhower. "So we can talk this out, man to man," was the quote. Around here, he had become the hottest thing since sliced bread. For me, lunch at the Coffee Cup was just a chance to overhear a whole room full of—mostly men—go on about this guy who was going to even things up for 'the Native.'

Well, I hoped someone would do something, but I wasn't ready to believe in Two Deer. Something about him just seemed wrong. And then, of course, he had lured away my girlfriend. Would I feel better about him if Evie were still here? I didn't think so.

"Oh well," I said to Andy. There was no sense going on about it. But just as Butch felt like he'd found the missing key part in his life, I felt like I lost the key part in mine. And that actually wasn't the worst of it. If she'd just fallen for another guy, that would be one thing. But now, in spite of my best intentions, she'd deliberately taken herself off with the one guy who could hurt her. And what could I do about it? Not a thing.

We made coffee and then later Andy cooked dinner. It was moose meat, like everything else, but chopped small and stirred into a skillet with things like onions and carrots, then served all piled on spaghetti with some kind of sauce. He smiled over the serving plate. "How the Eye-talians do it," he said. It was delicious.

We agreed Andy would sleep on my couch, instead of going home at minus twenty-something to start warming his cabin. And then we sat and talked guy stuff, moose hunting, a possible new rifle for me, his restaurant, and finally Richard, who hadn't been seen since he walked away—or was dragged away—from William, out at the rail car.

"Somebody must be holding him," Andy said again. "I keep thinkin' if he could call, he would."

In that silence, we both heard someone knock and both looked at our wristwatches: 10:47. *Evie?* It was maybe a little late, but a guy could always hope, though so far in vain. Andy probably hoped it was Richard.

I left him on the sofa in the living room and went to answer. I flicked on the porch light just before opening the door.

I saw the gun first, a large handgun, maybe a .44 magnum, in a leather-gloved hand. This close up, the barrel loomed so large I might have been staring down a railroad tunnel. With his head pulled way back in the shadow of an oversized parka hood, I didn't recognize Edward Two Deer until he pushed forward into the light. I put up my hands and he waved me back down the hall to Andy, thumbing through a *Saturday Evening Post* he'd already read.

Andy looked up at him, surprised, set his magazine aside and raised his hands. "Not votin' for you," he said.

Two Deer waved me to the sofa next to Andy. "Nobody has to get hurt here. I know you have the oil lease papers and a big pile of cash. Those things are mine and I want them. Now."

I looked at Andy who looked at me, then up at Two Deer.

"Whad' ya do with Richard?"

"What did *I* do?" Two Deer nearly shouted. Having switched the gun to his left hand, he lunged at Andy, landing a sweeping, open-handed slap with his right. Even with the glove it made a loud sound and left a red mark.

"Ow!" said Andy, in an exaggerated way, clearly baiting Two Deer. It made me wonder if he hadn't noticed the gun.

"What have you done with Evie?" I asked him.

170

He thumbed back the hammer on the .44 and fired a round into the sofa pillow at my side. The impact against my eardrums hurt like a punch, and the room filled with sulfurous, acrid, gunpowder smoke. Both of us jumped to our feet.

Two Deer flipped his parka hood back. Seeing his eyes didn't help. The whites showed all around and he looked equal parts determined and crazy. "What part of *gun* don't you two understand?" He looked at me. "I don't care if you're a priest." Then he looked at Andy. "I know what you are, and I don't care about that either. The salient fact is, I have the gun and I'm here for oil documents and cash. You have them. You either hand them over now or I kill you now."

"Sure you will," said Andy. "Already shot heck out of a sofa pillow."

Two Deer hit him hard with the barrel of the .44 and Andy dropped as heavily as a gunnysack full of dog chow. Bending, Two Deer put the gun barrel into the small divot just behind Andy's eye socket, thumbed the hammer back and looked in my direction. "I think you know I'm about to shoot your friend. I should mention, I'm about to shoot him with his lover's pistol—fingerprints still on. Nobody's going to wonder too much about this crime. If it is one."

"And what about me?"

"Collateral damage. Some poor schmuck in the wrong place at the wrong time. Now," he said, "my stuff." I could see the small movement of his gloved finger tightening. "Last chance."

"Hidden in the church," I said. The finger relaxed.

"Get them."

"You're not worried I'll take off?"

171

"And leave your best buddy to take a hole in the head? Not a bit worried. Get it, now," he said, the finger tightening again. "Any reason you can't be back in sixty seconds?"

I looked at the gun barrel. "Guess not," I said, and went to put on my parka. I didn't have much hope for the two of us getting out of this alive. I wondered fleetingly if I had left my .38 in one of the parka pockets. I hadn't. I thought about just running. What were the chances he'd really shoot Andy if he knew he'd lost the papers and cash? Probably pretty good at this point. Two Deer seemed to almost want to shoot Andy, just because.

Although I'd thought of hiding a gun with the other stuff, the idea of a gun behind the altar seemed wrong—was wrong. Of course everything I'd ever hidden here was stolen stuff, but always for a good cause. How much worse could a gun be?

I wondered, fleetingly, how much time it would take me to dash to Evie's, get a gun and get back. Too long.

In the end, I pulled out the envelope of lease documents and the bundle of cash. I quickly removed about three-quarters of the documents—along with one of the cash stacks—to stuff back in the hidey hole, replacing them with a clutch of like-sized old mimeographed church bulletins to pad out the envelope. If Two Deer grabbed the envelope and ran, we were in good shape. If not, we were probably both dead. I admit I hesitated. *Do I really want to do this?* Sure, why not. We might both be dead anyway.

Certain I'd used up my minute, I came back through the rectory door and went directly into the living room where Two Deer seemingly hadn't moved, the purpling of Andy's forehead the only change I could notice. If he lived, that would be a nasty bruise. Two Deer straightened, his gun arm hanging more neutrally. It seemed a good sign. "You got what you came for." I held out his stuff. He waved it to the sofa. The scuffled envelope looked kind of shabby and not very valuable laying there next to the shot cushion. Last summer I got to see gold, real gold bars. These oil documents must be the new gold, as if they'd been anointed. What these documents represented was no longer just oil, but now some kind of holy oil, blessed by whatever it is that excites unstable people with greed and the willingness to steal or kill to get what they want.

"You don't have to kill us," He looked startled.

"I have my stuff. Why would I kill you?"

"Because we're witnesses."

He waved the gun barrel off-handedly. "Well, that's true. But I'm a rising star, and you're a man with no future—whose girlfriend recently threw him over for someone who has a future. And this guy," he actually kicked Andy, "he's a pathetic, love-starved pervert. He's not really believable, either. So," he met my eyes, "guess I'm not worried about anything either of you have to say."

He looked around and I could see him shifting gears. "Get his parka and mitts," he nodded in Andy's direction. "I need to park you two where you won't be a problem for a few hours. I did notice how quickly you were able to get poor dumb Lonnie picked up after he managed to screw up shooting you." I went to the coat hook and grabbed Andy's parka. "Get it on him," said Two Deer, even helping a bit with the hand not holding the lethal weapon. It's not easy getting an unconscious man into sleeves.

"You got a shed with a padlock?" he asked.

"Out back. You do realize it's minus thirty-something out there?"

173

"Lucky you have your cold weather gear then, right? All you have to do is hold out until morning. I'll call someone over at the general store to come let you out." He made as if to raise the pistol. "It's the best deal you're going to get." He turned and started toward the kitchen and the back door. I looked down at Andy. "Come on! Drag him," he said.

But it took both of us dragging, him one-handed, and I thought the whole way about trying to get the pistol. I knew if I did, he'd end up shooting one of us. Being locked in a meat shed overnight wasn't the worst thing that could happen. We could survive, but we'd be darn cold by morning.

Or, if he had crushed Andy's skull with the pistol barrel, one of us would be cold in the morning and maybe one dead. If Two Deer was concerned about that as a possibility, he managed to not let on.

With difficulty we dragged Andy down a too-narrow snow path the sixty feet or so to my meat shed. With this fall's moose all butchered, paper-wrapped and distributed to indoor freezers around town, the shed stood empty except for a few tools Oliver had asked to leave here while working around the place. It made more sense than hauling everything across town every time, since he walked everywhere.

As we dragged, I caught a glimpse of the sky, deep and black with a fingernail of gold moon just rising, and a vivid, writhing green curtain of the aurora borealis. Some people claimed to be able to hear it hiss. The *shushing* sound of Andy, dragging along through the snow, made that impossible.

At the shed, we wrestled him up the two steps into deeper darkness and the smell of old blood.

"Back!" warned Two Deer from the door—as if reading my mind. We both knew it was now or never. He waved the pistol, all but invisible in the gloom, to help make his point. "Don't want to screw up now," he said. "By morning this will all be just a chilly memory—and a headache."

So he closed the door and I let him, relieved, if truth be told. We'd live to tell about this. Two Deer snapped-shut the padlock, which had been hanging open on the hasp. I heard his footsteps faintly, as he walked away, just the smallest crunch of snow under his stateside galoshes. I stood there in darkness, thinking about Evie, again—still. The loss of her ached as badly as a hammered thumb. It hurt all the time and then sometimes—like when I banged up to a moment that might have had her in it—hurt more.

I wondered if she were here or in Fairbanks, maybe studying or sleeping, or maybe locked up somewhere too, a captive like Andy and me.

There were no chairs in the meat shed, nothing soft to sit on or warmer than the minus thirty-something hard, splintery floorboards. Andy groaned.

Then I heard footsteps coming back. He'd changed his mind, come to his senses. I remember feeling briefly very glad, until I heard the surge and splash of liquid all around the shed perimeter and smelled gasoline.

CHAPTER 22

"U-u-uh." I could feel Andy sit up, his movement brushing against my legs in the darkness. "Can't see," he said. "Hit me too hard. I'm blind! Shit!"

"Relax. It's pitch dark and you're in the meat shed."

"Oh," he said, calming. "That's good, I guess. Explains the smell."

"Only for another minute or two. That liquid you hear pouring?"

"Yeah?"

"Gas! Two Deer is planning a barbecue."

"Us." He sat silent for a moment. Outside I heard the gurgle and soft *bloop* of the last gas from the metal can, the clank of the thrown can against the shed side, then the rattle of the match box—probably matches from my kitchen, which irritated me. I heard one, and then another scratch and break, and then the metallic ping of the Zippo lid flipping.

The explosive, soft *whoosh* of the gas igniting and almost immediate crackle of shed wood catching fire brought Andy to his feet. Flickering yellow-orange light shone through cracks and knotholes, revealing the shed interior with a dim glow. No wonder I had trouble with mice in here!

"What we got for tools?" Andy, still wobbly, did a quick circle of the eight by twelve space.

"Nothing!" I said. "It's a meat shed." I turned a full circle in place. Sure enough, flames all around, the dim shed interior already turning hazy with smoke.

"It's something," said Andy from a back corner. "Some stuff stacked here. Something yellow. Oh, goody."

"Goody, what?"

"Found a can of gasoline. We can burn our way out!"

"Funny! No sign of an axe? We could chop our way?"

"No axe," he said.

I heard a switch click and a pulling, ratcheting sound. "Guess we'll have to make do with Oliver's chain saw. Hope it's got fuel in it. Not gonna be able to gas it up with flames all around."

The engine caught immediately, filling the too-close space with raw, brutal racket and fuel-sweet two-stroke exhaust. It seemed hopeful. We didn't have too many minutes left alive in here. Andy stepped to the wall, revved the saw hard and pushed the spinning chain against one of the wall studs. The engine stalled immediately.

In maybe a minute, the temperature inside the shed had gone from icy cold to stifling and airless. My hopes plummeted as rising panic made me want to run in circles and jibber.

"Choke," muttered Andy. "Forgot to close the choke." He yanked the pull rope again and the saw caught immediately, quickly biting into the wall, throwing a spray of coarse chips that showed yellow by firelight.

"Get down," he shouted over the roar of the McCulloch, bending to work his cut around, both of us crouching and coughing as smoke from the fire and from the exhaust forced us toward more breathable air near the floor.

I experienced a brief, brutal moment of déjà vu, flashing back to crawling on my belly through the burning cabin, searching for little Rosemary. And I wondered if I was going to destroy this parka too, a loaner from Grandma Susie as she mended the last one I barbecued.

The saw stopped again. Andy clicked it and pulled the cord. Nothing. He looked at me through the dark haze, eyes round.

"Out of fuel." He didn't say it very loud but I heard him clearly. He pointed at the fire-lit line of mostly cut out escape hatch. "Time to kick."

On "three," the two of us kicked as one, like some kind of desperate can-can routine. But with the last part of just one two-by-four stud uncut, the wall held. It didn't help that both of us wore soft-soled mukluks.

With the air becoming too hot and thick to stand, both of us crouched, and I even tried sitting-down kicking, lashing out as hard as I could, ignoring intense pain in the soles of my feet. That one fragment of cut wall had become either our cell door or our escape hatch—either letting us out, or sealing us in to die. It waggled a little, but held.

Andy made a noise and snatched up the chainsaw. "You're out of gas," I reminded him, not making enough sound to be heard, but he lip-read. He stared at the heavy saw for a long moment, then turned it around, getting a grip on the chain bar instead of the handle.

Drawing a breath, rising to stand in a crouch, he swung the heavy saw engine like a massive hammer, crude and clumsy but effective, on the third swing, splintering the hold-out stud, driving the ragged rectangle of shed wall out into the flames and snow beyond. He waved me to get out. I waved him to go first. After all it was he who hammered out the wall.

He set down Oliver's saw, then picked it up and gave it a heave-ho toss out through the hole, something Oliver would appreciate. Stepping back, he managed a clean dive through the hole, appearing to miss the flames, somersaulting through deep snow to end up mostly on his feet, but holding a head that had to ache.

As I stepped back for my jump, I heard an explosive *whump* behind me and turned to see the lid blown off Oliver's gas can and the rising vapor from the spout blow-torching into what had already become an inferno. Andy said later I erupted through the hole in the shed wall like shot out of a cannon, imitating his somersault and rise, but then bending to gather mitts-full of snow to bath my again-seared face.

Off in the distance I heard the spooky growling windup of the fire siren, how it quivered and amplified off all the frozen surfaces, vibrating in the clear cold air.

I admit I was thinking about Evie, but this time it was Andy who spoke her name, like he'd been reading my mind. "Just glad Evie wasn't here, too, to keep her out of it."

"She's not out of it," I told him. "Far from it. Two Deer only wanted her to make sure he got his maps and money from us. Now he has them."

Neither of us spoke the next thought. *Now he doesn't need her.*

CHAPTER 23

I took about thirty seconds to smear Noxzema on my face, even offering some to Andy. "Stuff stinks," he said. It did. And the pungent odor transported me instantly to other places—Tennessee—and other sore skin, most notably sunburn, and even other times. The last time I opened this jar, it was Mary smearing it across my back and shoulders, clucking at me gently for staying out too long while also murmuring sympathetically. With effort, I shook myself back into the moment.

Andy did splash cold water on his face. I'd managed to get the worst of it.

"What do we do?" Andy gingerly patted dry his sore face with a towel. "Can we call someone?"

"You mean the marshal?" I asked him. "And say what? That the probable next governor of the Territory locked us in a meat shed and tried to burn us alive? Think he'd run right out and arrest Two Deer on our say-so?"

"Maybe not. Well, we need to call Evie, at least, warn her." We had gone so far as to walk down the hall into the office, and I had even picked up the phone, listening for odd static and buzzing, hearing none.

"No," I said, making up my mind. "We need to drive there. Warn her in person. If she's in trouble …"

"Haul her out of there." Andy finished my thought.

The drive to Fairbanks took us the usual hour. We saw two moose, cantering easily along on the packed-snow roadbed, only vaulting the five-foot snow-plowed shoulders at the last possible moment as we eased past.

We drove with the radio off, the heater on full, brains buzzy with sleeplessness, leftover adrenalin, overlaid with

180

vague dread about what kind of trouble Evie might be in when we found her. If we found her.

"Trail starts here," said Andy, as I parked the truck at the Denali Lodge.

I knew the room number, fifty-six, so we decided to start there. We found glass doors to the lobby still unlocked, a bit surprising at nearly 2:30, by the large-faced lobby clock. The paunchy night clerk eyed us blearily, his eyes rounding slightly at the sight of us, but he said nothing. I imagined he'd seen worse in Fairbanks in the middle of the night. Then I caught sight of our reflections in a lobby mirror. Well, maybe he hadn't seen worse.

Our faces were sooty, except where we'd wiped them down with water or Noxema. With hoods tossed back, Andy's hair, also sooty, stood up stiff and I had to believe mine did as well. Our blackened parkas had been charred in places, and the hood and wrist ruffs singed, frizzled or burnt away completely.

We spotted a sign indicating rooms twenty through sixty and headed down a long, narrow, turquoise-painted hallway, the line of cream-colored room doors and baseboard stretching off into the distance. Number fifty-six would be way off down near the end, close to the lit, bright-red-lettered exit sign. We moved silently down an expanse of gray-brown seashell-sculpted carpet, interrupted only by the occasional brass stand-up ashtray and severe chrome-and-vinyl easy chair. The thick carpet simultaneously soaked up sound while emitting an odor of stale cigarettes, maybe a hint of vomit, and an aggressive deodorizer.

"Classy place," murmured Andy, just as we reached door fifty-six. Without much hope, I knocked.

"Who is it?" Evie's groggy voice called out from inside.

I leaned close to the door and tried to speak quietly. "It's Hardy ...and Andy."

"Who?"

"It's Hardy!" I suppose I was trying to whisper loudly, but found myself hissing.

From inside I heard a solid thump. "Ouch!" She'd walked into something. "This better be important." She opened the door, first on the chain. "Oh no," she said, getting a look at us. She closed the door to slip the security chain, then opened it wider. "What happened? You two look terrible! Was anybody hurt? And what's that smell?" She leaned forward to sniff the air. "Smells like burnt dog and ...Noxzema. Ugh!" She stopped to lean down and rub the shin she must have knocked trying to make it to the door in the dark.

I admit I was hoping she'd ask us in. Wrapped in her pink chenille bathrobe, she had that half-asleep, hair-tousled, adorable warm look that always made me want to hold her, though I didn't expect to be doing any holding in my current condition.

"Are you guys okay," she asked, blinking and squinting, rubbing her eyes.

"We ..." I began. That's when the adjacent door opened, to room fifty-eight.

"What's going on out here? *What* happened to you two?" Edward Two Deer stepped out into the relative glare of the hall lights. I had to give him points for sounding surprised.

"That's what I was just asking," said Evie. "What *did* happen?"

182

I found myself swallowing hard. This couldn't turn out very well. The last time I tried to just tell Evie the truth about Two Deer, we went from acting sort of distant with each other to complete romantic break up. The way things kept going, any more truth could get me a restraining order.

So I hesitated, but Andy jumped in.

"This guy happened," he said, indicating Two Deer with a thumb. "Came to the rectory, pulled a gun, shot a sofa pillow ...you know that one you made with the fireweed stitched on it with pink thread? Blasted that to pieces. You know what a .44 magnum does to a defenseless little sofa pillow, it ..." I elbowed him.

"Yeah," said Andy, not slowing, "he shot the bejeezus out of that pillow, then he walloped me with a gun barrel. Just look at this." He hiked the side of his head around so she could see the purple green mess the gun barrel made of the side of his head. No refuting that.

"Then he locked us in the meat shed, poured gas all around, and torched it. Damn near toasted us like marshmallows!"

Evie swung on me. "Is any of this true?" she demanded.

I admit I swallowed hard. "All of it."

She turned to Andy. "Have you been drinking?"

"Have I ...? No!"

She turned to Two Deer. "Edward, you've had a busy night."

"Sounds like it," he said. "But, the truth is ..." he hesitated, shrugged, "I've been here the whole time." He said it well, smoothly and with gathering confidence. "Evie can vouch for me, right?

"Of course!" But then she hesitated, too, just a beat. He lied, and she lied to cover. All of it playing out just as he predicted back at the rectory in Chandalar, with him the rising star and Andy and me as insignificant collateral damage.

"You've got to leave here," I told her. "Let us take you back to Chandalar. You're not safe here."

She looked at me, didn't say anything, but I saw her eyebrows lift ...like, "You must be kidding. I'm here with the next governor of the Territory of Alaska." That's when I began to add up the time it took her to answer the door, the dull *thunk* we heard. A door closing? Were the rooms connected? In that instant I would have bet yes.

"This is fun, but ..." Edward looked at the watch he still wore—in the middle of the night—his eyes shifting to something behind me.

I turned to see a heavy-set man with a rolling gait approaching soundlessly down the long hallway. His dark green suit didn't fit him well, the material almost shiny, with the jacket a little long and the pants cuffs a little short, and black shoes with thick crepe soles on his feet. He wore his hair short in a pomaded flattop and clenched several inches of soggy-looking cigar in the corner of his mouth. It made him look like Popeye from the Sunday funnies, with the left side of his face pulled up on account of it and the eye squinted slightly from the smoke. The cigar smelt like a burning cat box.

"Trouble here, Mr. Two Deer?" He shifted his jacket to make sure we saw the butt of a large revolver protruding from under his left arm.

Edward looked at Andy, then at me. "No trouble, Ron, but these two gentlemen were just leaving."

"Great," said Ron, like he really thought it was. He grabbed each of us by the upper arm. "Show you the way." Andy tried to shake loose but Ron had a grip like a gorilla, and it didn't happen.

My eyes met Evie's, hopelessly, but instead of the distain I expected, in that instant made an almost palpable connection. The single glance took me from feeling lost about her, to feeling something inside me drop rightly into place. I saw something in her eyes I couldn't make out, but when I opened my mouth to speak, she made the slightest head shake, *no*. I took a breath and allowed Ron to haul me down the hallway—instead of punching him in the nose—turning my head to keep looking at Evie until Two Deer moved between us, stepping out into the hallway to talk to her.

Just short of the main entrance, anticipating Ron's 'bum's rush' out the door, I stepped sharply toward him, making his grip relax, then jerked my arm loose. Not looking for a fight I stood still, raised my hands slightly, passively—no threat. "We're good here," I said. He went for his gun.

I put my hand on the front of his jacket, pushing him smoothly back against the blue burlap-patterned lobby wallpaper, pinning his hand under the jacket and the gun to his chest. He tried fleetingly to reach around with his left hand to his right side pocket, probably for his blackjack, but it was no use.

"We're *good*, Ron, unless you want to make this into some kind of big deal?" We stood looking at each other until I felt him relax.

"No," he said, "no need. Not here, not now."

"Glad we agree." I gave Andy a head jerk toward the door and we left Ron like that, standing quietly against the wallpaper, his head wreathed in a cloud of his own noxious smoke. Going out the door on our own steam felt good, a small victory, although tonight's significant victory was still us not being burned alive.

We climbed into the truck and drove away quickly. There was still the chance Ron might have called the cops. And at nearly three a.m., it was long past time for a shower, maybe a bit more Noxzema—my scorched skin felt too tight for my face—and maybe there would still be time tonight for the chance to sleep.

Later, stretched out on Andy's couch, I saw Evie again, saw her clearly, saw that long last look, telling me ...something ...I didn't know what. But the one solid thing I knew, in spite of everything happening around us, was that she and I were connected. I couldn't shake the surety of it. And when I did go to sleep, slept soundly.

CHAPTER 24

"Edward Two Deer did this?" said William, not really a question, as he and I and Andy circled the charred remains of my meat shed.

"And more," I told him.

"Darn," said Andy. "Now we gotta build a new one. That was a good shed."

"It was full of holes, anyway," I told him. "No wonder I had mice!"

"And Two Deer did this?" said William again.

"Yeah," Andy said.

"Are you sure?"

Andy rolled his eyes. "We were there!"

"But we didn't really see him," I added. "He locked us in, walked away, then came walking back with gasoline and matches. I admit it surprised me." William didn't say anything, just pressed his lips together.

"You should have told me about the money and the documents," he said. By then we were walking back along the narrow snow trail to the rectory, seeing drag marks left by the unconscious Andy.

"Yes," I said, "I see that now."

With coffee perking and Andy building moose-meat sandwiches for lunch, I went next door to the church and removed the bank-banded stack of bills, which turned out to be hundreds—so ten-thousand dollars—and also the pile of oil documents I'd held back from Two Deer. Standing in window light in the church's heavy silence, I scanned some of them again, still not taking much meaning from them.

Each had a number, a date, geographical coordinates, and a generic-sounding bidder—like Southwest Oil Consortium—instead of something like Standard Oil. And each had the word 'Awarded,' rubber-stamped in large unmistakable, red print on its face, but with a small space below—Date Registered—left blank.

So maybe they *hadn't* been awarded, since I appeared to be holding the very documents in my hands. No wonder people were willing to kill for these. There were about fifty of them here. What were each of them worth? Five hundred thousand? A million?

I'd heard of people around here, not so long ago, who would kill you for "a hundred bucks and a shot of whisky." How many people would someone kill for just one of these pieces of paper? I didn't want to find out, especially since Andy and I were two of the candidates.

I took the documents and the money back to the rectory and handed them to William, mid-sip of his coffee. He looked surprised, but not nearly as surprised as Andy.

"Wait a minute," said Andy. "You held out on him?"

"Yes."

"With a gun to my head, you decided to play a trick on him?"

I shrugged. "It worked."

"Well what if he shot me?"

I made an apologetic face.

"You did take a big risk." William set down his coffee mug to shuffle through the documents.

"I *know* this claim," he said. Then he looked at each of us and closed his mouth. We waited.

"But you can't say anything," said Andy. William did a face shrug but didn't say anything more, sliding in that instant, back into enigmatic spy mode.

"I can tell you this," he said. "This is bigger …goes deeper, and is more dangerous than we knew. And I promise you Two Deer will return for the rest of these. He *will* kill you, if he has to, to get these. These documents, along with their links to the Senengatuk murder would put him and his friends away for a long time."

The three of us sat silent for a long moment. I could hear my kitchen clock ticking and, from across the street, the snow-muffled roar of one of the town's electric generators.

"See if you can answer this," I said. "Could that stack of papers be worth a lot of money?"

He considered for a moment, then nodded. "Many millions."

"Shit!" said Andy. "I'm so lucky—we're both so lucky—to be alive."

I looked at Andy. "We've got to get out of here, but I have no idea to where."

A sudden buffet of wind against the cabin drew Andy's gaze out the kitchen window. "Looks like we got weather comin' in. Not the best time to be out wandering around."

"Or maybe it is," said William. And that's when the phone rang.

Let it be Evie, I thought, walking down the short hall. Not a prayer. I don't believe in praying for such things. Just a …longing. No such luck.

It was Frank Jacobs. "Hey, Father," he said, friendly but something else, too.

"Frank."

"Wondering if you've been to Fairbanks recently? I should mention, this is an official call."

"Well then, officially I was there last night, or early this morning, more accurately."

"Ah," he said. "Care to tell me where you were—who you might have seen? Someone who might confirm you were there?"

"Sure," I said, "no secret. Andy and I were at the Denali Lodge, about three a.m., saw Evie, Edward Two Deer, and someone who was probably the house bouncer, a heavy-set guy named Ron with a flattop. Oh, and a night clerk, but we didn't speak to him. Any of them should be able to confirm we were there.

Frank exhaled, long and slow. If it's possible for the simple act of breathing out to sound worrisome, this did.

"Okay, well, you need to know that Police Chief Kellar, along with a couple of cars full of his Keystone Cops will be on his way to Chandalar pretty quick to arrest you and Andy. I shouldn't be calling, as you can probably figure out. I had in mind to fly down there and arrest you myself, but we've got a bad bit of weather just coming in— no flying, maybe for a couple of days. So I'm calling to tell you to get out of there. Go into a hole somewhere until I'm able to work this thing out. You don't want to let Kellar get hold of either of you!"

"But …I don't get it. Any of those people should be able to vouch for us—Evie at the very least."

"Well that's the thing," said Frank. "Evie is missing— possibly kidnapped, but who knows—along with the probable next governor of the Territory. So, there's alot of people worked up around here."

"And they suspect Andy and me for it."

"Bingo," said Frank. "Someone tipped them."

"Probably Ron, the bouncer. We didn't leave him on the best of terms, but it sounds like Ron's not talking."

190

"Bingo, again. Ron's *not* talking. In fact, he's the main reason they're coming after you. Ron won't be talking ever again. He's dead."

CHAPTER 25

"We have less than an hour to get out of here," said William. He looked energized. I felt disheartened and drained.

After yet another face scorching, being up half the night, and the news that the woman I love has either been kidnapped by a man I believe will kill her—or worse— she's gone off with him intentionally. I must have looked as low as I felt.

"We will find her," said William. "Do you have a parka you have not worn into fire?"

"I do," I said, without much gusto.

"Here is what we will do," said William. "Andy takes the truck to get his rifle and trail gear. Yes?"

"Sure."

"You get your unflamed parka, snow shoes, overnight pack, and your revolver."

I gaped at him. "Overnight? What about sleeping bags, a tent, food, fuel?"

"The Lord will provide," he said, which surprised me because he had never seemed particularly religious. Then he added, "or the Government." I started to ask, but he waved me off. "Better not to know much."

About thirty-five minutes later, we walked out my front door, closed it firmly—didn't lock it, so Kellar could feel justified kicking it in—and walked away. We headed out of town on the river, downstream, walking briskly but easily on a mix of packed snow and glare ice, heading west into the setting sun and a lowering sky.

Wind gusted in our faces, bearing tiny ice pellets, that rattled on my store-bought parka, stinging my cheeks and eyelids. The knot in my stomach hurt worse. Instead of starting out to find her, to rescue her if it came to that, we— *I*—was just running away. Although I certainly couldn't help anybody by allowing myself to be locked up in jail or beaten to a pulp while allegedly resisting arrest. *Keep her safe*, I prayed.

After walking about an hour, we stopped, turned and peered through twilight across a wide shallow bowl of gently rising valley. It felt a relief to turn my back on the wind and driving snow.

"Trail disappears," said Andy, peering back through his Zeiss scope. He pushed the rifle toward me and I took a look. Sure enough, wind and blowing snow had already wiped away much of our trail. By tomorrow morning, or when this weather slacked off—the absolute earliest any kind of posse could come out—the slate of our passing would be wiped clean. "Take that, Kellar," Andy said, and we turned to slog on.

By storm-filtered moonlight, leaning into the wind, we followed William across barren, gently rising terrain up over a rounded ridge and into the trees. Birch and alder stood widely spaced, none of them more than thirty feet tall, with only an occasional shorter evergreen. We weren't following anything like a trail or track. Drifts stood three to four feet deep, undisturbed, and we had long since stopped to fumble-on snowshoes. Snow fell more heavily now, small flakes but plenty of them, not so wind-driven in the trees but still blowing into my eyes.

"Are we there yet?" I asked, not expecting to be.

"Nearly" said William, which surprised me. We had probably not walked much more than five miles from Chandalar. I admit I'd been expecting to go a lot farther out, to be safely hidden.

"Think he knows where he's going?" I asked Andy, William striding ahead confidently, although he did risk an occasional light to check his compass.

"I think it's the spruce trees," said Andy, behind me. "Don't grow here usually. The single evergreens are trail markers. Bet he turns when he sees two."

Within another ten minutes, a pair of spruce, both about fifteen feet tall, set us off on a right turn up a steeper grade. It was rougher-going on snowshoes, leaving me sweating and panting, feeling out of shape. The trail stopped abruptly, totally blocked by angular boulders and a near-vertical rock rise.

William turned back to face us in the gloom.

"Lost?" asked Andy. William mostly ignored him.

"Raise your right hands," said William. We did, but I admit it all seemed pretty strange. "Repeat after me: I hereby declare, on oath, that I will support and defend the Constitution and laws of the United States of America against all enemies, foreign and domestic."

"Huh?" said Andy.

"Just swear," said William.

"I swear," I said, and Andy echoed.

"Follow," said William, whispering now, which also seemed odd. There shouldn't have been anybody for miles around to overhear. He led us in a circle around a huge, rough, geometric slab of boulder and out of the deep snow. Switching on his flashlight he ducked—and we followed—under a stone outcrop into a three-sided stone hollow with a small dark crawl-height opening at the back. "Snowshoes off," he whispered, our snowshoes rattling on bare stone, as he shucked his.

I shook off my heavy mitts to fumble with my straps. "Why are we whispering?"

Andy sniffed the air. "Bear in here?"

"Sometimes," said William, with a meaningful look at me.

He took one of his snowshoes, turned it butt down and began to tap around the floor, which except for a layer of dirt and leaves felt like stone. *Tap, tap, thunk!*

"And," said William, "we are home!" He brushed clear a sturdy wooden trapdoor built with heavy metal-strap reinforcing, and a steel ring inset to lay flat. The door opened smoothly, looked heavy, and it was—a layer of steel plate lining the underside. No wonder the hinges creaked! "Oil hinges," William said, making a mental note. "Wait," he said to us, disappearing down the ladder. We heard a kitchen match and saw a perfect square of warm, yellow lantern light appear, inviting us in out of the cold and the storm.

"Go ahead," said Andy. "I'll get the trapdoor" I must have looked incredulous. He shrugged and shook his head. "Government," was all he said.

We descended into a square room constructed with concrete blocks and mortar, with a flat, poured-concrete floor. I couldn't even imagine the amount of time, trouble and brute labor it must have taken to construct and outfit this place—secretly—this far out in the Bush. Not to even mention the cost!

The room was almost filled with supplies and equipment, such that the three of us standing at once, used up most of the floor space. Narrow bunks lined two walls, three on each, more like people shelves than beds. A fold-up table next to a small, kerosene cookstove made food prep and eating possible. I noticed a sealed, steel box marked 'radio,' and some kind of hand-crank generator apparatus, plus a rack holding six rifles—war-surplus .30

195

caliber M1s—secured by a locking steel bolt. Shelves stuffed with military rations and medical supplies occupied the rest of the available bunker real estate.

"Army food," said Andy, not happily, as he studied the shelves. I strongly suspected there would be no Italian coffee to wake up to.

"What is this place?" asked Andy. "A fallout shelter? *Here?*"

"This is," said William, with an exaggerated hand sweep, "Operation Washtub. Do not ask me why. This is what happens when the Pentagon and Mr. J. Edgar Hoover prepare to resist the invading army of the Union of Soviet Socialist Republics. There is talk now of abandoning the program, partly because it has been five or six years and Russians have not attacked, and partly—I am told— because Mr. Hoover does not want people to know he was connected with this."

"Political liability," I said.

"Exactly." William glanced at the bunks. He looked around, nodding. "This will do very nicely for us, for tonight, at least. And," he hiked up his parka sleeve to glance at his wristwatch, "we need to get sleep.

I struggled to get into the mummy bag on the narrow hard shelf, still wearing most of my clothes, as did Andy. It was warmer in the bunker than outside, about ten degrees below zero, or maybe even zero, but still pretty chilly.

No struggling for William. He sat on the edge of his bunk, put on the bag like a pair of baggy coveralls, pulling it up to chest height before sitting, turning, and kicking up his feet. He almost made it look easy. *I'll never sleep*, I remember thinking, and nothing more.

❖

A wooden match striking, igniting the heater cooker, snapped me awake in what seemed like the next second. I fumbled for my Timex. Four a.m.

"Stay put," instructed William, climbing the ladder and flipping back the trapdoor to get snow to melt for coffee, flooding the underground space with heavy, cold air. While generally bustling around, he wanted us out of the way.

"No problem," muttered Andy, his voice muffled. Somehow he was able to climb all the way into a mummy bag, pull the top shut and sleep that way. Not me. I had to have at least my nose out, to not feel claustrophobic, no matter how cold it was.

So I lay there, trying to sort through our options. It didn't take long. We really didn't have any. Kellar would be expecting us to turn up in Chandalar or Nenana, watching the trains there. They'd be watching my truck, or have it disabled by now. We wouldn't be taking a boat with the river frozen solid. None of us had an airplane in our hip pocket. So we'd walk to somewhere, Fairbanks? Sixty miles across country? I didn't think so. To the highway and hitchhike? *So, okay, we don't have any options,* I concluded.

Still, William whistled cheerfully to himself as he opened cans, mixed and poured. About the time I decided we had no options, I smelled coffee perking, and something like ham frying, and remembered the one option I'd left out. We could eat! I was hungry.

Stuffed around the table, we ate and enjoyed scrambled powdered eggs, canned Canadian bacon, pilot bread—William smeared his with lard, the Russian way—and drank a pretty fair cup of coffee, especially when you consider it had probably been resting here in its can for about five years. With something in my stomach I felt more optimistic about having no hope for the future.

"Nearly as I can figure," I said, "we're stuck here."

"Could be worse," said Andy. "Food, heat, a roof. Good here 'til spring!"

I ignored him. "We can't go back."

William shook his head. "No."

"I don't think you're planning to wait it out here." He shook his head again.

"No."

"What, then?"

He sipped his coffee and wiped his drippy nose on his sleeve. "We need to get to Fairbanks. We can pick up Evie's trail there."

"How?"

"There is a highway, about a mile off this way." He pointed east. "You'll see."

In about an hour, breakfast finished and the bunker put back right, we turned off the heater and lantern, climbed the ladder, and pushed up cautiously into the bear cave. William stuck up his head first, in darkness, to look, listen and sniff for whatever might be about—before risking his flashlight. It was just a little after 6:00 by my watch, sunrise a good four hours distant. We emerged into a clear, bitterly cold morning, the storm blown out and gone, and the temperature probably minus thirty-five or forty. From out of the hazeless sky, the nearly half moon shone clear, along with layer upon layer of stars. They lit the landscape an almost-daylight filtered blue, trees casting long navy-colored shadows on pale blue snow.

Morning has broken, like the first morning, I sang in my head and my heart—an old Presbyterian children's hymn—as we started down what I imagined would be a long trail leading to …I didn't know where. Except that I knew—believed—the trail would lead to Evie.

So even though we still had no options that I could figure, no clue how we'd get to Fairbanks, no idea how we'd pick up her trail, no idea how we'd rescue her—or anything else—I felt a rising bubble of hopefulness. As we reached the end of the trees, ready to start down the long, open valley and away, I felt almost giddy.

The bullet hit a small tree just as I passed, about two feet above my head. It startled all three of us so badly we froze in place long enough for the echoing racket of the explosion to wash up around us from below.

CHAPTER 26

A second shot cleanly nailed another tree, again a bit above our heads. I watched as William, wearing his scoped Russian rifle strapped over his shoulder, did some kind of twist and turn with the gun, and dropped cleanly into a firing position in the snow. Flipping off his heavy mitts, he sighted, ready to shoot.

"Hold up," said Andy, still standing in a cautious crouch. "Warning shots," he said. "Nailed both trees, could have nailed us just as easy." Still frozen in place, we watched and listened. Then a distant cry.

"Help!"

William twisted up to look at us. "What do you think? On the level?"

"Andy's right. He could have just picked us off."

"I see him," said Andy, peering through his scope. "In a sleeping bag, leaning against a tree. Rifle in his lap."

"We cannot just walk down there," said William. "This could be trickery." He peered through his own scope.

"I'll walk down," I said. "You two can cover me."

"No, I'll go," said Andy.

"Too risky." William picked himself up. "We can take another route, head west, and avoid him. Keep low, and eliminate the risk." As if he'd been listening in, we heard the voice again.

"Help!"

"We're burning time here," I said, straightening. "I'm going down. You two cover me." I didn't give them time to argue, just turned and started snowshoeing down the easy slope.

200

At first I couldn't make him out, just a deeper blue shadow under trees on the far side of this slight scoop of valley. But from about the halfway point I could see him, a man wearing a parka, sitting in a sleeping bag, leaning against a small tree, his rifle still across his lap—which didn't mean he wasn't holding a handgun. I came down and approached him slightly from the side, to avoid blocking Andy's shot. Then I knew him: Lonnie Holden.

"Thought you were gone," I said.

"Shoulda been. Wanted to be. It's about fifty degrees *above* zero in Tulsa today. I could be walkin' around in a T-shirt, mowin' the lawn—if I had a lawn. About ninety degrees warmer than this god-forsaken place!"

We looked at each other. "What happened?"

"Followed you guys out of town; figured I could pick you off easy with the rifle. Wasn't counting on the storm and losing the trail. He looked at my feet. "Had no snowshoes. Finally, nothing I could do but climb into this bag and hole up. Too cold to sleep. No trail forward or back. Just been sitting here, shivering. Started thinking about my mother. Decided I don't care about the money. They said they'd kill me if I screwed up again. But I'm not afraid of them. If you'll help me this time, you'll never see me again."

"Are you hurt?"

"No, just colder than I've ever been! I piled this snow up around me to stay out of the wind. I just hoped— prayed, really—you'd come back this way."

"Okay," I said, "just hand me your rifle, butt first …very slowly."

"The Injun has me in his sights, doesn't he?"

"You bet."

"He's good."

201

"He was a sniper in Italy."

"Shoulda known. Nearly put a bullet in my eye out there on the riverbank."

"So that was you," I said. "Now the handguns. Just toss them away. By the barrels," I cautioned. I noticed he didn't have to dig for them. They were ready in his lap. He tossed them, then held his hands up.

"Can you walk?" I extended my hand which he caught in both of his and levered himself to his feet, leaning against the tree to step out of his sleeping bag. He made as if to toss it away. "Let's roll that up," I said.

He looked at me. "Easier to travel without."

"You're not out of the woods yet."

"No," he said, looking around. "You bet I'm not!" By the time we had the sleeping bag rolled and tied, Andy and William had made it most of the way down.

Lonnie turned to me. "I'm sorry," he said, his eyes two tiny pricks of light in the blue-black shadow of his parka hood.

"Change your life," I told him.

"I can't."

"Has there ever been anything in your life you really wanted to do, but couldn't?"

"No. You're right, I guess."

"This way," called William, and we turned, following him down the grade, three of us on snowshoes breaking trail for Lonnie. Instead of heading east toward Chandalar, we turned more north toward—I didn't know where. But William knew, stepping along confidently. In less than an hour we made out pinprick window lights, then distant vehicle lights passing and finally we clambered over a snowplow mound to pull off our snowshoes and stand on a packed-snow highway. We came out about a hundred yards from a tiny false-front store with "Wally's Mile 35 Trading Post" discernible in moonlight. I knew the place on the Fairbanks highway but had never stopped. It was just the store, attached to a small garage with a log cabin set farther back in a small stand of evergreens. Instead of approaching either the store or the cabin, we made new tracks through drifts to the garage.

"Snow shovelers are needed," said William, grabbing two shovels hanging by nails alongside the garage door.

"I'll take one of those," said Lonnie. I took the other. He was a good shoveler. Still it took about fifteen minutes to clear a path to open the garage doors and connect with the road.

"It's forty below," said Andy as we opened the doors and switched on an overhanging light bulb, revealing a maroon-colored Willys station wagon. "You can't think you're gonna get this thing started." William didn't say anything, just grabbed the electrical connection hanging through the squares of radiator grill, unplugging the engine oil heater from its extension cord.

"I will wager I can." He opened the driver's door, turned the engine over smoothly, easily, quickly starting it, the rich gas smell permeating the tiny garage.

"This more of that 'washtub' stuff?" asked Andy, getting a *shush* look from William for speaking in front of Lonnie.

"Loose lips sink ships," he cautioned.

"Sorry." Andy quickly brightened. "I call shotgun," and without waiting vaulted into the front passenger seat.

"We'll get the doors," I said, Lonnie waiting with me to push the doors to and snap the padlock.

"Where to?" With all of us aboard, William shifted into gear.

203

"The airport," said Lonnie. "I'm ready to be somewhere that's *not* forty below."

"Definitely head to Fairbanks," I said. "Maybe the Denali Lodge?"

"Lookin' for your girl, right?" asked Lonnie.

"Well," I said, "used to be my girl."

"You think she's got something going with Two Deer?"

"Well ..."

"She don't," said Lonnie. "Not happenin'. I think she gets him pretty well. Thing is, she *really* wants an Injun governor." He laughed to himself. "Also not happenin'." He looked up. "I'm pretty sure she's not at the Denali."

"Where, then?"

"I'll tell you when you drop me at the airport."

"So you want us to just let you walk away?"

"Well," he said, "yeah."

I looked at William and Andy as they looked at me. "Okay, but I want one more thing from you before you go. A phone call." He heard me out.

"Okay," he said.

We made Fairbanks just before sunrise, about nine o'clock, and the airport a few minutes later.

"Mind you," Lonnie said, as we pulled up to the terminal steps, "I can't be sure where they are. All I heard was something went bad at the Denali and they had to skip."

"Yeah," said Andy, "we heard that, so skipped to where?"

Lonnie climbed out of the Willys into the frosty, gusty air, puffs of wind softly moaning around the building's crannies and downspouts, driving and drifting bits of snow and ice. It even *sounded* cold out. Nevertheless, Lonnie took the time to fish deep in his parka for his pack of Luckys, to shake one loose and light it while we waited, all eyes on his leathery, impassive face.

Sucking a great lungful of blue smoke, holding it, exhaling he said, "You know that new mall they're building out north of town, the Great North Star Mall?"

"What's a mall," asked Andy.

"*Shopping* mall," said Lonnie. "You don't get out much, do you? They built one last year in Minnesota, all kinds of shops, completely inside. Like a little town that's all roofed and heated."

"Now they're buildin' one here?"

"I said so, didn't I? Anyway, it's being built by Midwest Investment Enterprises ... by oil money ... and the first section, mostly complete, includes their office, around on the far end. Can't miss it. Okay?" he asked, like, 'Can I go now?'

"Okay," I said, "thanks. Good luck."

Lonnie ducked his head, as if to say 'aw shucks,' then reached in windows to shake hands all around. "You guys saved my life. I owed you one." He looked around. "Tried to leave a week ago, but there were cops all over. Hope they got better things to do now. So long!" He turned to walk up the shoveled concrete stairs and into the terminal, trailing a cloud of smoke. An electric sign set the time at 9:13 and the temperature at minus forty-two.

"Think he can do it," asked Andy, "change his life?"

"No," said William.

"Maybe," I said. "It starts with wanting to, in his case, maybe needing to."

"Tell you what I need is coffee," said Andy.

"And another breakfast," I added. "I need food!"

205

"You need," said William, "to not get arrested before we can find Evie."

"Yeah," agreed Andy. "That too."

CHAPTER 27

"Even fugitives need to eat," I said. It had already been five hours since the day's first breakfast—much of it spent snowshoeing or shoveling—so I felt famished. We chanced our second breakfast at a tiny greasy spoon called Sourdough Johnnie's down near the river behind the rail yards.

Everything about *Johnnie's* had a worn, tired, pre-war look, from the frayed linoleum to the flyspecked wartime pinup of Betty Grable wearing only a swim suit and a come-on smile over one shoulder. Hers was the shapely bottom that launched a thousand wartime air sorties and helped make military life overseas bearable.

A small bony waitress looked up from her magazine. She had corrugated ribs visible above several buttons undone and dishwater blond hair bunned back in a net. She parked her cigarette in a glass *Olympia Beer* ashtray on the bar, tucked menus under her arm and headed our way. "She ain't Rosie," Andy commented.

"No one is," I said.

"Out of the hash," said the waitress. The story of my life.

We ordered, and she hung the ticket on the smeared chrome kitchen wheel, spun it and went back to leaning on the bar smoking her cigarette. Music from KFAR, Pat Boone singing *Love Letters in the Sand*, played on a cream-colored, dusty, greasy Bakelite Motorola—another remnant of the '40s. The smells of cigarette smoke, bacon, and coffee mingled in a familiar, homey, early morning scent.

She came carrying the three heavy plates, laden with food, plus ketchup, two of the plates balanced expertly on one skinny arm. There were enough greasy, crispy hash browns on each plate for all three of us, but we soldiered on and it was all delicious. We saluted Betty with heavy mugs of surprisingly hearty coffee.

"Rosie needs this cook," I said, between mouthfuls.

"This cook needs Rosie," said Andy, eyeing the waitress, lost in a *Photoplay* magazine article about he-man hunk, Rock Hudson.

"That guy's a homo, you know," said Andy.

"No!" said William, with feeling. "How do you know that?"

"I heard around," said Andy. "We homos have our sources. Surprised you didn't know, bein' a spy and all."

"We do not spy on everyone," said William, with frost.

On the radio, the song ended. *Singing the Blues*, by Guy Mitchell, said the announcer, his rich voice filling the small, nearly empty place. "Warmer by tonight, with highs in the low minus twenties."

"A heat wave," said William, pushing back his plate, sipping his coffee and sighing. He'd eaten *all* his hash browns.

A jingle came on: women singing, "Nothing else comes near, when you're out of Schlitz, you're out of beer." And then news at the top of the hour.

First in national news: A southern Negro man, Martin Luther King, Jr., had made the cover of *Time* magazine. King wasn't the first Negro on *Time* but it didn't happen often. Nearly two years earlier, King helped to spearhead a bus boycott in Montgomery, Alabama, effectively emptying buses, costing the municipal bus service a fortune and worse, illustrating that Negroes could be a significant economic force.

Andy made a face and sniffed. "About darn time."

"Locally," the announcer continued, "three Chandalar men, one of them an Episcopal priest, are wanted for questioning in connection with a body discovered early this morning at the Denali Lodge in Fairbanks."

The waitress looked up from her magazine, stretched for the radio knob to turn it down and nodded toward the parking lot. She drew on her cigarette. "Highway Patrol," she exhaled. "They come in for Cook's cinnamon rolls. If you boys're them they're lookin' for, you got about two minutes to get out the back door." She jerked her head in the direction of the short hallway that led past a lit *Olympia Beer* clock and a grimy restroom.

We stood as one and William dropped a five on the table.

"You may keep the change," he said.

She smiled, mostly with eyebrows, appreciating a tip that didn't jingle. "I'm off at four," she called out behind us, hopefully.

A frozen, stamped-down path in the snow, punctuated with cigarettes and yellow urine stains—indicating not everyone smoked or peed inside—led us around to the Willys at the front. We were just in time to see the two gray parka backs of the Territorial highway patrolmen disappearing into the restaurant wannigan.

"Close," muttered Andy as we climbed back into the Willys. It hadn't stayed warm.

"Where to?" asked William, cranking over the engine, which quickly caught, grabbing the column shifter, poised.

"North of town," I said. He nodded and shifted into gear, lurching us out of Sourdough Johnnie's lot and on our way.

"What if Evie is not out here?" William asked over his shoulder.

"Then we'll go on to the next place she might be," I said.

We saw the nascent mall in minutes, several acres of perfectly flat, cleared space. It was all punctuated by plain lengths of galvanized pipe standing up at regular intervals through several feet of drifted snow. At the ends of what appeared to be rows, stood very tall aluminum light posts, the actual lights uninstalled, with just the wires visible at the top.

"What is this place and what are all the pipes?" asked Andy.

"They are signposts and, I believe, this will be a parking area," said William.

"Yeah," said Andy, "like they're really gonna ever fill acres of space with cars."

We hesitated at the mall entrance, an unfinished thirty-foot-tall offset rectangle, curved over on the top outside corner instead of square. Constructed of brown-painted plywood, a huge, blue plywood star intersected with the top inside corner, and again, wires stuck out here and there in anticipation of future lighting.

A single snowplowed lane led in, with a four-car plowed space near the building and a City of Fairbanks patrol car plain to see.

"Fairbanks police," I said. "Keep going," and William accelerated smoothly past. In another quarter mile we crossed a bridge over a small creek with a turnout just beyond.

"Here," I said, William already making the turn.

Gaps of several minutes between passing cars made it easy to climb out of the Willys armed, unseen. Not that men walking around with rifles, even near town, would be considered unusual. In minutes we slogged our way through thigh deep snow up the frozen gorge of streambed, well protected from the chilly, gusty wind and, even in daylight, completely hidden from view.

I'd never seen a building quite like this so-called mall. For one, it had been designed completely flat roofed, with flat porches, entries and overhangs as well, giving it that long, low, modern southwestern look that had suddenly become so popular everywhere. And it was huge, as long as an airplane hangar!

The building's front, adjacent to the parked cars, appeared to be small shop spaces, most of the doors still plywood covered, as were the display windows. Alongside each door stood a sidelight of stacked and mortared translucent glass blocks. In some places, a façade of stacked rock had been added. It all looked very modern, very 1950s and up to the minute—and completely out of place in Alaska.

We climbed up out of the creek bed, back out into the gusty wind, and approached from the windowless, doorless side. Andy crept forward to peer around to the front. "More cops," he called back, hushed. Then he disappeared.

"Where is Andy?" William hissed, alarmed. "I looked away then looked back. He is gone."

I saw him go. It looked like he sprinted away, heavy rifle and all. Rushing to peer around the corner, I found Andy, about fifty feet farther down the wall, holding a door just slightly ajar. We quickly caught up.

"Self-closing, but the wind caught it," he explained. "I got here in time."

William pulled one of his .45s out of a parka pocket and cocked it. "We will go in, then."

"No sense standing out here in the cold," I said, suppressing a shiver.

On William's signal, Andy yanked the door one man wide and we darted in, William, me, and then Andy.

Inside was just as cold and also dim, lit only by daylight oozing through the glass blocks. We'd entered a store space, about thirty feet wide and fifty deep, littered with shop tools, sawhorses, ladders and construction debris. A path led down through the center of it to what would eventually be a wide outlet at the rear, into the mall proper. For now, it presented another plywood door we'd need to make it through without getting shot.

A voice, suddenly very close, sent us ducking for cover. In another instant the inside door pushed wide, heavy spring squeaking, then banged shut behind as three of Kellar's pet cops came hustling through. "At the airport?" one said. "Then we've missed 'im. Plane to Anchorage left a half hour ago."

"Got orders to check anyway," said another as they pushed open the door to outside. We heard their car doors slam, the engine start, and the tires spin.

"They're gone most of an hour," said Andy. "That's three less people we have to get past to find Evie."

We came out from our hiding places and approached the inside mall door. The glimpse I caught, as the three came through, and the fact that it seemed like more unheated space, made me believe it would be empty, that we had farther to go. So I eased the door open slowly, enough to stick my head through, without squeaking the

212

door spring, then beckoned to the others, slid through and stopped, stunned.

The room had been set for a party, a big one. We stood in a blocked-off section of mall hallway, nearly two hundred feet long and sixty or seventy feet wide with ceilings probably sixteen feet high. Hanging all around the walls were maybe twenty black-and-white portraits of Edward Two Deer, each of them about-four-by-eight feet. Some of the portraits included Evie, smiling, close to the candidate in domestic-appearing situations. There was even one photo of the two of them that looked like it had been taken in Washington, D.C., though I knew it hadn't. Or I believed it hadn't. *Did they travel together?* I didn't think so.

There were bars for drink service on all four sides, draped nearly to the floor with long white cloths, lacking only ice and alcohol. At one end of the room stood a speaker's platform with a lectern and microphone.

In the half-light, at less than zero degrees, the room had a frosty, surreal look, like something you might find in your refrigerator that's gone "off," no longer viable, no longer consumable. Or maybe that was just me.

"Somebody's got big plans," said Andy, at my elbow. He stared at a poster of Evie with Two Deer. "That's weird," he said with feeling, "but probably means she's safe. He needs her."

A telephone rang, distantly, from an office space beyond the podium, and we all ducked. The office had a real door and brighter light filtering around window shades and as we drew closer, we could hear someone typing— too slowly to be Evie. An engraved doorplate read 'Edward Two Deer Campaign Office.'

213

With my eye to the window crack, I could see the reception area of a mostly-finished office space with pink and gray patterned wallpaper and darker gray carpet. As far as I could see to the left, six upholstered chairs waited around a low coffee table, magazines neatly arranged. On the right, a taller reception counter with a glass vase and fake flowers stood empty, much of it covered with a layer of floury construction dust. Sounds we'd heard came from four smaller offices, doors all open, arranged to one side. "Looks like a dentist's office," I whispered.

"I will go in," William whispered. "You wait."

I started to protest but he waved me back with the .45. "Cover me," he whispered, turned the knob and eased the door in.

I heard Evie's voice clearly, insistently, from one of the offices. "Don't do this, Edward," she said. "You're better than that!"

I seriously doubt it, I thought, uncharitably.

That's when somebody sapped William from his left side, dropping him nearly soundlessly to the carpet, his unconscious face the last thing I saw as the self-closing door pulled shut.

CHAPTER 28

We had just seconds. I motioned to Andy and we took off running—silent in soft mukluks—looking for places to hide. One of the wet bars, with its long, draping white cloths, would have to do for me.

I barely made it. The extra second I took to slide under from behind paid off. The cloth still trembled as a couple of Two Deer's goons burst from the office, revolvers drawn, Two Deer following right behind, pushing Evie.

I heard her sharp exclamation. "William!" She tried to bend to him but one of them shoved her forward into the unheated hall where she wrapped her arms around herself in the subzero temperature.

"So Lonnie lied," said Two Deer, uncocking the same big pistol he'd used on Andy. "No wonder he headed for the airport."

"Or he missed this one," said one of the others.

"Maybe." Two Deer gestured with the handgun before sliding it into a concealed shoulder holster. "You two circle the place, look for parked cars, footprints, broken doors, anything not right."

"Right, Boss," said one, and the two went off together.

Two Deer turned to Evie. "I need an answer from you now. No more 'think' time. I'm gonna be governor of Alaska, first Native-American governor appointed then elected—in the country! Admit it. You're ambitious. I know you want this. No more stinking little town, stinking little shack, no more *dead-end preacher squaw man.*"

He'd gone too far and I saw her wince. Still, I knew she *was* ambitious and he really was offering her the world.

"I'll only consider it," she said, shivering, "if nobody else dies."

Two Deer jerked around to give her a hard look. What am I supposed to do with this guy? Some kind of Federal agent. He's been on me from the start. I don't see him rolling over for this."

Evie gave him a hard look back. "Offer him a lot of cash and a cushy job in Juneau. Make him the first director of the State Highway Patrol or your security chief."

"But don't kill him?"

She shook her head. "No!"

He finally noticed her shivering. "You're cold. Let's get you back inside." He pushed the door open and stepped over William. "How about I kill him and give you the money I would have given him. How does one hundred thousand sound?" I didn't hear her answer.

We didn't have much time. The two goons in their stateside overcoats couldn't take more than five minutes to make a quick circuit of the place and hurry back to get warm.

Andy, climbing out from under the speaker's platform, met me at the door. He carried his rifle in one hand and one of William's .45s in the other.

"Can I kill him?"

"Tempting," I said, "but try not to."

We walked in like we owned the place. "Find anything," Two Deer called out.

William rolled to his feet as we came in, clear-eyed, apparently playing possum, bending to pull a small pistol from his mukluk.

We followed Two Deer's voice to a small kitchenette squeezed between a pair of the other rooms. He leaned on the counter watching Evie crouch to pull ice cubes from a

216

small under-counter refrigerator. "You're gonna like Juneau," he was telling her. Something I doubted.

Andy got to him first. Two Deer gaped. "You?" he said, incredulous.

"Darn straight." Andy swung, knocking the politician all the way to the floor with a round-house pistol whack to the side of the head, down but not out.

"That *hurt!*" Two Deer groaned and squeezed his eyes tight shut, still on his hands and knees on the carpet. "You're supposed to be dead. Lonnie promised you were dead!"

"Lonnie lied. Get over it."

Evie stood to face me, ice bag in hand. "You came," she said. "You're alive." A single tear overflowed each eye, making tracks down her cheeks. "We got the call. They said you were all dead. I ..."

I felt the room recede as our eyes connected."

"You knew I'd come for you."

"If you could, but ..."

I pointed at Two Deer, now rolled up to a sitting position against one of the cabinets, holding his narrow head in both hands. "This guy's a loser."

"I know," she said, quietly. "He was never you. But for a while I thought he might be what Alaska needed ... and what *I* wanted. A Native American who could go head-to-head with whites in the political arena. Our savior," she finished wryly.

"There's a bigger problem," I told her, and turned to Two Deer with the phrase I'd been practicing. "*Dove e il bagno?*"

Without looking up, he answered me in fluent Italian. I had no idea what he said, but how he said it, how he looked saying it, spoke volumes.

217

He reached up to take the ice bag from her, figuring he needed it more than William. She yanked it away, nearly snarling. "You're *not* Native!" she shouted. Her voice ringing in the small space. "You're probably not even American!"

He looked up at her. "Does it matter? Does it really matter? I've lived in this country most of my life. I *look* Injun." He pointed to Andy. "More than he does!"

"*Injun!*" she shouted. "Injun?" She looked around, wild-eyed. I saw her eyes fix on something but wasn't quick enough to stop her. She snatched up a wooden-handled kitchen knife, about ten inches long with a sharp point and what looked like a very good edge.

Too late, Two Deer's survival instinct kicked in and he began struggling up from the floor.

With the knife in her right hand, she grabbed his braid in her left and yanked his head back, exposing the throat. Before I could stop her, she leaned in and slashed hard. There was nothing anybody could have done.

Two Deer gave a heart-rending cry, falling back down on the carpet as she stood over him, the freshly cut, two-foot braid dangling like a dead serpent in her hand.

When the two henchmen came back from their circuit, they opened the door and looked down to the carpet where William should have been. When they looked up, they were eye-to-eye with Andy's .45 and my .38. They knew the drill. They bent to put their revolvers on the carpet and straightening, put up their hands.

William, in his mild way, confronted Two Deer. "Where are the oil documents?"

"Go to hell!" snarled Two Deer, the smooth-politician veneer peeling away to reveal the oil-field tough guy.

218

William whacked him with an open hand on the already-sore side of his face, bouncing his head off the wall. It had to hurt.

"I don't know! Ask these guys," he said, indicating Andy and me. "I went down there and asked nice—didn't kill 'em—and only got a couple of the contracts and a stack of church trash." He winced in my direction. "Ask him."

"That part's true, except for the asking nice," Andy exclaimed. "You tried to burn us alive!"

"That's a lie," he said, not to me but to Evie, his eyes pleading. "I never."

"Well somebody did," she said. "I saw them. You saw them. They showed up all singed and stinky."

"That guy is a lying suit of shit!" said Andy, with feeling. It was hard to argue the point.

In the end, all we could find were the several contracts I'd given to him. We couldn't find any of the bundles of bills. I had a feeling a lot of it had gone into setting up the banquet hall and the huge photomurals.

William used the kitchen knife to cut lamp cord to hogtie the three. Then we waited. When the three cops returned from the airport, we did the same with them. They came swinging through the door to find four handguns at face level, and as one simply raised their hands. We relieved them of a pile of weapons—multiple handguns, knives, blackjacks and brass knuckles—and added the three to our thug collection.

When it was all done, Evie and I looked at each other and she walked into my arms. "I'm so sorry. I didn't want to get you involved in this. That's why I told you we were breaking up. You were supposed to back off, stay out of harm's way. Why didn't you?"

"I didn't believe you," I said. "Well, maybe at first. But then I just guessed it, that you were trying to keep me out of trouble."

"And you couldn't just back off?"

"I couldn't," I said, "not with you in danger."

"Oh Hardy," she said, and she kissed me. And something inside me that had been disarranged for too long, dropped back where it belonged.

❖

"You're still wanted," said William. "We need to get out of here."

Evie looked up. "You're wanted? By the police?"

"Kidnapping and murder," said Andy. "Now that we got you, we can at least prove we didn't kidnap anybody."

"Well, then, whom did you murder?"

He gave her a look. "*Accused* of murdering that security guy at the hotel. Hoping *you* could tell us who killed him. My money's on Two Deer."

"Ron? Ron's dead?" Her hand went to her mouth and her eyes grew large. "He was alive when we left the hotel. He couldn't do enough for Edward, hoping to get a job in Juneau with the new administration. He helped carry Edward's and my luggage to the car." She broke off and shook her head. "And now he's dead. I can vouch for Edward, at least. We've been together here, since then."

"We can't let Kellar grab us," warned William.

"I have an idea," I said, explained it to them, and we set Evie up to make two quick phone calls.

Kellar arrived alone. After all, his three best men were already on duty here. He came blustering in, cigar in hand, found only Evie at first and gave her what was supposed to be his seductive look. He came up short when he saw

220

the six men: shorn Two Deer and his two thugs, plus his own three cops, tied up and arranged against one wall.

"What the …?" He assumed a pose of astonishment, grabbing the cigar out of his mouth and squinting suspiciously at Evie.

"Cut those guys loose!" he demanded.

"But Chief," she said, "they've been stealing oil leases, receiving and spending stolen cash from the Naval Oil Reserve! They may even have been in on the plot to kill Peter Senengatuk."

He wrinkled his forehead at her and threw his arms out, palms up, foul cigar set between extended first and second fingers.

"Tell me somethin' I don't know!"

That's when Frank Jacobs and his deputies—the other phone call—arrested the whole bunch of them. He took statements from Andy and me, cancelled our warrants and turned us loose. "Go and sin no more," he said. And laughed.

CHAPTER 29

Days later, President Eisenhower appointed an Alaskan, Mike Stepovich as the new Territorial governor, there being no evidence that the President ever seriously considered Edward Two Deer.

Though not a Native American, the villages celebrated Stepovich as the first native-*born* Alaskan, especially as word of Two Deer's Italian ancestry began to reach the villages.

After a day of interrogation from Frank Jacobs and others, and a promise to return on demand, Evie, William and I drove home to Chandalar. Two significant questions remained: who killed Ron, and who had Richard?

Andy went back to his restaurant. We all knew the more time went by, the more likely Richard wouldn't be found until the snow melted—the Alaska way. Either that or the eventual postcard from the tropical vacation hideaway. "Would be better than nothing," said Andy.

Evie went back to teaching. "I miss my kids," she said. They missed her, too. Their substitute, one of the CAA wives, was a "monster," they told her.

When we showed up at the Coffee Cup for Saturday breakfast, Rosie looked us over and sniffed. "About darn time." Holding the coffee pot safely out to one side, she hugged Evie and then hugged me. "Out of the hash," she whispered intimately. It figured.

I turned over the rest of the stolen oil leases to the marshal, glad to be rid of them. Without Richard's side of the story, it was difficult to figure who to blame. Since Lonnie had skipped—thanks to me, as William pointed out—blame for the murder of Ron at the Denali, and suspicion about the Senengatuk murder leaned to him. I didn't like him for either one, but had no better suspect to offer.

I slid easily back into the mission church routine of visiting the sick, trying to make sure nobody froze or starved, and helping my parishioners figure out their income tax and other government documents. It all went back to ordinary in a matter of just a few days, until I received a phone call—one I'd been expecting.

The next Saturday morning, I picked up Adele at her cabin and brought her back to the rectory where we met Evie and walked together to the depot under a cloudless brilliant blue bowl of sky. With the temp up to about minus twenty and no breeze, it felt like a spring day, sunlight glittering off a million diamonds in the snow.

The blue and gold train came ringing, hissing and clattering into the station exactly at 10:10, and we edged forward with the small crowd to get a look at who was arriving and who departing, most carrying their belongings in doubled, string-handled, Coghill's shopping bags— Chandalar Samsonite—we called it.

With the crowd pressing around, small Adele briefly lost sight of the train steps, the brakeman, and the arriving passengers. "I can't see," she said. But then she could. Like the Red Sea parting, the crowd split cleanly to reveal an impossibly tall figure wearing his familiar silly porkpie hat, with a shopping bag in one hand and bouquet of daisies in the other.

A murmur ran through the crowd. Not just about the return of Butch, but about the flowers, something none of us had seen since way last summer, now only the dimmest memory.

She saw him, hesitated, covered her mouth with both hands, her eyes bright. Then she ran for him, launching herself like a child at the last minute, into the air. He caught her, clutching the small woman, the bag and the flowers with ease, and he kissed her on the mouth.

She may have hesitated, retiring her dreams of motherhood in the fleetest sliver of a second. Then she kissed him back, gratefully, joyfully. Most of the crowd melted away, us too, leaving them just as they were.

"I predict an enthusiastic homecoming," said Evie as we walked back.

"I think you mean sex," I said to her.

"Oh yes," she said, "lots of it." She blushed a little, took my arm and squeezed it hard. I admit I wished we were going home, too. "I know what you're thinking," she said.

A few days later I asked her, over coffee, "Ever think about us being married?" She looked at me a long time and took a deep breath, releasing it slowly before she answered.

"Only about all the time."

"And about making love?"

"Even more."

"The thing is," she said, "when I think I've lost you, drowned in the river, shot by Lonnie, I realize I can't …I don't want …to live on without you. You're my …" she hesitated, "everything."

"So we should get married," I told her, "if it's like that."

Her eyes met mine. "It is, and we should."

In that moment, hopefulness reappeared, just suddenly *there* the way the very air turns to gold when a breeze lifts a shimmer of snow catching the low sun.

Within a day or so I caught sight of William and Alice through my window strolling along the frozen river, holding hands. Well, holding each other's bulky mitts, anyway.

And a strange kind of double-knock at the parsonage door, half rap and half bird scratch, brought Adele and Butch in to announce that they would be married, "When it is warm," said Adele. Sounded good to me.

Evie and I began to imagine ourselves living together here, her not going back to her chilly cabin at night, about waking up together, having a life. In one of those conversations I told her about the little girl.

"I've been dreaming about a small, dark-haired girl."

She looked at me. "Do you know her? How old is she?"

"I don't know her. Don't think I've seen her anywhere, except in my dreams. She's probably four or five."

"How long has this been going on?"

"Gosh, about six months."

"Walking along a stream?"

"Yes!"

"Then I've seen her, too," she said, frowning a bit. "I wonder what that means, both of us dreaming her?"

"Something good," I assured her. But it seemed strange, very strange. And over it all hung a cloud. I didn't see it at first. Or I did see it but let myself forget.

The phone rang: Andy. "Somebody trashed the restaurant. Turned it upside down looking for something."

"Think Lonnie came back?"

"Nah. Never saw a guy so happy to leave Alaska. Don't know what to think. But if it's somebody still looking for lease papers, you're next."

"I gave them all up," I said, something he knew anyway. And then, remembering my previously tapped phone—although I wasn't hearing any of that static—I said it again. "I gave them all to Marshal Jacobs."

"Yeah," said Andy. "Watch your ass."

February became March with temperatures climbing to near zero and sunrise a bit after seven instead of halfway through the morning. *Almost summer*, I told myself over coffee.

Friday night, Evie and I, along with Butch and Adele, appropriately saw *To Catch a Thief*, the Cary Grant and Grace Kelley academy-award winner from a few years back—movies take a while to get to Chandalar. No one wanted to sit behind big Butch.

"He's so dreamy," sighed Evie as we filed out, after ninety minutes with Cary Grant. "Almost," she said, with a sidelong glance, "as dreamy as you!"

"Nice save!"

Butch and Adele said their goodnights and headed off while Evie and I strolled companionably under starlight, down the snow-packed streets to my place for coffee. Off in the distance we heard one wolf howl, then others, followed by a smattering of nervous husky barks from here in town.

Andy had been right. When we got back to my cabin, we found the place torn apart—again—turned upside-down. They'd flipped my mattress, emptied all my drawers, even kitchen drawers, and when I swung closed my medicine chest door I discovered a note taped to the newly cracked mirror: "Last chance," it read in large block letters.

"What is it about creeps that makes them always want to tear your place apart? How many times is this?" Evie asked. I hadn't even told her about the last time. She peered over my shoulder. "Last chance for what?"

"I dunno," I told her, though pretty sure I'd find out.

Evie didn't turn up for coffee the next morning, Saturday, which wasn't too unusual. We'd stayed up late putting my place back together and she insisted on walking herself home. I didn't call her and didn't go over early because I knew there was little she liked better than the chance to sleep in, something her teacher schedule didn't allow any of. But about eleven o'clock, I put on my parka and mukluks to walk down to her cabin. With only coffee for breakfast, my stomach was already pondering the possibility of the two of us and Coffee Cup cheeseburgers for lunch.

She wasn't there. What's more, she hadn't been there. I could feel my heart thud up as I found the door ajar and I pushed in to discover the fire out and the bed unslept-in. I tried her phone, to call Andy, but found the line cut. Feeling frantic, grasping for alternate possibilities—there weren't any—I began jogging back to the rectory, only to be intercepted by Butch, also wearing a frantic look.

"Adele's gone," he said, looking wild-eyed. "She walked to Coghill's for lard this morning. She never made it there, and now I can't find her."

"C'mon," I said, and we hurried back to the rectory, me struggling to keep up with Butch's long strides and adrenaline-fueled pace. I called Andy.

"On the way."

227

I also called William, who didn't answer. On a hunch, I dialed Alice at the Bide-A-While. She answered on one ring. "I can find him," she said, leaving me with the distinct impression she was actually looking at him as she spoke.

"Tell him Evie and Adele have been taken," I said. She repeated it. "He's on his way," she said, and he was, knocking quickly and walking through my door within about ten minutes.

"What do we know?" He nodded at Butch, his face grim. William treated Evie like a favorite niece, taking her loss personally. "Andy on the way?"

"Yes," I told him. He cut right to the chase. "You have any of those lease papers or money, you are holding back? Anything at all?

"Nothing," I assured him. "I held nothing back."

"That may be too bad."

"Huh?"

"It means we have nothing to bargain with. The four of us sat down to strategize, but made little progress. We didn't know who, where, or why.

Just then, Andy walked through my door and took a stool.

"Borrowed a car," he said, in answer to the question I didn't even voice. "Anthony's."

At four o'clock the phone rang. Although we'd been sitting around the kitchen table, I made it up, down the hall, and into the office to answer on the second ring.

"You ruined me," said the voice.

"Who is this?"

"Shut up and listen. I don't want to kill these women but I will."

"I'm listening," I said, actually sharing the handset with Andy. When the voice spoke again, Andy's eyes got round.

He mouthed, "Richard!"

"I'm going to make this easy for you," Richard went on, "so you don't get confused. I'm pretty sure you turned over those lease papers, and I know you managed to get Injun Ed locked up. That's funny! You know what his name is, really? Edward Leonardo Morelli …Ed Lee, to his hick family. You've been busy—and lucky—but it all ends here. I want you to know I'm serious, but fair."

"Sure, fair," I murmured back at him. *This guy's missing dots on his dice*, is what I was thinking.

"And get this, if the marshal shows up, your girl is dead. Period. Dead. Bullet through the head, dead. You get it?"

"I got it," I assured him. "Look, this is between us. Let her go."

"Oh, you bet it's between us, and whether or not I let her go is completely up to you. Remember that."

"I will."

You know the railroad bridge at Nenana?"

"Sure."

"About ten minutes ago I had your little friend Adele tied out there, right next to a red line I painted on the catwalk. You don't have a lot of time to get to her because, darn it, we forgot to leave a parka for her." He laughed, but there was no humor in it. "I'll call you back with more details, when you know the exact spot I'm talking about." And I heard a distinct click as he broke the connection.

"Adele on the railroad bridge at Nenana," I said, grabbing gear, heading out the door, adding, "No parka," back over my shoulder as I went.

229

Leaving William and Butch, who was not happy to be left, Andy and I ran for the truck—him carrying the sniper rifle—making the twenty-minute-or-so drive to Nenana and to the bridge in record time. All the while I found myself trying to calculate how long Adele could be up there without losing so much body temperature she'd go unconscious or suffer severe frostbite on fingers, toes and ears—maybe losing them. I will never forget first Alaska stories of toes frozen so badly they just broke off, to be dumped—like black, irregular-shaped marbles—rattling out of the sock.

We almost missed seeing her there as we approached, a tiny figure up maybe sixty feet, the equivalent of a five or six story building above the frozen river at just about dead center. A stranger, someone from "the states," might be already unconscious in the cold. But she'd lived every winter of her life in this cold, was used to it, and knew to wrap herself small, back turned to the slight breeze to conserve body heat.

With the sun molten in the clear sky, intense yellow light poured in sideways from behind us, creating both impossible brilliance and deep, dark shadows while projecting the geometry of the bridge on the nearby hill.

"If this isn't a trap then I'm a dog turd." Andy worked the bolt to chamber a round, "You lead, I'll cover. No trouble knowin' where they'll be." He jerked a thumb at the intense sunlight. If they happen to miss you the first time, I'll see they don't get a second chance."

We parked at the south end of the bridge, the town side, and I scurried up the steep earth embankment on a narrow tramped-down footpath through about two feet of snow. Not walking the footpath wasn't an option, there was no other route. So I couldn't duck, dodge or do anything to diminish the itchy way the bullseye felt between my shoulder blades.

When I reached the railroad tracks at the top, I turned to hurry along the narrow catwalk out onto the bridge. I couldn't bring myself to jog this far up on thirty inches of plank. Meanwhile, behind me and just before the bridge, Andy pitched himself flat between the rails, scanning for the shooter we both assumed would be there.

We weren't wrong. I saw movement out of the corner of my eye and pitched flat as two shots rang out, almost as one, the noise hanging and echoing in the bridgework and against the hill.

But they weren't shooting at me!

Two shooters rose as a pair and each fired a round at Andy! Shooting as one was smart, but rising was their mistake. Andy, prone and steady, picked one of them off while the first shots still echoed. I heard the shout of pain and surprise. I took it for my signal to get up and start moving, but still couldn't jog.

Granted, the rail looked sturdy, but it assumed someone just walking erect, holding on. I could easily be shot, or slip and fall flat, simply rolling under to fall a very long way. I sneaked a look over the edge, all the way down to snow-covered river ice. Just looking made muscles clench all the way back to my sphincter.

The bridge, still a landmark after nearly forty years, ran a bit over seven hundred feet from pier to pier. So I had what amounted to a three-hundred-fifty-foot shooting gallery to cross to get to Adele. Just because they hadn't shot at me yet, didn't mean they wouldn't.

He hadn't lied. Adele wore no parka—at about minus-twenty degrees—but I saw with relief that she did still wear her hat, gloves and mukluks. She sat tiny, knees pulled up tight with arms wrapped around, conserving her core body temperature. She saw me coming, but stayed put, stayed as warm as she could, and resisted the urge to jump to her feet and become a larger, colder target.

They were shooting at Andy, not me, so mostly a trap for him. How could that make sense?

Approaching Adele, I used my folding pocketknife to quickly saw away ropes that held her. Then, unzipping my parka, I beckoned her up and off the catwalk to step over to the scary place between the rails. I lay down, across heavy creosoted ties with six or eight inches of nothing but air between them. Then I pulled her down and tight against me, warming her small body against mine, wrapping the rest of my parka around behind to try to keep her warm.

The shooter had no angle on us but it didn't mean he wouldn't try. It wouldn't be an easy shot. The steel rail and heavy timber ties between us would deflect or absorb gunfire. He still had the sun on his side, clearly spotlighting Andy's head whenever he tried to get a look up over the rail. I sneaked a peek as the shooter squeezed off another round, zinging a ricochet off heavy steel just inches in front of Andy's face.

Other than that, the shooter had little ambush advantage here. No cover. From the narrow road to river ice stretched an expanse of several hundred feet of shallow, open riverbank and flood plain, no rocks, trees or stumps to hunker behind.

Back in the late twenties and early thirties—I'd seen photos—there had been boatbuilding here, big sternwheel river boats arranged on long timber slipways—ways, they called them—for easily sliding the big boats to the river. But time, and the river itself, had taken everything, leaving only a smattering of sparse willows and one cast-off cable reel, about three feet in diameter, half-buried in snow. I remember seeing kids balancing on it, rolling it out the road last summer.

So there, behind the reel, the shooters had set up.

Andy followed the ricochet with two quick shots, counting on the time it would take the remaining shooter to cock his rifle and be ready to fire again. Andy fired, and in what seemed like a single continuous motion, yanked the bolt to cock and then fired again. His second bullet plowed through a section of the cable reel, blowing away a big chunk of it. That was enough.

The shooter jumped to his feet, face bleeding from splinter hits, shouting, tossing his rifle off into the snow, standing with hands up and spread. His surrender noted, he quickly checked his buddy—apparently dead—then sprinted away down the road, trusting, hoping, maybe even praying Andy wouldn't backshoot him.

Andy didn't. "Tempting," he said later. "An easy shot."

So we had Adele back, seemingly no worse for wear. "Living here my whole life," she said, "I don't notice cold much."

That morning, she had only walked a block or so from her cabin, still out of the main part of town, when a big black and white car pulled up alongside to ask if she wanted a ride. "I told them, no thank you, I like to walk." That was when one of them jumped out of the car, snatched her up and stuffed her in the trunk. The next time the trunk opened, she was in a warehouse, unheated and dark. They did bring her inside a small heated office, gave her lunch and later let her use the toilet. "They weren't mean," she said. But they wouldn't answer any of her questions and wouldn't let her leave. After a couple of hours, they stuffed her back in the trunk, drove to the bridge, pulled her out of her parka and tied her there.

The man who tied her said, "You won't be up here long. They're coming to get you." And in just about a half hour she heard an engine, peeked over her shoulder, and recognized the church truck.

"I knew you'd come," she said to me.

"I'm glad *you* didn't come along," she said to Butch.

"How come?" he asked, I think a little miffed that we went to rescue his girl without him.

"They were shooting!" said Adele, taking one of his huge hands in both of her small ones, holding the back of it against her cheek.

"There is one thing I do not get," said William.

"I don't get *any* of it," said Andy.

"What?" I asked.

"The red line," said William. "He went to the trouble of painting a red line up on the catwalk, and he went to the trouble of mentioning it to you."

"So?"

"So it has to mean something."

CHAPTER 30

We waited. Through the long evening we sat in my living room, the five of us, plus Alice Young, who showed up about ten o'clock. Reading listlessly, planning fruitlessly—with no idea what to plan for, drinking too much coffee, jittering. Only Adele, curled up with her head on Butch's thigh and snuggled under a down parka, managed to sleep.

"Making us wait is part of the plan," said William. At about midnight, he and Alice got up to go lay down on my bed. But they didn't sleep much either, and now and again I could hear them talking.

Very late at night, with just the two of us still sitting up awake, Andy said, "I thought I was in love with this guy. No, I *was* in love with him. Now I want to shoot him!"

"Alaska makes some people crazy," I reminded him. "So much wealth seems so possible. To find …or earn …or steal."

Andy looked up. "Richard told me once that he worked in the Texas and Oklahoma oilfields, and he hated it. That's what this is all about, isn't it—oil?"

"Maybe in the beginning." I didn't tell him the rest.

Sometime between three and four I think we must have drifted off. I know I did. I dreamed that dream again, walking along a stream somewhere, trout rising, jumping. The little girl walked with me, the one I often saw in dreams. "I don't know your name," I told her. I had told her this before, but it never got me anywhere.

"But I know yours!"

"Okay," I said, testing her, "What is it?"

She giggled. "It's Daddy!"

I jerked awake, startled, dazed. Seconds later the phone rang and I stumbled to it, bleary eyed, my stomach doing flip-flops. I tried to say hello, but croaked and cleared my throat. "Hello?"

"So here's how it goes," said what I now knew to be Richard's voice—very upbeat and frankly sounding more and more crazy. "This is simple. I know you'll get it. You want to save your precious Evie, right?"

"Of course."

"So tonight, you go to the red line on the bridge in time to be there when the 10:10 comes by. Got it?"

"So far," I said. "What then?"

"'What then' is, when the headlight shines full on you—like a theater spotlight—and I can clearly see you from wherever I am, you jump."

I was sure I misheard.

"I ...jump?"

"Yep. Just make sure the headlight has you. I want to see you go over. Then I," he hesitated so I'd get it, "*drop* Evie, unharmed, on a street in Nenana and drive out of this frozen hellhole."

"You want me dead." Saying it aloud didn't make it any more believable or understandable.

"Not just you. I have a plan for our little buddy, Andy, too."

"Andy was your friend, your ..."

"Lover? But he's not now, is he?" I didn't know what to say.

"I'm giving you the chance to give up your life to save another. It's the 'Jesus way.' The shepherd gives up his life for the sheep, and all that. You'll be famous. A martyr. Isn't that what you people dream about?"

236

"Never have." It was all I could say in the face of such extreme absurdity.

"So, you got it?" he asked, wrapping up. "Any details I can clear up for you?"

"Let me speak to Evie."

"No," he said.

"How do I know she's alive?"

He snorted. "You know. I kept my word about Adele; you have her all safe and sound."

"Look," I said, "Evie hasn't harmed you. I haven't harmed you ...Andy hasn't. Why can't you just let this go, let her go, and leave?"

"See you tonight," he said. "Break a leg, at least." He laughed at his joke and I heard the click as the line closed.

❖

"You can't jump off the bridge," said Andy. "There's gotta be another way."

"I'm all ears," I told him. We were all awake, back in the living room, yawning, craving coffee. But when I went to the kitchen to make some, all I could find was the empty can. Last time I looked I had about half a can and I didn't remember finishing it. *Did someone break in and steal my coffee?* Nothing made sense this morning.

"We have about fourteen hours to figure this out," I said. "And there's more. He plans to kill you, too."

Andy screwed up his face in disbelief and pointed an index finger at his chest. "Me? How?"

"I don't know."

"Well, I can't figure out how to save you *and* me on an empty stomach—without coffee. Let's go get food."

We set out for the Coffee Cup, *en masse*, just before sunrise, the sun already lighting just a gold rim along the top of the near hill. Instead of taking roads and walking around the long way, like adults, we walked single file on packed-down kids' trails around cabins and sheds, across vacant lots, more or less as the raven flies.

The clear cold air and growing predawn glow helped settle me. In the space of just a few minutes of walking along, listening to snow crunch and the distant growl of a slow-starting truck, it all fell into place for me. I went from wild desperation about what I *might possibly do*, to an exact sense of what I needed to do, and would do. Even though what I decided seemed crazy, in the end I felt the bizarre calm that comes with knowing I'd settled on the only solution.

We were first through the door when the restaurant opened, Rosie greeting, waving us to find places in a room full of empty chairs and loud music. I recognized Joe Bennett and the Sparkletones' frenetic *Black Slacks*, playing on the Crosley, which, mercifully, Rosie reached up to turn down. "Too early," she said. She looked at our faces, looked for Evie. "Something's wrong!"

There's a cover illustrator I like, working for the Saturday Evening Post. His name is Norman Rockwell, and he is famous for arranging and painting a scene in a way that sets it in my mind and makes it unforgettable. That happened just then, as I imagined the six of us around our table posed for the cover of the March, 1957 issue.

William and Alice sat next together, leaning in to one another, two secret people saying what they say. He, polishing the lens of his rimless glasses on a napkin, Alice taking a deep draw on her Tareyton, then waving it for emphasis. I'm sitting by myself, as is Andy—only I look calm—at least that's what I think. Andy looks tired, frazzled, maybe confused. Butch and Adele just look happy to be together, especially after yesterday. Adele has just told Rosie about her rescue, and about Andy saving her. Rosie, not yet knowing that Evie "has been taken," is just turning to focus the golden light of joy on Andy, the only man she's ever cared to love in her whole life. She looks proud.

In this Rockwell scene, Rosie has a yellow pencil tucked behind her ear, bright in a froth of dark, shiny hair. She's wearing the white-framed glasses, a mint-green waitress dress with "Rosie" stitched above her left breast, hence the local joke, 'Hey, Rosie, what do you call the other one?' She hasn't had time to change out of the caribou mukluks she put on this morning to walk to work.

Typically, she's holding a round, glass coffee pot— full and steaming—in her right hand, shifting ceramic mugs on the tabletop with her left for one of her quick pours. It all fixes in my brain.

The door opens and closes; the small brass bell at the top of the frame tinkles. A swirl of frosty air sweeps past our knees. The neon sign next to the door is lit and spells "Open" backwards, 'nepo,' from my perspective. We all must have glanced around at about the same time to see who came in, because as one, we went silent, seeing the man with the gun.

CHAPTER 31

The gunman saw Rosie first and recognized her: the Italian bombshell. The one who planted the big one on Andy at the restaurant in Fairbanks. "You!" he said, and his jaw dropped, but not the barrel of the Colt semi-automatic.

"Bob," I said, recognizing the congenial policeman, though I suspected not on duty now. Today he wore what seemed the standard issue oil-thug uniform: good quality, medium-brimmed fur felt fedora with no ear cover, a long dark overcoat, and unsnapped black rubber galoshes.

He tipped his head in greeting. "Father." Then he looked at Andy, the gun following his eyes. "You and me need to take a walk."

Andy's eyes narrowed and his jaw muscles knotted. "Don't think so."

"Sorry folks," said Bob, shrugging regretfully. He raised the pistol, sighting, trigger finger tightening.

We all froze. William and I had guns we couldn't get at. Butch sat on the wrong side of the table, same for Alice and Adele, who were probably too small to do anything anyway.

But still I rose, knees flexing to jump, arms reaching, all the while knowing I couldn't possibly get to where he stood, couldn't possibly stop him. I knew I'd hear the deafening roar, feel the thudding impact on my eardrums, of one, two, probably three shots delivered "center mass," as the Army firearms trainer used to drill. I'd see blood-ringed bullet holes blossom and spread across Andy's tan, plaid flannel shirt. I remember fearing that bullets passing through him would hit someone else, maybe the cook, at the back of the restaurant.

Rosie spun, lashing out with her Pyrex coffee pot, steaming, scalding coffee drenching Bob's gun hand. He pulled the trigger reflexively—it had to hurt like blazes—the gun fired, missing Andy widely but grazing Rosie's new Crosley radio. He shook the pistol out of his hand, skin already blistering, red and raw-looking. "Damn," he shouted. "Damn!"

But Rosie wasn't finished. She whacked him hard on the side of the head with the pot, knocking his hat off, splashing his head and neck with the remaining hot liquid, the impact making a resounding *bonk!*

"Ow!" he said petulantly, like a schoolboy being switched, ducking and covering with his arm, trying to protect the burned, tender parts.

By now, we were all in motion, ducking, jumping, protecting. Butch reached Bob first, clubbing him with a forearm and fist that took the man all the way to the black-and-white checkered tile floor. Butch snatched up the .45 with what looked like an expert hand, thumbed back the hammer, and thrust the muzzle to the side of Bob's head in a way that made me know it was all over for Bob.

"No-o-o," said Adele's soft voice, as she had followed around the table to put her hand on his forearm. Butch shook his head, like a man sleepwalking, waking back into the room and the moment. He gently lowered the hammer, expertly dropped the clip out the bottom of the grip and ejected the live round.

Adele stretched up to pat him fondly below one big shoulder, and he turned his head to smile at her.

Rosie looked up from pursuing Bob with the coffee pot, her eyes seeking and finding Andy's. She set the pot on the table and met him halfway around, the two folding into each other's arms, holding on hard. "I love you," she said. "I'd be lost without you in the world."

"I'd be lost without me, too," he said, ever the smartass.

William crouched with his .45 muzzle nuzzling Bob's ear. "Where," he asked, in his deceptively, mild-mannered way, "is Evie?"

Bob raised his hands above his head, even though lying on the floor. "I don't know. I got a call. Somewhere near here—someplace with a telephone."

William looked around at the group. "Should I kill him?"

"Not here," said Rosie over Andy's shoulder. "I got customers coming in anytime. They're not gonna want to eat if it's all bloody."

"Wait," I said. "Let me bless him first." I hoped we were kidding—trying to scare him. Color drained from his face.

"I …I *really don't know* where she is," he said, with emphasis. "And if you shoot me, I still won't know."

"Yeah," said Andy, stepping away from Rosie's embrace, turning. "But you'll be one big thorn out of our asses. I say take him out in the woods and shoot him. I'll do it."

"I am afraid," said William after a moment, rising from his crouch, "that I have already shot my quota this month. We will have to turn him over to Marshal Jacobs and let the Federal Government deal with him. "I would say fifteen to life at McNeil Island."

"I'll see your fifteen and go twenty," said Andy.

William caught Alice's eye. "Handcuffs," he said. She reached around to where his parka hung on the chair back.

I couldn't help noticing she knew exactly which pocket they were in. She tossed them and he caught them easily, cuffing Bob's hands behind him, not much minding the injured one.

More intimately, he asked Bob, "Is there anything else you can tell us?"

"Only that he's a nut job," said Bob. "This all started out like business. You know, change some stuff on oil leases, put them out to our own companies. It was a sure thing, money in the bank. Then," he shook his head, "something went sideways." Bob looked at me.

"I like Evie," he said. "Heck, I like *you*… love the way you whipped Chief Blowhard without even working up a sweat. I'd tell you if I could. Looks like I'm out of this and I'm not sorry about it. But I just don't know anything."

The restaurant door opened, tinkling the bell, and some of the 'usuals' began filing in. If there were anything odd about guns and handcuffed people amid the scent of gunsmoke in the place, they didn't show it, just headed to their accustomed chairs, lighting up their smokes.

"Coffee, Rosie," one of them called.

She peered into the empty pot like there might be some left. "I'll make a fresh pot," she said, moving away, resuming her routine.

So we ate and drank our coffee, but I can't tell you what I ordered or if I enjoyed it. I remember looking up from my daze to see Rosie looking at me, her hand on the back of Andy's neck, fondly. And he didn't seem to mind. When she had the time to ask, "So where *is* Evie?" the others filled her in. When it was time to go, she came and knelt in front of me, setting the coffee pot on the table. She put her hands on my knee and leaned close, looking into my eyes."

"You'll get her back," she said. "It'll be okay."

"Thanks. I hope so."

As she kissed me on the forehead and stood up, someone called, "Hey Rosie, where's my breakfast?"

"It's cookin'," she called back and, snatching the pot, spun away.

❖

I don't know where everybody else went, but I went home. I couldn't stop thinking about tonight at 10:10 on the bridge. I'd made up my mind. I knew the others, particularly Andy and William, would be out following any leads, beating the bushes to find and save Evie. Maybe they would. But if they didn't it would be on me.

Does anybody who is going to die really *think* they're going to die? I mean, I've lived my whole life without dying yet, though I could have several times. Now I'm actually making plans to die, yet still don't believe it.

I'm planning to jump. That will be the hard part, stepping off the equivalent of a five-story building in the dark. *Can I do that?* I had a hard time parachuting out of an airplane during the war. I'd still be in the darn plane if the sergeant hadn't both bullied and cajoled. Knowing I was doing this thing for Evie, the one person on the planet who lit the light in my life—would that make it easier? Maybe, but I remained unconvinced.

I felt strangely calm. I wrote a few letters, to be mailed later. I wrote one to the Bishop, expressing thanks for taking me on here, one to Mary's parents. I hadn't kept closely in touch with my in-laws after she died, after I came up here. I always felt just a little like they blamed me, like maybe I didn't do enough. Maybe they thought a man in seminary had a hotline to God that would somehow save their daughter, cure the polio—make her able to breathe and walk again.

I also settled a few small debts, wrote a quick will, leaving everything I personally owned to Andy, and then did some house cleaning. I didn't want my parishioners to come in here after they scraped me off the ice to find the place a pigpen.

When darkness fell, I fixed a small meal of canned bacon, eggs, toast, and hash browns, what Mary used to call breakfast-for-dinner. It was tasty. I lingered over a second cup of coffee, wondered where my friends were, and if I'd be seeing Mary tonight. Somehow it didn't feel odd to die for one woman and go directly to another. I had thought it might. Maybe it's all just love and the mistake we make is the kinds of different boxes we try to stuff it in.

One thing puzzled me. I admit it: the little girl. Presumably she's my daughter in the future, and now it seems I don't have a future. *How does that add up?* I wondered. Of course, it didn't.

At about 9:00—as I was pulling myself together, getting ready to drive out alone to the place I'd die, feeling more than a little sorry for myself—Andy showed up.

"Thought I'd drive ya, bring the truck back after." I must have looked at him oddly.

"What?" he demanded. "You're *not* dying out there. Forget it! Not if I have anything to say about it."

"Do you?"

He looked sheepish. "Well, not just now." He hesitated. "Except this," he added, making not much sense. "Just make sure you jump from the red mark." As if I wouldn't.

245

After I got my parka and mitts on, ready to walk out the door, I hugged him. He hugged me back. It felt a little strange. "This will be okay," he said.

Easy for you to say! "Drive?" I asked him.

"Sure," and I pitched him the keys.

He brought along the Mauser, just in case. But I thought it unlikely that Richard would show himself, to be picked off. This whole thing was designed to give Richard the front row seat to my death, in a way that didn't expose him at all. Then, hopefully, he'd drop Evie in Nenana, unharmed, and drive away—though I knew the Highway Patrol was probably out there looking for him already. I didn't care much for his chances of really getting out of the Territory.

We got to the bridge at about 9:30 on the first overcast night we'd seen for a while. On other nights I'd seen it so moonlit here that the bridge threw a latticed moon shadow on the near hill. Not tonight. I needed a flashlight to pick my way up the foot trail to the tracks, then to follow the narrow catwalk out the three hundred fifty-some feet to the painted red line. It looked like nothing so much as blood, by the light of my Eveready.

Off in the far distance I heard a train whistle, so far away it might have been the wind or a wolf howl, except that I knew it wasn't. In my mind I could see the crossing they were blowing for. In a couple more minutes, they'd blow again at the crossing just below town but still across the river. Then the train would run along the hill just a few minutes more to get to where it turned toward the bridge. From here I'd see the headlight and the lit passenger windows, maybe make out the people smoking, chatting, reading, in the seats and in their compartments. Warm, snug, safe.

246

I don't believe in praying for 'favors.' I've never thought it was how God works. I don't believe God cares if our basketball team wins, or even our country. I don't think God saves the king—or now the Queen. This sounds like heresy, but I don't think God cares if we live or die. If God created Heaven and earth, which I do believe, then it seems to me He would be equally comfortable with our existence in any of his created realms.

So I didn't pray to live. I prayed for strength. And I prayed for courage, for myself and for Evie. These had been hard days for her, too.

I'd read that suicides, ready to jump, would remove their eyeglasses. But I didn't wear any. I could hear the hum and rattle of the southbound, rising. In another few hours the people on that train would roll into Anchorage, dispersing into the night, to home, to the airport, to the hotel. And I—what was left of me—would be in Andy or Oliver's meat shed, frozen stiff and solid by morning, waiting to be measured for one of Oliver's pine boxes. I could almost smell pine shavings on the wind.

A wolf howled, not so far away. Sometimes they still came into town. I knew that Evie and Richard were watching the bridge, waiting for the light. *Aren't we all?*

The whistle blew, suddenly very close, the train starting the long curve to the bridge. It startled me. If I'd been hanging on the outside of the guardrail, the noise might have shucked me right off into darkness. It would be just my luck to fall all the way down unseen. Richard would think I'd run away, as any sensible person would—any sensible person without someone to really love.

So I thought about Evie, her dark eyes and soft voice. And as the train came out on the bridge, I imagined her here with me, even as I climbed over the rail and hung on the outside. When the blinding, blue-white spotlight hit me full on, and I'd double-checked to make sure I was jumping exactly from the red line, I let go with my hands while pushing off with my feet, falling backward, waving my arms to stay vertical, flexing my knees for landing, just like in the paratroops. Never mind that I didn't have a parachute this time and would be falling to solid ice. So far, it was all easier than I expected, at least until I hit the ice. I remember thinking how startled the engineer must be to see me jump.

In that last instant, leaping into darkness, I thought I heard Evie's voice, like a benediction.

"Oh, Hardy!"

Chapter 32

Falling happens quickly. I had calculated that falling sixty feet takes about two seconds. It's true. One second I let go of the bridge, the next—instead of smashing myself to pulp on ice, hard as concrete—I sank to my chest in soft snow. I let out an involuntary *ooof,* but the fact is, it felt a lot like jumping out of the boxcar the last time I got my grocery shipment. Survivable.

The *ooof* helped Butch find me in murky darkness and extend one muscular arm to help me pull free. As he did, a cloud shifted and filtered down enough moonlight for me to make out the snow pile I'd jumped into, at least twenty feet to its summit. A steady procession of about thirty of my parishioners bearing shovels, filed by, whispering good wishes, shaking my hand, patting me on the back. Rosie hugged me. "Glad you made it safe," she said, as though I'd been traveling. They'd all been out here since just after dark, shoveling like mad, by the looks of it.

Alice, ever businesslike, took me by the arm. "William wants you over here," she said, also in an undertone. She led me to William, who turned out to be only one of six spotters arranged in a circle, all facing outward.

"We are certain he is watching," said William, "and that once he believes you are dead, he will do something to give himself away."

"It won't be much," Andy cautioned as I drew close. He gave a quick glance in my direction. "You okay?" I nodded and he went back to his task. "Nice of you to drop in," he added.

"Funny," said a familiar voice. Oliver's. Then he said, "There's a light! On the hill ...cemetery overlook."

"Everybody keep looking," cautioned Andy, "in case it's not them." Adele handed him the Mauser and he dialed it into focus. "It's a car ...door light ...late model ...pretty sure it's them. Anybody got anything else?" No one answered. Standing, Andy grabbed me by the sleeve. "Let's get!" He led me, not to the shore and the Ford, but out toward the middle of the river. "Meet you there," he called back, apparently to William who waved us away.

"But ..." I said.

"Hurry!"

I almost tripped over the dogsled, tied to a stake, hammered deep. Andy bundled me in, handed me the Mauser and a rope end to hold, "In case you fall out." He yanked the slipknot calling, "Hi you huskies, mush!" A big thirteen-dog team—picked for speed—ran like their tails were aflame.

"Says he's gonna drop Evie downtown, unharmed. Myself, I think he has other plans. But it's all we got."

It felt like flying, racing through darkness, nearly soundless, with just the occasional snow crunch and scritching of dog claws on ice. I could still feel my heart thudding—as if I'd just jumped off an impossibly high bridge. Would we make it? Could we save her? I hardly dared hope.

The town lights came up fast, the team not slowing at all as we raced up the incline of riverbank, across the railroad tracks and onto snow-packed city streets, the sled fishtailing as we made the turn.

I twisted my head around to look at Andy. "Do you know where they'll be?"

"I think so. Think they'll be down on the main street by the railroad depot."

"Why there?"

He laughed, grimly. "Streetlight! I checked. It's the only one lit now. The rest are out." Jumping off the runners he ran to gain the extra bit of speed. "Thinks it's a spotlight on him."

We pulled up short of Main Street, tied up the team and followed a footpath trail alongside the Pioneers of Alaska hall to sneak a cautious peek at the street. We found it empty.

Nenana's wide frontier-town main street came down to a *'T'* at its north end, to a right or left turn instead of crashing into the railroad depot, which some drinking drivers had been known to do.

"We beat 'em," said Andy. "Advantage of traveling in a straight line."

It would be nearly five minutes before William showed up with Butch and Oliver. "Five, maybe ten more minutes," said Andy. "If that really was them. Pretty curvy comin' down that hill."

Sure enough, in five more minutes, a new Chrysler Imperial—likely the same car Lonnie had been driving the day he came to kill me—nosed cautiously into the bright circle of streetlight. Andy called it—like center ring at the circus.

He looked at me. "You're on. You go and I'll back you. Love to see his face when he sees yours."

Jogging down the alley, I passed behind the Pioneer's building and several other small storefronts, past lines of garbage cans wearing tall snow hats. The alley brought me out on Front Street—paralleling the railroad tracks—just about fifty feet from the depot. From there I could spot the

Chrysler in its pool of bright light. Seen through the windows, the chrome, swooping-bird hood ornament faced away, glittering.

They were talking in the car, then Richard swung his door open sharply, got out and hurried around to open the passenger door, dragging Evie out by a handful of her parka. I could make out her hands bound in front of her. Roughly, he dragged her around the car, out of the shadow of the depot overhang into better light. From the standpoint of Andy's shot, he dragged her right into his sights.

I jogged across the street, darting from object to object for cover, to power poles and behind a parked, snowed-in car. Then I sprinted along the depot on the platform side to emerge on the building's far end, now behind Richard.

Evie stood unsteadily, parka hood back, sobbing, with remains of makeup smudged around her eyes and her nose running. Her lip looked swollen, and her left eyelid, like she'd been hit. I could feel anger rising in me, like a vessel filling, and with it, the desire to punch Richard to pulp.

Then, as often happens, I heard that other voice. "Who would Jesus punch?" *Drat!*

"Hardy," she sobbed, "jumped off a bridge for me, because you said you wouldn't kill me."

Richard appeared to consider this, then laughed. "So I lied. I really didn't think he'd jump. Actually, I've been planning to kill you the whole time."

"But ...why?"

"Because of Edward," he said, as if that explained everything. "Because," he drew a deep breath and then let it out, "because, he thought you were the missing piece in his great plan to be governor of the Territory, to make statehood happen, and turn things around for all the

252

Indians. So he threw me over for you! What a schmuck! A pretend Indian! We had such a good thing going."

I took a step, then another, moving slowly into the light, though still outside the hard edge of streetlight.

She gasped when she saw me, eyes widening, , and she might have given me away but for Richard's total immersion in his moment of triumph. He reached into his overcoat pocket to pull out a revolver.

"Down on your knees," he said, and grabbed her by the hair to force her down, both for the power of it and for the easy headshot, I imagined. "This is where women like you want to be anyway, isn't it?"

I had to hand it to her. She took one step and threw a knee toward his groin, unfortunately just grazing him, but I could tell it hurt. He drew back an arm and slapped her so hard she staggered and fell, the bare-handed *whack* of it echoing off nearby buildings on the cold empty street.

"Hit her again and I'll kill you," I said, noticing that small 'voice' didn't argue this time. He spun.

"You're dead," he said, clearly astonished, wiping a sleeve over his mouth, disbelief making him jibber. "I watched you go over! You *can't have survived that!"* The idea of it seemed to confuse him. But then, I saw him get the next idea.

He jerked himself sharply erect, eyes traveling from side to side. "He's out there, isn't he …Andy? And he's got me in his sights." He smiled to himself. "But I tell you what. We were lovers," he said, with particular emphasis. "Andy *won't* shoot me."

I dropped my heavy mitts, took a step and punched him hard on his cheekbone. He fell all the way to the street, but rolled, and rolling, fired off a round—missing me widely—breaking glass that tinkled, dribbling down somewhere behind me.

Still on his side, he aimed a fast kick from the ground that I didn't anticipate but managed to sidestep. It helped that we both had frozen snow with a skim of ice beneath us. Trying to climb to his feet put his face at about my belt level. I slapped him hard, my knuckles still sore from the impact with his cheekbone. His head battered back and I moved in.

Bracing himself with both hands, he scrambled to his feet, quicker than I expected. Although he "cleaned up" well, there was a good bit of the oilfield brawler left alive in there. He made to hit me, swinging the pistol barrel toward my head, an unmistakable roundhouse that I saw coming. Then he jumped back, almost theatrically—like a Victorian actor. Turning sideways to me, he dramatically raised and then extended the pistol—a western single-action—the hammer thumbing back as the muzzle moved into line with my right eye.

"Well then, die *now*," he shouted and I saw the trigger start to pull, cylinder start to turn.

Andy did shoot him. He put a clean round through his ex-lover's right shoulder, the slug passing through Richard, hitting, and likely penetrating the depot wall behind.

Richard fired reflexively, the bullet ricocheting off the hard, slick surface of the street and away. The wounded arm fell to his side.

"*Ah-h-h!*" he shouted, grabbing his wounded shoulder. "He shot me! Andy *shot* me! The *bitch!*"

Furious, Richard shifted the gun to his left hand, turned, aimed, and with a look of triumph, squeezed the trigger.

So Andy shot him again, cleanly through his left shoulder. Then Evie grabbed Richard and spun him, kneeing him—so accurately—that he fell hard, curling himself tightly around his groin, bleeding from both shoulders, moaning in real pain, and all the while muttering in disbelief.

"The bitch *shot* me."

CHAPTER 33

"You're not dead," she sobbed, tears falling freely. "I saw you jump, too. How can you be ...?"

I took her in my arms, held her, patting her, kissing salty tears as the crowd surged around us. Andy, William, Butch, Rosie, Alice, Adele, and Oliver—everybody who had been out at the bridge shoveling snow for hours in darkness came to mill around, give and receive hugs, and watch Richard bleed.

Somebody called Maxine, a bit regretfully, I thought, to come and patch him up. When she heard what he'd been up to, she said, "Do I have to?"

As Andy explained, "Had no idea where Richard would set up to view the kill. If we'd known he was all the way up on the hill, coulda had live music and appetizers!"

Andy picked up on Maxine's theme. "We don't *have* to call Frank Jacobs." He jerked a thumb at Richard. "We could let him *escape*," using two fingers on each hand as quote marks to show he didn't mean it. "Tie him to a tree somewhere and come out to pick up his frozen carcass in the morning. Remember Frankie?"

I did remember Frankie, my first murdered corpse here, spread-eagled and frozen solid. I remember we had to balance him on the sled, and one icy blue hand kept coming uncovered, making it look like Frankie waving to the crowd as we brought him in.

"Tempting," I said. But we made the call anyway. "Be there in the morning," the marshal promised. "Sure you don't just want to tie him out somewhere?" He laughed and clicked off, likely not realizing how close he came to the prevailing sentiment.

256

"Any regrets?" I asked Andy, finding him standing off a bit, staring at Richard where he lay in the street.

"A million," he said softly.

"I mean about shooting this guy."

"Oh that! None. Only wish I coulda shot him more."

I watched as Rosie came and stood over Richard. Though her pretty face appeared placid, inside she had to be seething. This guy had made a pretty good effort to kill everybody she cared about. After standing above him a long moment, she delivered a vicious kick to his upper thigh, which had to hurt, even delivered wearing soft mukluks.

"Probably shouldn't kick a man when he's down," I said dutifully, but with zero conviction.

We loaded moaning Richard into the back of my pickup truck, drove him down the street to a room at the lodge. Since he had both arms shot, we scooted his bed over to the wall and used two padlocks and a heavy dog chain to secure his ankle to the iron radiator.

"Won't be goin' anywhere a radiator can't go," said Andy, and laughed, but without humor.

It was well after midnight when the last of us ended up squeezed around my kitchen table, on the tippy stools and anything else that would sit, brewing coffee from the red can which Rosie poured while William and Andy filled in the missing pieces.

"He told us exactly where you would be jumping," said William.

Andy picked up the story. "So we just had to shut down some of that distance and give you something soft to land on. My idea was for all of us to stand around with a big canvas, kind of like an Eskimo blanket toss. Snow was Butch's idea."

"Good thinking, Butch," I said, deeply grateful to be alive.

Butch ducked his head modestly, and Adele beamed. "There was plenty of snow handy," he said. Of course I'd seen him shovel snow, so had a pretty good idea who moved most of that mountain.

"But," said Evie in a lull, after having said almost nothing since the streetlight, "why did you jump?"

"Because," I said, slowly, searching for the right words. "he said it was you or me. I was reasonably sure— at the time—Richard would let you go if I jumped, so I did."

"And you weren't afraid?"

"I was terrified."

"But you did it anyway, knowing you'd die."

"That's the thing. I expected to die. I couldn't see any alternative—certainly couldn't imagine all these people down below, shoveling snow for hours—but a part of me expected to live anyway. Somebody—sort of—told me something that made me think I *would* live, even though it didn't seem possible. It was all I had, so it had to be enough."

"Since nobody *did* die," asked Alice, "can the law *really* do much to him?"

"Peter Senengatuk died," I said. "Probably not directly by Richard's hand, but by his orders."

"Conspiracy to commit murder," offered William. "He will go away for a long time, to some Federal prison in the States, with high walls and very nasty cellmates."

"I wish," I said, "that one of you—I looked at both Evie and William—had told me you two were working together."

"They were?" said Rosie. "So you *didn't* break up with him? Here I was feeling all sorry."

"No," said Evie, "we *did* break up, sort of. I admit I was pretty hung up about Edward's chances to be appointed a Native American governor. When William told me what he needed, someone to work on the Two Deer campaign and feed back information, I thought, *This is my chance*."

"How did you get information back to William?" asked Rosie, a big reader of spy novels. "Was it a dead drop? Secret passwords? Disguises?"

"Newsletter," I guessed. "It was Evie's job to send out the campaign newsletters and she just added a fake address and name to the list, typed up her report and included it into the pile to be mailed. Right?"

William nodded. "Easier," he said to Rosie.

"So he *hired* you to be a spy?"

"No, I volunteered. I *wanted* to work on the campaign. I wanted Edward to succeed—that was before I knew he was a crook and wasn't even Indian. "I also wanted to prove William wrong.

"But I soon figured out Edward and Richard were in this together," she said. "Apparently it started well, but then something went wrong. They had a falling out. Part of it was, Edward really wanted to be governor." She smiled ruefully. "He *said* he could make a difference for Alaska Natives. I guess I just kept focusing on the side of him that seemed caring."

"Caring?" said Andy, "So caring he knocked me nearly cuckoo with a gun barrel? Offering to shoot me with a gun he claimed was Richard's? Then promising we'd be safe in the meat shed, but actually meaning to burn us alive? If he even *has* a caring side, he forgot to show it to *me*."

"He didn't actually mean to burn us," I said. Andy looked surprised.

"You told me he came back with matches and gasoline. We sure nearly died!"

"I was wrong," I admitted. "When we surprised him at the Denali Lodge that early morning, he looked as shocked as Evie to see us all charred. That's when I realized someone else came along and tried to burn us to a crisp."

"Richard!" said Andy, "Boy, can I pick 'em."

"Yeah," I said, "Richard followed Edward, hoping to retrieve his lost documents. Then he watched Edward lock us up tight and decided to make the most of it."

"But why kill us? He already had money—already had his plan in place. His companies would get their leases, probably find *big* oil, he woulda made millions. Coulda bought the whole Territory himself. Why kill us?"

I looked at him, looked at the others. "Don't you see?" He shrugged, took a sip of his coffee and made a bad-coffee face.

"No."

"It was jealousy."

"Huh?" Andy said it, but the whole group looked stunned.

"They were, um—in bed together."

"Oh funny," said Andy. "Kick me while I'm down."

"No, really, they were lovers. I didn't realize it until Evie cut his hair, but there's actually an old photo at Richard's, of Edward—with a mustache—standing beside, probably Richard's mother.

"And the book I found out at the railroad car, *The Maltese Falcon*, the one Richard had been reading, had the initials ELM, erased but visible. Of course they didn't mean anything to me at the time: Edward Leonardo Morelli."

The two must have worked out an elaborate plan, encouraged—maybe funded—by one or more of the drilling companies, to fake leases in the Naval Oil Reserve. With Richard actually working on the inside for the Federal government, and with some access to the process, I doubt they had any trouble setting up dummy companies to receive the most oil-rich claims.

"Then, what I think happened was, Edward got intrigued by the power to do good, his new role as statesman, and the opportunity to improve Native lives. In its way, admirable. He was able to raise himself from an Italian immigrant oilfield roughneck to a distinguished Native American with what seemed like a real political future. Suddenly he saw himself as somebody. He faked a college credential, bought some good clothes and for the first time in his life, had people like Evie admiring him, wanting to work with him, be around him, help him. It went to his head." I looked at her. "It would have gone to mine, having you hang around. Wait a minute, it has!" Evie gave me one of her large-eyed, adorable smiles.

"So Richard gets something going with me ..." said Andy.

"At least partly to make Edward jealous," I surmised. "But it didn't work. Then, you and I found the leases and money and moved them. And he decided ...I don't know what. That you and I had thrown in with Edward, or that *we* were lovers, or oil partners; there's no telling. And that's probably when he kind of lost it, bashed William on

261

the head, and started paying Lonnie and others—like Chief Kellar—to watch us, bug us, scare us, and ultimately try to kill us.

"I kept wondering why first we were bugged, then we weren't. And where all the heavy artillery at the Hazel B came from, and then why it disappeared."

Evie cocked her head. "Why did it disappear?"

"Because the jealousy and craziness between the two finally scared away the oil companies, scared away the big money. Edward had already moved on to imagining a political future, probably with you, jilting Richard, leaving him all the more desperate and crazy to recover the money, and especially to get revenge."

"So wait a minute," said Andy. "When Lonnie phoned in to say he killed us, who did he call?"

"I thought he called Edward," I said, "but he didn't. He called Richard, who then called Edward to gloat, so the message got through anyway."

"It stunned Edward," said Evie. "And when he passed the word that all three of you had died, I thought my life was over."

She turned to me. "How did you know you wouldn't die on the bridge?"

"The little girl told me," I said.

She cocked her head, curious. "The little girl by the stream?"

"A little girl …by a stream …told you?" said Andy.

"Well," I said, reluctant to divulge, "a little girl I sometimes meet in a dream."

"Aaah," someone said. And then, this being Chandalar, they all nodded knowingly, and because it was about three a.m., began to drift off home to bed.

262

Evie left last. "You could stay," I said. "My place is warm."

"It is," she agreed, casting a longing glance at my sofa. I knew she had to be exhausted, only massive amounts of caffeine keeping her in motion. "But I have some thinking to do, some deciding, and I need to do it by myself. And then she kissed me, warmly, wistfully, for a long time, put on her parka and went home.

CHAPTER 34

The morning of March 22, 1957, I spent folding deceased people's used clothing in the Quonset hut. Some joker, or maybe some one-legged man, sent us one cordovan loafer in brand-new condition. It almost always sat in splendor at the top of the shoe pile and one of the local entertainments was to watch people discover that lone shoe.

The hopeful would pick it up, admire it, and begin to hunt for the mate. But also, realizing that someone else *could* find the other and start looking for this one. So, he'd casually conceal it while searching in vain for its mate.

Having found that shoe myself, tried it on and hunted for the other, and watched others hunt for it for two years, I am certain there is no mate. For all I know, it may be a little joke that God plays. Or the Tlingit Natives in Southeast Alaska may be right— the joker may be Raven, the Trickster, who does such things to men.

Feeling in that moment, a bit like the lone shoe, I saw movement at the glass front doors and turned in time to see Adele and Butch arrive, step in, draw a breath—it smelled like old clothes and moth balls in a giant closet—and move toward me, hand in hand.

"Can we talk to you, Father?" asked Butch, his warm breath clouding in the frosty air—almost as cold inside as outside.

"Of course," I said. "It'll give me a chance to get out of here to someplace warm." I finished folding a pair of striped, seersucker shorts, consigned them to the "totally useless" pile and went from light bulb to light bulb, hanging by their twisted fabric cords, turning switches to "OFF."

We came out of that dim, silent world of the deceased into a bright, springish day, the temperature about zero, the sky perfectly blue and clear. Soon icicles would hang to five or six feet from eves and start to drip. Snow would begin to melt and the river ice soften, eventually breaking up and sweeping downriver, spring flowing in behind.

It's hard not to love spring in the north, hard to not be excited by each little sign or portent. This, my third spring in Chandalar, I should have been nearly giddy at spring changes, but instead, felt a little flat.

I hadn't seen Evie since that night. I knew she was here, knew she was well, knew she was teaching her classes and going about her life. Andy had stopped asking, when he called from Fairbanks, "Have you seen her?" I hadn't.

I showed Butch and Adele into the rectory, got them seated in my office and went to make fresh coffee. They seemed good, relaxed, friendly, affectionate, so I frankly couldn't imagine why they were here. Even sitting in my uncomfortable office chairs, they were holding hands—a good sign. The coffee perked and I took them each a cup, returned for a cup for me, and walked back down the hall to my office, still without a clue.

"How can I help?" I asked them, settling into my creaky chair.

She looked at me and smiled. He looked at me and smiled. And then I knew, before he even spoke. "We want to get married, and we want you to marry us."

And that's how it ended, the long, dark time.

They had a date in June that we marked on the church calendar, and they reserved the parish hall for a big celebration. They even brought a guest list—virtually everyone in town. Later, I watched them walk away, hand in hand, him huge and her tiny, and I felt a small bubble of joy stir in me and begin to rise.

Afternoon brought Rosie to my door. "We need to talk, *Father*," she said, putting me on notice that this was business.

"I'm happy to," I put her in the chair, fetched a mug, and poured coffee for her, for a change. "How can I help?"

"I've decided to have a baby," she said, tossing her dark curls and smiling. "I want someone to love and to share my life with."

"I can't help you with that," I said, after all we'd been through together, daring to be a little flippant. Fortunately, she smiled. "Some people get married, first," I told her.

"Yes," she said, "they do." I heard a knock at my front door, then heard the door open and someone stepping in. I started to climb out of my chair when Andy appeared.

"Sorry I'm late," he said, mostly to Rosie. He hesitated, then bent to kiss her on the lips. Rosie turned to me.

"We want to get married," she said. "Are you going to be okay with that?"

I looked at them both, frankly a little stunned. "Do you love each other?" I asked, "And will you both work your whole lives to protect and guide your child—your children?"

"We do," they said together. "We will."

"This won't always be easy," I told them, mostly her.

"Is anything?" she asked. "Any marriage? Anything worthwhile?"

❖

266

I had finished dinner, washed up the dinner dishes, and sat at my kitchen table on one of the tippy stools, lingering over my dinner coffee and basking in the glow of a warm and happy day.

I heard the knock and the quick door-open, a rhythm I recognized as Evie's. A part of me still tends to believe that if too many good things happen, some bad thing will likely occur to hold the happiness average down. Maybe this would be it.

Still, no matter what she'd come to tell me, Butch and Adele, Andy and Rosie, all had made up their minds to move forward hopefully and lovingly, and nothing discouraging that Evie could tell me now could diminish that.

She came in and kissed me, which seemed hopeful. She pulled off her 'spring' wool jacket and hung it on a nearby hook. Snagging the 1953 Anchorage Fur Rendezvous mug off the rack she filled it about half up, adding a bit of sugar and canned milk. She settled across the table from me, looked me in the eyes and took a sip.

"I heard," she said, in answer to the question I didn't ask. "Andy came by to tell me the whole story. I am …awash …with joy."

I admit I just smiled.

"Is it wrong?" she asked.

"Because he's gay?"

She shrugged. "Yeah."

I shook my head. "I don't know. I don't think so. My fallback is to try to imagine what Jesus would say if Rosie and Andy came to him. I think he'd say, 'Love each other and take good care with your kids.' And they do love each other. They've loved each other their whole lives."

She took another sip. "What about us? I want to know what really happens to us."

"We love each other, too," I said. "For richer, for poorer, in sickness and in health, in a big parish or in the wilderness, I don't think that will change. I think we …end up …together. At least I think we should."

"Is that what the little girl told you?"

I looked up, looking out the kitchen window at the last of sunset. "Hah! She won't even tell me her *name*."

She took my hands in hers across the table. "You're in luck, then. I know her name, I've always known. Emma."

ABOUT THE AUTHOR

Photo by V. Judy

Raised in Alaska, Jonathan Thomas Stratman infuses his novels with all the excitement, color, and adventure of life in the rugged 49th state.

Whether in his acclaimed *'Cheechako' youth series,* or in his *Father Hardy mystery series,* Stratman's characters call on reserves of courage, stamina and resourcefulness—not just to prevail, but to survive. No wonder so many readers say, *"I couldn't go to bed without finishing the book!"*

A NOTE FROM THE AUTHOR

Dear Reader,
If you enjoyed this book, would you please go to Amazon.com, or Goodreads, under Jonathan Thomas Stratman, and write a quick review? I'd appreciate it very much!

You can also check out my Facebook page:
'Jonathan Thomas Stratman, Author.' A "LIKE" would be very helpful, too.

Thanks,

*P.S. **The Old Rugged Double Cross—Book 4** in the Father Hardy series is available at Amazon.com under Jonathan Thomas Stratman.*

270